FLOORED

A Ward Sisters Novel

KARLA SORENSEN

Chapter One

LIA

THE FIRST TIME I saw Buckingham Palace, I had a surprising thought.

This is bullshit.

Not the palace. The palace was great. It was beautiful, all stately and whatnot with gleaming gold fleur-de-lis on each black iron fence post that protected the royals from us mere mortals.

No, the thing that was bullshit was me.

For two weeks, I'd been in the place I'd dreamed of for as long as I could remember. Great Britain, with its monarchs and history and architecture and ugh, just everything. And as I sat on the steps across from Buckingham Palace, surrounded by people snapping selfies and chattering on with their fellow travelers, I was lonely. I missed home.

How freaking annoying was I?

I should have been ecstatic. I should have been on cloud nine. Ten, even!

After snapping a picture of the building behind me, I sent it off to my twin sister, Claire. She wanted to see everything. And if this had been a normal trip, a week or two to sightsee, she probably would've ditched her snowboarding-god boyfriend to come see the Brits with me.

But instead, I was here by myself because my sightseeing was a package deal with time spent studying at Oxford for the Michaelmas term, which ran from the end of September to December. I'd arrived a few weeks early to settle in and see all things before my researching began in earnest. It was what I'd dreamed of as I started my Masters in English Literature, this type of immersion in British culture and education with a rock star professor whose work on the Brontë sisters was akin to a religious text to me.

Yet I was the sad sack wandering around London, staring glumly at the beautiful sites.

As I tucked my cell phone into my front pocket, it started buzzing.

Claire.

"Hi! What are you doing?" I winced after it came out because even to my own ears, I sounded cringe-level excited to be talking to someone.

My sister laughed. "Calling you because you're at Buckingham Palace, you bitch."

"I was." I stepped to the side so a group could pass me as I meandered through Green Park. "I'm walking through the park just by it now."

She sighed audibly. "And here I sit, working on my monthly budget. Which sister is cooler?"

My chest ached at the sound of her voice. "How's life? "

Claire laughed. "We talked two days ago."

An eternity in twin-land, especially when—prior to my trip over the pond and her moving in with her boyfriend Bauer—we lived together.

Taking a seat in the grass, I tipped my face up to the sun. "I know, but I miss knowing everything that's going on. No one calls me with random updates anymore because of the time difference."

"Well," she drawled, "it's still early, but so far, I've made my bed, cleaned out the litter box, and now I'm sitting down to work on the budget. Yesterday, I went grocery shopping and got on FaceTime with Logan. He couldn't figure out something on his computer, and he refused to ask Paige for help because she told him he wouldn't be able to figure it out on his own."

I smiled at the mention of our older brother and his wife, the people who raised us. "See? I'd know this shit if I was at home."

She was quiet, and I knew that kind of quiet from her. She was thinking. Analyzing. And I knew I'd admitted too much. Again, total bullshit.

This—the mopey, wish I was home, missing the mundane normality—wasn't me. It was the opposite of me. And if Claire thought I was undergoing a personality transplant just as I was starting the biggest educational opportunity I'd ever had, she'd worry herself sick.

So, I did a mental reset and flipped the switch.

"And I'll know it again when I get home," I said brightly. "I told you about the gowns we need to wear to eat at the dining hall, right?"

There was a smile in her voice when she answered. "Yes. You told me about the gowns."

"Three-course meals at a frickin' college dining hall. This is the kind of posh shit that only the British would think up." I tilted my head. "Or the French."

"Are you bored, Lia?" she asked.

I pinched my eyes shut. Twins were the worst sometimes. "No?"

"Are you not sure?"

Flopping back on the grass, I stared up at the towering trees. "What makes you think I'm bored?"

"Well, you haven't started your class yet, and you're sight-seeing alone, and you're having FOMO for the life you lived for the first twenty-two years of our life. That usually means you're bored."

"I can't be bored," I cried. "I'm in *London*! I've got this adorable flat in Oxford, and the whole town is adorable, and the campus is amazing, even if they have really strict rules about not sitting on the grass, and how on earth could I be living a life where I can come spend the day in London because why wouldn't I and somehow still be bored and missing the normal life I left behind."

Claire laughed under her breath. My cheeks burned a little hot at my outburst, and I looked around to make sure no one heard me. I couldn't even handle the idea that some lovely Brit who might become my best friend for the next couple of months would hear me and think I was just another crazy American.

"Lia"—she sighed—"promise me something."

"What?"

"Don't be so consumed with what you're missing that you stop paying attention to what's in front of you. Okay? Go eat a scone. Or that beans and toast and bacon thing you told me about."

I smiled. "That's for breakfast."

"Fine, then go get a beer in a pub and enjoy your time. Flirt with a cute British boy. Then go back to your flat in Oxford and get a good night's sleep. Don't you meet with Professor Atwood tomorrow?"

My fingers plucked at a blade of grass. "Yeah. I'm so freaking lucky she's letting me do this." I watched some clouds drift across the sky, a dark enough gray that I frowned. "You're right. I'll go get some food."

"Be careful on the train home, okay? Make sure to head back before it's dark."

I smiled. Claire was so *Claire*, she couldn't even help herself. "Okay, Mom."

"Love you."

"Love you back."

She hung up first, and for a few minutes, I laid on the grass and stared up at the slowly darkening sky. When the breeze held enough of a chill, I stood and pulled my wadded-up jacket out of my crossbody purse.

I wandered for a while. Taking pictures. Looking up at buildings. Reading placards. I hopped on and off the Tube, allowing for spur-of-the-moment decisions in what I might discover. It helped take that edge off, the one I desperately didn't want to feel again.

As I did, I tried to take Claire's advice to heart. Be in the moment and not think about what I was missing. I did pretty well until the first fat raindrop hit me on my forehead.

The rain came out of nowhere, and like a rookie, I'd left my little umbrella back at my flat.

Even though I pulled the hood of my jacket up, it didn't do much to protect me from the sudden downpour, so when I looked up and caught sight of a dark wooden sign for a pub off a side street, I smiled, thinking of what Claire said. I quickly jogged around a group of tourists on a sightseeing walk, hooked a right onto the quiet street, and ducked through the heavy wooden door.

It was quiet inside, decorated with dark wood, glass-covered sconces, and burgundy booths that had seen better days. It was still hours before the post-work rush would have a place like this packed to the brim with men wearing tailored suits in want of a pint.

God bless London, because really, British men knew how to wear suits. It did not take long to recognize how far superior they were to American men in that regard.

I slipped off my jacket and ran a hand through my hair. After a day of sightseeing, it was beyond tangled. The only other people in the pub were huddled in one of the corner booths, and for a split second, I wondered if the beer was poisonous or something, because honestly ... it was really, really empty, considering what time of day it was.

An old man wiping down the dingy wood bar nodded to me as I slid up to a stool. "What can I get for ya?"

I glanced behind him at what was on tap. "I'll have a Stella, please."

He nodded, deftly pulling a glass under the correct tap. "Be wanting anything to eat, dear?"

I smiled. Would the accents and the casual endearments ever get old? "Just the beer for now."

He set it in front of me. "Cheers."

After my first sip, I glanced around the pub again, wishing that even one other person would've been sitting at the bar with me.

Alone.

My first two weeks here had been a whirlwind, yes, but I'd still spent a lot of my time alone. Which was ... weird for me. The busyness and exhaustion of adjusting to the time zone change had kept that loneliness from swamping me.

But sitting alone at the bar, I felt that same visceral pain in my heart, missing ... well, everything. The rest of my family. My best friend, Finn. Since I'd already talked to Claire, I started to pull my phone out to see who else I could talk to when I heard his voice behind me.

"Don't tell me my brother's actually taken the night off, Carl."

The bartender nodded, giving a quick smile to whoever that deep, glorious, accented voice belonged to. "I'd reckon he never expected you to stop in."

Mr. Accent made an *oof* sound, full of amusement, and I smiled into my Stella.

"Need anything to drink?"

"I shouldn't," he answered dryly, "but after this week, I think I'll take one."

"Got a new IPA, if you want to give it a taste."

"Sounds bloody perfect," he murmured. "Though anything with alcohol does right about now."

What *was* it about the accent?

After taking the pint glass from Carl, the nice bartender, Mr. Accent made a noise that was quite delectable.

"Lewis coming back?"

"Not tonight."

Mr. Accent sighed heavily. "Is he home? Suppose I could pop 'round there while I'm in town."

Carl shook his head. "Out to the farm. Had to help your parents with something."

"No wonder I didn't know," he answered.

The sip of my Stella was slow, and I swear, I wasn't trying to eavesdrop. I couldn't help the fact they were right in front of me.

Mr. Accent sat back on his stool, spreading his large hands out over the bar. "Well, it's quiet enough. I'll stay for a bit. Can you turn on the match for me?" he asked Carl.

Internally, I smiled, feeling a lot less bored and a lot less alone.

Flirt with a cute British boy. Isn't that what my sister had told me? My very smart sister.

As Carl flipped on the TV, I kept my eyes on my beer, careful not to turn and gawk. Because he sounded hot—really, really, grade A, level ten hot—and I didn't want to visibly pout if he turned out not to be what I envisioned.

Leaving a seat open between us, he slid his tall, broad frame onto a stool and folded his large hands together in front of him on the bar. Ink crawled up his forearms, as did ropey muscles and strong veins.

Excellent signs, all around.

Have you ever tried to check out a man without him noticing? It takes skill, people.

His attention never once wavered from the soccer game on the screen—the emerald green grass and brightly colored jerseys of the players passing the ball back and forth before the start of the game.

Match.

Whatever.

I snorted into my beer.

"Not a fan of football?" he asked me.

Straight, unfettered energy pulsed under my skin, and it took everything in me not to look too eager for interaction. But honestly, I was. After the icky feelings of the entire day, I probably would have been this excited if Carl, the old bartender, had made small talk.

Instead of turning fully to see if his face was as hot as his voice and hands and forearms, I kept my eyes forward, just as he seemed to do.

What had he asked me again? An exclamation from the announcer on the screen, something about offsides, pulled my attention back.

"Am I a fan of football?" I mused. His finger drummed lightly on the side of his glass. "Yes," I said. "The *real* one."

He whistled at the jab. I tried to hide my grin by taking another sip of my beer.

When he replied, his voice was dry, mild amusement hanging off every deliciously spoken syllable. "Hate to break it to you, love, but that sport you Americans call football is *not* the real one."

Oh boy, Mr. Hot Voice and Muscley Forearms didn't want to go down that road. Not like he could know the brother who raised me was a Super Bowl winning football player, now one of the best defensive coaches in the league. If he wanted to talk football, I'd run his ass into the ground without breaking a sweat. So, I turned slowly in his direction, and when I did, I froze.

The face matched the voice. The hands. The muscles and ink. It matched, surpassed, blew the voice and the hands and muscles out of the water.

And when a slow smile pulled at the edges of my mouth, he did some turning of his own. It took everything in me not to climb into his lap where he sat on that stool.

I'd been around some hot men in my day. Kissed a bunch. Slept with a couple who I really, really liked.

And Mr. Hot Voice with the Hot Face and dark hair and knife-sharp jaw just made every single one of them fade into oblivion.

His gaze studied my face carefully for something. Whatever he saw caused him to relax. "What?" he asked.

I pointed at the TV. "I don't think this is an argument you want to have with me."

He licked his bottom lip, and reflexively, I felt my thighs clench together. His eyes, an indecipherable color in the dim light of the bar, never strayed from mine. "Carl, put another drink for the lady on my tab, if you please."

I raised an eyebrow. "Who said I wanted another one?"

Under the guise of looking out the street-facing windows, he slid to the stool next to mine, his shoulder brushing my own. "Well now, it's raining out, so I reckon you won't be in a hurry to leave. Besides, I think this is exactly where you need to be right now."

Lifting my beer to my mouth, I took a sip to hide my growing smile, but his eyes dropped to my lips regardless. As I set the pint glass down, I crossed my legs and set my chin in my hand. "Why do you think that?"

"There's a look on your face that intrigues me."

I snorted. "Is there? I can't wait to hear this."

"You're missing something."

My face went slack with shock, but I blinked, recovering in the next breath. "Why on earth would you say that?"

When he lifted his chin in a blatant study of my face, the light of the room caught the hard edge of his jaw. Seriously, a man who looked like him should be illegal.

"Because any time a beautiful woman is drinking alone in a quiet bar, and she has the terrible misfortune of telling me she hates the beautiful game, then she's clearly missing a screw or two."

A shocked laugh burst out of my mouth. His answering grin was belly-flipping gorgeous.

I did a little leaning of my own. "And let me guess, you're just the man to help me find them."

His thumb tapped the surface of the bar. His lips curved into a devious smile that made my toes curl inside my shoes. "No."

My eyebrow lifted in question.

What he said next were words I'd replay a thousand times over the next few months, when I had no idea how true they were. In a rough voice that pulled goosebumps up along my arm, he said, "I'm the man who's about to give you an education, love."

Chapter Two

JUDE

THINGS I DID NOT NEED tonight:
- Beer.
- My brother to be out of town the one night I was in London and felt like stopping by to see him.
- A cheeky American woman with big blue eyes and long dark hair.

Yet knowing the safest course of action would be to not drink the beer, go back home and pretend I'd never stopped by, and ignore the invitation in her eyes, I damn well ignored it.

The woman laughed at my blatant come-on, revealing straight white teeth and a dimple on the right side of her face. But after a shit day, a shit week, indulging in something that I wanted—not needed—sounded perfect.

Like me, she must have been caught in the rain, which was heavier than I'd expected it to be when I came to see Lewis. The ends of her hair looked damp where they curled against her back.

But the smile was all I got in response, which only intrigued me further.

"Educate me on soccer, huh?" she mused quietly, leaning back on her stool and folding her arms over her chest. Those big eyes focused on the match, one I'd wanted to watch from home, except I had an appointment with my agent, something I couldn't ignore. Looking at her delicate profile in the dim light of the pub, I couldn't even regret that I wasn't at home, watching Tottenham and Bethnal Green, the latter who I'd be playing in short order.

"Football," I corrected with a grin. When she rolled her eyes, I laughed. "Been in London long?"

"About ten days." With graceful fingers, she traced a line of condensation along the surface of her glass. "I'm here to study at Oxford for Michaelmas."

I nodded. A smart, cheeky American then.

"You probably meet many interesting people," she said carefully.

"Why's that?"

She gestured at Carl. "I assumed you worked here or were here a lot or something."

He lifted his bushy gray eyebrows in question, probably wondering if I'd answer her honestly.

I was a footballer, and my brother was the pub owner. And not only did I not spend a lot of time here, but it was the first time I'd ever stopped by without my little brother asking first.

"My brother owns it," I said. "While I do meet some characters in my job, I'm sure Carl has me beat for good stories."

Carl snorted. The American smiled.

"Let's say I'm interested in this soccer lesson," she began, turning slightly on her stool until her knees touched my legs under the bar. I didn't move. Neither did she.

My elbow bumped hers. "For the sake of argument, and since the *rest* of the world calls it football, can we dispense with the s-word, please?"

She grinned. "That really bothers you, doesn't it?"

"Well, it's the wrong name, so yes." And not that I'd say it out loud, but playing that game—the one she was currently disparaging with her American label—was the center of my entire universe. If we sat at those stools long enough, or Carl flipped to the right channel, a replay would likely come on showing me on the pitch, doing what I did so well. The only thing I did well, it felt like, even as my body was trying to tell me I was getting too bloody old to keep going at it the way I wanted.

Thirty-one felt a decade older some days, especially given the young talent.

She gave a magnanimous wave of her hand. "Fine. When in Rome and all that."

"They call it football there too," I pointed out.

Carl walked past and shook his head when he saw how closely we were sitting together—the American and me.

"What's your name?" I asked.

She licked her lips, pulling my attention to her mouth. It was a bloody marvelous mouth too. When I tore my eyes away and met her gaze again, it was knowing. It was also full of banked heat. The pretty American girl had no problem with me staring at her pretty lips.

"Lia," she answered.

I held out my hand. "Jude."

No last names were offered, which was fine by me. If she didn't live here, and paid no attention to football, my last name wouldn't mean anything to her. But all the same, I decided not to risk it.

The past few weeks, the pressure of being me—Jude McAllister, who was carrying his team on his slowly aging back and trying desperately to keep them out of mediocrity, who was trying to keep his younger brother from meddling in his life, who was making sure his family knew how wrong they'd been about him—was a slowly growing millstone around my neck.

For one night, I didn't want to feel any of those things.

Each day that I poorly juggled my responsibilities while balancing a high-demand career was another day that I craved an escape. One night, like this one, where I could pretend no one wanted anything of me. One night when I could flirt with a beautiful woman, a night when I could indulge in something harmless and only for me.

When she slid her cool fingers up my palm, I felt the charge of it up the length of my arm, like she'd plugged me into a socket.

"Jude," she repeated slowly.

Lia was tasting those letters on her tongue, and fuck all if it wasn't the sexiest thing I'd ever seen. I wanted to hear her gasp it into my ear with her nails digging into my back.

Because I was feeling particularly turned on by every facet of this brief interaction, I did the same back. I licked my bottom lip and met her eyes. "Lia," I murmured. Her pupils dilated, a pulse fluttering wildly at the base of her slender throat.

"We are definitely having a moment here." She glanced down at my hand, still holding hers.

Slowly, I pulled mine away, using the tips of my fingers to curl along the edges of hers, and she swallowed.

I watched her face as she settled her hands back around the pint glass in front of her. "How very American of you to point it out."

She lifted her beer, and I clinked my glass against it.

"Don't worry," she said. "I'm about to ruin it."

"Are you now?"

Lia set her chin in her hand, like she had earlier, only she fully turned on her stool, so I had no choice but to either bracket her crossed legs with mine or be turned away.

I chose the former, stretching one arm along the back of her seat. That long, curling hair brushed against my forearm, and I fought the urge to see how it felt tangled in my fingers.

We both took another pull from our drinks, and as I was setting my glass down, she said, "I think your football is the most boring sport in the entire world."

My entire body froze. "I beg your pardon."

Glancing over his shoulder, Carl whistled under his breath.

She shrugged. "They just ... run all over. There doesn't seem to be any strategy that I can see."

Was my jaw on the floor? My heart pulsing in a bloody heap just next to it? That was what it felt like.

I took a moment to recover the absolute heartbreak that anyone would say those words to me, but when I caught a flash of anticipation on her face, I knew she was looking forward to my reaction.

Lia was an unlit match, simply waiting for someone to provide the friction she needed to ignite.

I'd provide that happily.

"I can see why it might be difficult for you to understand the grace and fluidity of the game," I told her quietly, leaning in just enough that her breath caught. "Given there's no smash, grab, graceless violence like you lot think is interesting."

A spark flared hot behind her eyes. "It's hardly graceless."

"Do tell," I drawled.

Lia took the challenge like a relay baton, and oh, did she run with it.

"Have you ever seen a receiver stretched out in the air to make a catch, so aware of his entire body, so in control of it, that he manages to get one"—she licked her lips slowly—"just *one edge* of his toe inside the line so it counts."

My voice sounded like I'd chewed glass when I answered. "Those games are like watching a car wreck that someone starts and stops a thousand times and you can't quite stop looking to see where it all went wrong."

In truth, I had nothing against American football. The opposite, really. As was true of most professional athletes, I had a thorough enjoyment of all sports. Yes, football was my favorite, and it was in my blood, but I watched the Super Bowl almost every year. I tuned in when the league played games in London.

But there was no way I was admitting that now. Not when it was triggering the strangest type of foreplay I'd ever encountered. She'd slid forward in her seat, foot curling around the back of my calf, my fingers were toying with the edge of her hair. It was soft and cool from the rain.

"Ahh," she said triumphantly, "but you can't quit watching. There's a structure to it. A framework that requires critical thinking and forethought." Lia glanced at me underneath her long lashes. "When they line up against each other, they're reading everything about their opponent. Each flinch, each flicker of the eyes, each word that's shouted. Will it be a run or a pass? Is that defender going to blitz? Every answer is a different option, and they're ready for all of them."

It sounded like she was talking dirty, in the hushed secretive tone to her voice. I couldn't tell if I wanted to laugh at what we were doing, or tear her clothes off on top of the bar.

From the look in her eye, she wasn't entirely sure either.

I chuckled under my breath. "Look at the telly," I told her, tapping the side of her leg. She turned her face toward it, jaw set stubbornly. Before I slid my stool closer, I glanced over my shoulder. The pub was still practically empty, which suited me fine at the moment. No one was watching us. My arm curled fully around her back as I moved closer, setting my face just over her shoulder so I could murmur in her ear. "Watch," I instructed. "Not just the ball. Watch all the players move along the field. It's like a chess game, see? You can't move too far forward or you're offside, you have to have total awareness of the people playing against you, and the people playing with you. Total awareness of where the ball is and how your body is positioned." My lips brushed against her hair and her entire frame shivered. "Watch the defenders hang back when the other team has possession. Now look, their striker has the ball, and they'll move up, in case they can help. They have to work as one moving piece."

"Mm-hmm," she managed. "I-I see it." Lia cleared her throat delicately, and from the corner of my eye, I noticed her fingers curl into a fist.

She smelled fresh, and I turned just slightly, placing my nose in the crown of her hair.

I inhaled.

She exhaled, a shaky gust of air as it passed her lips.

"The back and forth of the game is what makes it so beautiful," I whispered. "It's like water. There's an ebb and flow, a movement that never quite stops. That's what makes it so hypnotizing."

Her knee pressed against my leg, a helpless gesture she may not have even realized she'd made because her chest was rising and falling so rapidly.

My voice got deeper. "That's why you can't look away for a single moment. Because that moment might change everything. See," I murmured, sliding my hand over her back until my fingers found the curve of her waist under the cotton of her shirt, "that pass was perfection. If one person hadn't paid attention, if one person wasn't exactly where they needed to be ..." I paused, watching a player dart up from midfield, watching one of the strikers hook the ball high in his direction, and the other drilled it into to corner of the net with a perfect header. The stands erupted, the players gathered to celebrate, and an unwitting smile curled my lips. Bethnal Green, the arseholes, would gain three points on the table today.

When I glanced sideways, Lia was smiling too.

"There it is," I whispered. Her face turned, and our mouths were a hairsbreadth apart.

"What?" She spoke so quietly I could barcly hear her.

I licked my bottom lip, and her navy eyes tracked the movement. "The moment you see it, how utterly perfect this game is."

Lia blinked, backing away slightly, and I fought a wave of disappointment.

Her hand reached for her pint glass, and as she lifted it to her mouth, the one I very much wanted to taste, the sound of a loud crash and breaking glass had her jumping. Beer sloshed over the lip of her cup, dousing the front of her shirt. She cursed, her face twisting up in frustration.

"Hold on," I said, leaping out of my chair to snag a bar towel from Carl.

Carl headed back to the kitchen to find the source of the sound, and I rubbed the back of my neck as Lia sopped at the mess all the way down the front of her black shirt. It wasn't even remotely supposed to be cut in a sexy way, but it clung to her chest nonetheless, making the line of her bra visible against the wet material

She laughed under her breath. "What a perfect end to this day," she said. "I'm going to smell like a frat house until I get back to my flat."

"No spare in that bag of yours?" I asked.

Lia shook her head. "Of course, I decided I didn't want to look like a tourist today and left my backpack behind." She continued to use the towel to sop up the beer. She looked miserable.

I glanced around again, making a split-second decision before I could think too hard on it. The couple in the corner had only looked up once but returned their attention to each other shortly after Carl had left the front.

"If you'd like a clean shirt, there's a spare room upstairs," I told her.

Lia's hands slowed, and it took a moment for her to look up. Her eyes studied my face intently.

"Only if you want," I said quietly. "Or I can get one for you and be right back down. There's a toilet downstairs where you could change if you'd rather."

She set down the towel and lifted her chin to meet my gaze head-on. "I like the upstairs option."

Bloody hell, I did too.

I took a deep breath and decided not to weigh the intelligence of walking this beautiful woman upstairs into the empty flat of my brother's pub, where I could close and lock the door.

Where there was a sofa. And a bed. Hell, a kitchen table would do at that point.

Carl returned from the kitchen.

"Everything all right?" I asked.

He nodded. "Vickie dropped a glass. All good."

"Right." I tilted my head at Lia. "I'm going to get her a clean shirt from upstairs."

His eyes narrowed. I narrowed mine back.

He'd worked for my brother long enough to know there was no point in talking a McAllister out of whatever course they were on. He held up his hands. "I'll be right here. Where I always am," he muttered.

I smiled.

Lia set her hand on my back, and I turned. Her head just barely cleared my shoulder as she stared up at me. "Shall we?" I asked.

She answered me with a lopsided grin, and I led her upstairs.

Chapter Three

LIA

Two options lay in front of me as I followed the hot man with the phenomenal ass up the narrow stairs that led to the space above the pub.

1- I was going to be chopped into a thousand pieces because he was a murderer.

2- I was going to get epically laid by the most beautiful man I'd ever seen.

And he wasn't even just beautiful. Considering I almost orgasmed just listening to him talk about soccer, I figured my chances of satisfaction were pretty freaking high.

"Do you live up here?"

He glanced over his shoulder, sending me a grin so boyish and delicious that I almost tripped.

Smooth, Lia.

"No, it's mainly used for storage, but there is a place to crash in a pinch." He stopped on the landing, sliding his hands above the doorframe until he found the key.

The doorknob was beautiful, as was the paneling on the deep red door. "That's beautiful," I murmured, touching one of the raised edges.

"Have a thing for doors, do you?"

I tell you what I had a thing for. British men named Jude with long legs and broad shoulders, a jaw cut like granite, and the kind of scruff lining it that made me feel downright naughty. But sure, we could talk about doors.

I smiled. "Don't you ever look at doors like that and wonder who made it?"

Jude unlocked the door and pushed it open for me. "Not particularly," he admitted wryly.

The room above the pub wasn't large, but it was clean. Plaster walls painted a soft gray had boxes stacked along one side. Floor-to-ceiling windows lined in beautiful trim looked out at the street below.

At the back of the room were two identical, white-painted doors with antique crystal doorknobs. He opened one door and stuck his head in, appearing with something large and white in his hand.

"It'll be big, but it's clean," he said, eyes holding mine steadily. Finally, I could see them clearly. They were a deep, clear green.

Honestly, I felt a little relieved I could see all of him clearly, so I took the shirt and walked through the second door, which wasn't more than a large closet. A closet it may have been, but it gave me a necessary moment to breathe. As I quietly tugged off my beer-soaked shirt, I studied a few pictures taped up on the wall. Jude had his arm slung around a guy with a similar face. Based on how Jude looked now—I'd pegged him in his early thirties—the picture was easily fifteen years old, both men wearing a team jersey in bright green. A soccer jersey, I thought with a tiny smile. No wonder. Maybe he played in high school.

Before I left the privacy of the closet, I took a moment to be completely vain. I tugged my phone out of my purse and used the camera feature to gauge just how shitty I looked after my run in the rain.

With a wince, I caught sight of my hair. Frizz-tastic. The phone went back in my purse, and I did what I could with my hands and an elastic band, trying to wind my hair into a bun and anchor it on the top of my head. With a pinch of my cheeks and a deep breath to gather myself, I had to take a beat. You know the kind. Where you recognize the ramifications of being alone in a room with a bed and a hot British man who made my thighs squeeze together when he said things like, *utterly perfect.*

"Would you like another drink?" he called out.

A metaphorical door opened with those five words. Sometimes, just by nature of studying what I did, I thought about situations as if they were playing out in a book. Was the character making a sympathetic choice? Could the reader understand why—based on previous history, cultural norms, established patterns in the narrative—why things were decided in the way they were?

In my silence, he spoke quietly. "We don't have to, of course. But I'd be remiss not to offer the opportunity for privacy in light of our conversation earlier."

He was giving me an out. We could go straight back downstairs, and he wouldn't hold it against me. We'd take our places where we sat earlier and probably engage in some heavy, harmless flirting until I left to catch my train back to Oxford. I'd never see him again, but I'd go home with a story about the night I wished I indulged a bit. I'd go back to my small flat, get in bed alone, and I'd wonder what would have happened if I'd stayed for an extra drink.

The strap of my purse bit into my skin where I clutched it in my fingers. On one hand, I was not a *sleep with a guy I'd met that night* kind of girl. No judgment, I had friends back in Washington who were that type. More power to them and all that. It just wasn't me.

Partially because I'd never met anyone who'd made me want to sleep with them on the night I met them.

And Jude just about had me panting on that stool, whispering naughty soccer things in my ear. Want wasn't the problem.

If I left, if I took the out, I'd regret it.

I'd wonder. I'd wish. And I'd lament the fact that I didn't take a chance and learn how a man like him kissed. And just about more than anything, I hated feeling like I'd missed out.

"What the hell, right?" I whispered.

I shoved the jacket back into my purse and took a deep breath before I left the tiny room.

His back was to me when I cleared the doorway, and Lord, his frame was glorious. Tall and broad with strong shoulders and slim hips. His hands were big where they held the whiskey bottle, his arms roped with muscle and a few tattoos that I couldn't make out.

"Sounds perfect."

For a moment, he froze, like he hadn't expected me to say that. But when he turned, a pleased grin covered his stupid-handsome face.

"It may be a rubbish drink." Setting the whiskey down, he crouched in front of one of the boxes on the floor. "I have ginger ale and soda water, both room temp."

When I grimaced, he laughed.

"I know," he said. "It's a tragedy, to be sure."

"Ginger ale, I guess."

Jude went to work, fixing two rubbish drinks while I wandered the space and trailed my hand along a small bar cart lined with bottles in all shapes and sizes.

Opposite of the boxes was a daybed, and I smiled at the sight of it.

"A thing for beds then too?" he asked. This question had his voice pitched lower, and the suggestiveness was obvious.

"I wanted a bed like that when I was younger." The comforter was basic blue and white stripes and adorned by a simple white pillow. But the frame, an ornate white and gold metal, was straight out of my ten-year-old fantasy.

"And your parents didn't oblige? The horror," he teased.

I sighed. It didn't feel like the kind of night when you said things like, *well, my dad was a shit ton older than my mom, he died of a heart attack when I was little, she freaked out and decided being a single mom wasn't her jam so she bolted, leaving us in the custody of my older half-brother.*

"I shared a room with my twin sister until we were fourteen, so bunk beds were pretty much a done deal."

He hummed, bracing one of those broad shoulders on the wall. His dark eyes tracked me as I continued exploring. "Twins, eh?"

I gave him a warning look. "If you make a dirty joke right now, I'm out of here."

"I wouldn't dream of it." He held out a lowball glass.

Approaching slowly, I realized that Jude had hardly moved since I changed my shirt. He'd let me move toward him, at my pace, in my time.

Our fingers brushed when I took the drink, and it caused the slightest lift of his chin, a slow inhale expanding his chest.

"The picture in there." I tilted my head toward the space where I changed. "That your brother?"

Jude lifted his dark eyebrows briefly. "It is. I forgot that was in there."

"He doesn't look much younger than you."

"Only about two years between me and Lewis," he answered. No other offer of information, but I suppose that wasn't the point of this little exchange. If all we wanted to do was talk, we could've carried our asses back downstairs.

"You were wearing a soccer jersey," I accused. "No wonder you got so touchy."

The smile that spread over his face after I said that could only be described as predatory. Anticipatory.

Yet again ... my thighs squeezed helplessly. Holding his eyes, I raised the glass to my lips and sipped slowly. Then swallowed painfully.

It was *horrible.*

For someone whose brother owned a bar, he made epically

shitty drinks. Or ... maybe I just hated whiskey. I'd never actually tried it before.

Jude took a sip of his own, licking his bottom lip as he lowered the glass. "You must enjoy a good sparring match to keep poking this particular bear."

I grinned. "Maybe I do."

He straightened to his full height, and flutters exploded in my belly. He'd cover me entirely should we stretch out on that bed. He'd blot out the light and be able to dominate me as he saw fit.

"I'm not surprised Americans en masse don't understand," he said. After another sip, he set his glass down. "You're not the best at it, so naturally, it's rubbish."

I took a sip too, but I kept my glass gripped in my hands because the gentle tone of his voice just before he took a prowling step toward me made me feel ... inexperienced. No, I was no shaking virgin at twenty-two, but Jude was clearly older. Clearly better at this than I was.

"Such a tragedy that we're not," I whispered. "All that flopping on the ground, pretending to be injured. Sounds like a tough game to master."

Jude emitted a shocked gust of laughter. But his eyes glowed. My cheeks felt warm.

"You are ..." his voice trailed off, but his gaze tracked down the entire length of my body.

I backed up a step, my shoulders hitting the wall behind me.

"I'm what?" I set my glass down on top of the box.

"Frustrating." He took another step.

"I've heard that a time or two." My hands curled into fists to keep from reaching for him.

"I'll bet you have," he murmured. His fingers picked at the hem of the shirt, which skirted my hips. He managed to wind some of it in his grasp without touching me. My skin burned from that lack of touch. I wanted his big hands everywhere. "I'll bet you love driving people insane."

My chest rose and fell rapidly.

"Look at you." He fisted the shirt, yet instead of tugging me toward him, he used that to anchor me in place. "It's right there in those blue eyes how badly you want to say something else."

I rubbed my thighs together. He noticed.

My chin tilted up in challenge. "You think you've got me pegged?" Now it was me who licked my bottom lip, and he huffed air from his nose, a bull ready to charge if I waved my flag just one more time. "You don't know me."

"Isn't that the appeal?" His other hand rose, just the pad of his thumb landing in the middle of my mouth. "Don't tell me it's not." He dragged my bottom lip down, and oh, my gawd, I was panting audibly. "The only thing you know right now is that you want me over top of you. You want me between those pretty, long legs." He dipped down and ran his nose along my cheekbone, his mouth ghosting over my skin. Just shy of touching me.

My hand shot out and grabbed the waist of his jeans, my fingers curling over the edge, hot, hard skin against the back of my knuckles. Jude pulled his head back and stared down at me, his forest green eyes unreadable, unfathomably deep.

His jaw clenched. "Am I wrong?"

"Do you have protection?" I asked. That was my answer to his question, and the way his eyes flared, he knew it.

"Back pocket."

My hand slid from the waistband, and I brushed against his length as it did. He inhaled sharply, and oh, more thigh squeezing because he was not wrong. I did want him over top of me and between my legs. I wanted this night of crazy after a day of feeling inexplicably sad and lonely. I wanted to find some physical comfort in the arms of this man who I'd just met.

Maybe it was irresponsible. Maybe it was ill-advised. But it didn't *feel* like either of those things.

Every so often, I felt an urge to do something insane like this. Normally, I could cap it. I could seek a safer comfort elsewhere in my life.

But no one was here to stop this impulse and allow me this outlet. Just me and him, about to tip over the edge together.

When I reached into his back pocket, I felt the foil packet. Okay, so he walked around with condoms. But if I looked and sounded like him, I'd probably do the same thing. It was a miracle half of London wasn't here tossing panties at him.

The hand on my lip trailed down my jaw, only stopping when he gripped the back of my neck. Hard.

His eyes flared at whatever he saw on my face. So what if he had a condom in his pocket? It was possible that this night was as strange for him as it was for me. A role was being played by both of us.

It was possible he didn't make a habit of sleeping with bedraggled tourists, just like I didn't make a habit of falling into bed with a perfect stranger.

But tonight ... the role was exactly what I needed. Maybe it was what he needed too.

I tossed the condom onto the bed and met his gaze straight on. "Are you going to stare at me all night or put your money where your mouth is?"

My words were swallowed immediately when he dived, his mouth taking mine in a fearsome kiss.

Arms wrapped around his neck, fingers digging into his thick hair like I'd done it a million times, and Jude angled his head, sweeping his tongue into my mouth like he'd done it the same amount of times. My hips angled out, his angled in, and then he boosted me up against the wall with one strong hand under my ass.

I wasn't entirely sure anymore who was the bull and who was waving the flag because as he sucked my tongue into his mouth and pulled a whimper from my lungs, it felt like we were charging headlong at each other, destined for a collision of epic proportions.

His hands ripped at my clothes, mine did the same.

There was very little finesse as teeth tugged at lips in sharp bites. He gripped the flesh underneath my leggings in big, grasping hands, and he muttered dirty words into the skin of my neck when I shoved his zipper down and wrapped my hand around him.

The clean shirt fell to the floor, and he tugged my bra strap off my shoulder, sucking kisses covering the hot skin he found underneath the black lace.

I writhed against the wall, trying, trying, trying to scramble higher, get closer, touch more of him.

His kisses were dirty, his tongue alone making me see stars as he pushed it rhythmically against mine. I tugged fiercely on the strands of his hair until he pulled back. His hair was a disaster, his lips swollen from my kisses.

"Look at you," he whispered. With surprising tenderness, he brushed his knuckles along my collarbone. "Bloody gorgeous."

Was it a cliché to admit in my head that a man like him, with the eyes and the smile and the muscles, saying I was bloody gorgeous in that accent had me ready to do backflips if that was what he asked for?

"Bed. Now."

At my command, he grinned.

He walked us over, and when my ass hit the bed, he didn't immediately fall on top of me. He towered above the bed, staring down at my half-naked form sprawled over the comforter.

"Leggings. Off."

I raised an eyebrow at his return command, but my hands slowly pushed them down my hips. He sucked in a sharp breath when I kicked them off. My fingers trailed a delicate circle around my belly button, and he bared his teeth like I'd just shown him something delicious that he couldn't wait to devour.

His jeans were shucked off quickly, and I tried to keep my eyes from widening.

Because hot damn, he was bloody gorgeous. No, it didn't sound as good in my head with my boring American voice, but when Jude covered himself and prowled over top of me, I didn't care if it didn't sound as good in my head.

I stopped thinking altogether and let him warm the parts of me that were cold, let him suck and kiss and taste.

I let him pin my hands down on the bed.

I let him push my thigh up over his shoulder.

I let him roll his hips in sharp snapping thrusts until I screamed in back-arching relief.

Say words and phrases into my skin that I'd never had a man say to me.

And before long, after he shouted my name and stared down at me like he'd just seen a glimpse of friggin' heaven, I let him sag on top of me, sweat-soaked back and muscle-covered arms slick against my own skin.

I let him kiss me softly as we both came down from an impossibly high peak. My heart hammered in my chest, and I had the thought that I should get up. That I should get dressed and go get on the train.

He pulled away from my body, and I winced, which made him grin unrepentantly. I slugged him in the arm, and he laughed, pulling me back into his arms.

"I should go," I whispered even as my arm slung over his abs, and I kissed the skin over his still-pounding heart.

"Just stay for a little," he whispered back. "I'm not quite ready for tonight to be done, love."

My eyes drifted shut. "Just for a little."

Everything caught up with me when I did. Exhaustion seeped into my bones, from the day and this unexpected evening, a lovely weight tethering me to that bed.

Just for a little.

It was my last thought until the sun rose.

Chapter Four

WHAT A CLICHÉ.

When you pry your eyes open to an unfamiliar room with the unfamiliar weight of an unfamiliar man's arm over your waist, it's one thing. But when all of those things hit you after you realize that you've spent the night somewhere you shouldn't have, jeopardizing the first meeting with your intellectual idol, it's enough to make a grown-ass woman break down into tears.

"Shiiiiiit," I muttered under my breath.

A quick glance over my shoulders revealed Jude, sound asleep in all his naked glory. In the bright light of the next morning, he was so beautiful it wasn't even right.

The blanket he'd pulled over us only covered him to his waist, and Lord, his chest and abs were enough to make me pause when I really didn't have time to be pausing. His pecs were the size of freaking dinner plates, and each neat square of muscle lining his stomach was holy shit perfect. What a waste to spend the entire night with a body like that and only enjoy it once.

I wasn't embarrassed that I'd slept with him because, after that experience, I don't think any woman would have doubts. That was *scream it from the rooftops* sex. But even with that knowledge, I inched my way out of the bed slowly, doing my very best not to wake the sleeping hottie.

What I didn't want was the awkward exchange. He'd said it himself; the appeal of the entire exchange was the anonymity. He knew nothing about me, and I knew nothing about him. And I wasn't particularly in any position to start anything, even if he wanted.

As I tugged on my leggings and looked back at him again, his big hand sprawled over his muscled chest, I wasn't sure my pride could handle it very well if he brushed me off upon waking. My shirt was in a heap by my feet, and when I bent over to pick it up, he moved, groaning deep in his chest before he rolled onto his side.

The groan. I had to close my eyes when I thought of him making that sound the night before.

Yeah, I'd be retelling the story of that night for generations because I'd earned the right.

At one point, I had a vague recollection of that voice groaning, *bloody perfect*.

A sound from the street below had me snapping out of the post-coital recollection because I needed to get my ass to Paddington to catch a train back if I had any hope of getting to my meeting with Catherine Atwood on time.

She'd offered me this chance when I met her at one of her guest lectures back home in Seattle, and no way was I going to blow it because a hot guy made me see stars.

Not only would I be a cliché but I'd also kick my own ass for my stupidity.

With my purse and jacket tucked tightly under my arms, I paused by the bar cart when I spied a napkin and a pen.

Just in case you need more sports tips, I scrawled, followed by my cell number. It was enough finality that I could walk away from the tiny room without obsessing. There'd be no questioning whether I should message or call or casually drop by the pub for another pint because I had no way to reach him. With a deep breath, I closed the door quietly and crept down the stairs. When I turned the corner, I froze when I spied the bartender sitting at one of the stools.

His eyebrows rose slowly, then he cleared his throat, turning his attention back to the white mug sitting in front of him.

"Good morning," he said.

"Morning." I motioned to the door. "I'm guessing you can lock up behind me."

He rolled his lips, clearly hiding a smile as he nodded.

"Good." I hitched my purse.

Carl, I think his name was, turned slowly on the stool. His cheeks looked a little pink, and I found his embarrassment more endearing than I should. His eyes could hardly hold mine as he stood. "Coffee for the train, dear? I've got a takeaway cup."

I smiled. "That would be amazing, thank you."

He nodded, tugging on the door that closed off the bar. He deftly poured the steaming, black liquid into a tan cup before he looked up again. "How'dya take it?"

"A couple of sugars if you have them."

He snagged a few packets from one of the table holders, then set them on the bar. Gratefully, I picked it up and tucked the sugars into my purse. "You're an angel, Carl."

His smile was soft. "That's the first time I've ever been called that particular name, but you're welcome all the same." His eyes darted back toward the stairs. "Far to go?"

"Oxford."

He whistled. "Best get moving then. It'll be busy first thing in the morning."

Holding up the cup, I smiled. "Thanks again."

For the coffee.

And not treating me like I'd done the walk of shame through an actual bar when, in fact, that was exactly what I'd done.

What a strange turn of events, I thought as I hustled my ass to the train station. The day before, I left my flat expecting a fairly easy day of seeing some of the sights I hadn't seen yet. I saw some sights, all right.

The station was packed, given it was a Monday morning, and the soaring ceiling of glass and iron was high enough that I never felt claustrophobic as I waited in a jostling line to hop on the train I needed. I was at the back of it, though, so by the time the doors slid shut behind me, I settled on the floor of one of the connecting cars between trains, my head resting on the hard plastic as I listened to the chatter around me.

People visiting. People going off to work. Or like me, on their way to school.

I hadn't traveled much, which most people found surprising, given my brother's job in the NFL. But when Logan played, we were in school, and his mom—our nana—stayed with us. Being in a place like this was a culture change that made my blood hum happily. Days like the one I'd had, feeling lonely, wasn't normal for me.

Maybe the night before, the hours I'd spent with Jude, was the reset I needed because my loneliness was long gone as I sat on the floor of that fast-moving train. I couldn't really see any of the blurred scenery passing because of where I was sitting—the buildings and cars and communities that sprawled out from London—but I felt at ease, all of the ickiness from before a distant memory. I sighed and took the last lukewarm sip of the coffee Carl had so generously given me.

My phone buzzed in my purse and I pulled it out. An email from Catherine Atwood caught my attention on the notifications, and I blew a gusty sigh of relief when I saw it.

Running behind. Will meet you thirty minutes later than we arranged.

Best, Catherine Atwood, PhD

Maybe the ghosts of the Brontë sisters, who I thought of as my patron saints if I had any, were looking out for me. They saw my opportunity for the epic shag and helped a sister out. It made me smile to imagine it.

The second notification also had me smiling, but for a different reason.

Finn: Second date with Keeley went great. We're going out again tomorrow.

My thumbs flew across the screen as I replied to my best friend.

Me: OMG I TOLD YOU

Me: Didn't I tell you she didn't actually think you were a nerd?

Finn: You did. She doesn't even mind that I'm working a thousand hours a week right now.

Me: An excellent trait for someone dating a doctor.

Finn: Future doctor. I hardly have time to sleep right now. Is it stupid to try to date someone I actually LIKE?

Me: Shut up. Go out with her again. I'll just never speak to you anymore because you'll be happy and busy and becoming a doctor and sucking face with her all the time.

Finn: True. You'll probably never see me when you get back either. I know how you feel about PDA.

Finn: Bauer and Claire are the WORST, btw. I saw them last week, and I swear, he forgot I was there at

one point when she kissed him.

That made me laugh softly because normally, I did hate PDA. I teased Claire about the fact that she and Bauer couldn't keep their hands off of each other, but in a strange way, her new relationship—and Finn's, for that matter—made it easier to be where I was. She had someone. Someone who loved her fiercely, no matter how caught off guard we'd all been by my quiet sister's relationship with the bad boy snowboarder.

Me: You'll have to manage them in my absence.

Me: Gotta go, my train is approaching the station.

Finn: ?? You're just getting back to Oxford??

Yeah, not touching that one with a ten-foot pole. I tucked my phone away as I hauled myself back up to my feet, following the flow of people who exited the train along with me at the Oxford railway station. The university of Oxford wasn't a typical college, centered in one place within a city. Depending on where you needed to go, it could take another forty minutes from the train station until you reached your destination.

After two weeks, I finally felt like I had a handle on the whole "getting around" thing. At home, it was so easy to just ... hop in the car. Here, it was like a whole *thing*. Figuring out the best/fastest way to arrive where you needed to go.

Oxford was smaller than London, obviously, though equally steeped in history. It still felt like I was walking through a movie set as I made my way back to my place. I skipped up the narrow stairs to my second floor flat and unlocked the bright blue door. With a glance at the clock, I had just enough time to change, run a brush through my hair, slap some mascara on, and get to Catherine's office at Oriel College.

The mirror in my tiny bathroom had me grimacing because

whoo boy, my hair looked like I'd spent the night having sex with someone and then bolting out the door. With a yank of a brush and a little product, I was able to braid it and wind the full length into a sedate bun at the base of my skull.

My black shirt still held a trace of beer smell, so I stripped that off and tossed it into the hamper in the corner. The leggings stayed, as did the flats, and I topped them with a soft chambray shirt and a simple gold necklace.

I shoved an apple from the tiny kitchenette into my purse, munching on it on my way to her office.

By the time I got there, I beat our postponed meeting time by three minutes. Just enough to have a nervous pit swirling in my belly.

I loved school. Loved learning. And I came this close to blowing off this first meeting with Catherine when she was doing me a huge favor by agreeing to allow me into the research cohort she was overseeing. My advisor at UW about cried tears of joy when I asked for the credits equal to a class for one semester in order to do it.

This was what you called a no-friggin'-brainer.

When I raised my hand to knock on her office door, I took a second to gather myself.

Whatever urge I'd felt yesterday, whatever feelings had swamped me during my day in London, those had to stay the frick away from me. Leaving my family, leaving my entire life for a few months had nothing to do with epic shags or morose palace viewings. I came to learn and get one step closer to figuring out what I wanted to do with all these years of education.

"You can do this," I told myself.

I knocked, and she called for me to come in.

From her seat behind her massive desk, Catherine glanced at me over her black-rimmed glasses. "Morning, Miss Ward. Thank you for being willing to wait for me."

"No problem." I took a seat across from her when she gestured to one of the leather chairs.

She set her pen down and leaned back in her chair, assessing me carefully. "Let me remind you, simply because you're not taking a typical class, this will be no walk in the park. I'll expect world-class work from you, Lia, because that's what I expect from everyone who learns under me."

"I understand." I took a spiral-bound notebook and my favorite purple pen out of my backpack. "And I am beyond ready to get started."

She grinned. "Good."

As she talked, I listened, I wrote faster than my brain could keep up with, and as I sat in the chair, my memories of Jude faded, disappearing like a fast-moving train.

Chapter Five

THE MOMENT I opened my eyes and found myself alone in that awful little bed, I knew the day would turn to complete and utter shit. A glance at my phone, left discarded on the floor in a pile of the clothes that had been torn from my body with surprising alacrity, showed a time that I hadn't slept to in years.

Sitting up, I felt aches in my back and grinned to myself.

Sore from sex at thirty-one. What a joke I was. Not just that but she'd snuck from the room without waking me like I was some drunken tryst she desperately wanted to avoid. I could hardly hold that against her, though, as it had been the driving force behind my impulsive actions. That woman, beautiful and bold and unafraid to challenge me, had no bloody clue who I was.

Not that I was someone who got mobbed on the streets, especially when I came into London. But when she looked at me, those big blue eyes held no expectation, no weighty anticipation of what I might be like because of what I did.

And in my life, it was glorious to have that moment of respite.

Made all the more glorious when I heard the heavy footsteps of my brother tromping up the stairs to the flat.

38

"Are you decent?" he called from the door. "Or do you have a bird balancing on your balls?"

I rolled my eyes. "Bloody Carl," I muttered, standing to tug my trousers back up over my legs. "You can come in."

Lewis shoved the door open, and I glared.

He laid a hand on his chest. "I'm gutted."

"Are you?"

"Imagine my surprise when I come in this morning, and Carl informs me that my paragon of a big brother took an American up to my flat for a shag in my pub. I've never even done that."

I raised my eyebrows.

"Fine. Once or twice before I married Jo."

"Where were you last night?"

"Had to go help Mum and Dad with something. I didn't know you were going to stop by. I always ask when you're here, and you don't actually come." He smiled. "If I'd known, I would've forced you to come with me."

Guilt had me grimacing. My brother, though I loved him, did have a terrible habit of trying to smooth over the rough, dysfunctional edges within our little family. I hardly talked to our parents anymore, a fact that bothered him immensely. But in fairness, they weren't complete arseholes to him.

"I think I like how I spent my evening better, thank you."

Lewis laughed. "She must have been fit as all fuck if you took a go at her. I haven't heard about you with a woman in bloody ages."

A flash of Lia, uninvited, swept through my mind. Back braced against the wall while she waited for me to kiss her. Yeah ... she'd been that and more. Not that I particularly wanted to discuss that with my arsehole brother.

I shoved at his shoulder. "Put a sock in it, Lewis. I'm allowed a night of fun every once in a while, yeah?"

"You'd be a lot more enjoyable to be around if you had nights like that more often."

Rolling my eyes, I decided not to argue that one with him. It was the great argument between me and my family. Our parents —humble, hardworking stock who came from humble, hardworking stock—couldn't understand sacrificing my life to playing a game. They were farmers, a cog in a wheel that kept the world, the very framework of society moving. And to them, my career was silly. Shallow.

But they'd never understood.

In that game, I found the great love of my life—the black and white ball and the green grass of the pitch kept me centered. Kept me driving forward and gave me purpose when everything else in my life felt uncertain. A place that I could carve out my legacy and make an impact that would far outlast my days playing the game.

Until the past few seasons, where age was catching up with me far faster than I would've liked. Lewis, who did love football, simply wished that I was more present with our family. Or at least put in an attempt, which was the same thing he wished from our parents, who were just as stubborn.

Tugging my shirt back on, I watched Lewis look down at the bottles on the bar cart. "You drinking my whiskey, you prick?"

"Sod off. It was already open."

He laughed. "I can't believe you actually drank during the season."

"I hardly finished either," I said, quite defensively too. "Less than half a beer and probably two sips of your whiskey."

Lewis shook his head.

"You're here early," I said.

His gaze snapped from the bottles. "Yeah. When Carl told me my big brother not only visited without being guilted into it but also *slept* here, I decided it warranted investigation."

My eyes rolled without any conscious decision on my part. "I don't have to be guilted into visiting."

"Don't you?" Lewis tapped his chin. "Yes, I vaguely remember that one time six years ago."

The truth of it pricked, just a little.

"It's not like you hop over to Shepperton much either, little brother." I wiped a hand down my face. "I'm pretty busy during the season, you know."

"Everyone's busy in their own way, Jude," he said evenly. "I worked all day on bookkeeping for the pub, then had to drive out to Mum and Dad's to help."

"With what?" Guilt, just as he'd said, had me asking.

"They got some new creep feeding pens that needed set up. Two of his workers are sick, so he needed an extra set of hands with that and measuring the lambs."

All the things we'd had to help with as boys, all the things I'd hated to do. "I tried to send them a check last year, told him to hire more people so they didn't have to work as hard."

"Some people like working hard on their own land," Lewis answered. "Not everything can be handled with a check, big brother."

"So I gathered when he mailed it back to me," I said with a wry smile.

My brother finally cracked a grin. "Feel free to toss any money you please at the pub. We need to replace the booths. Can't have cracks in the seats if your sainted arse is going to grace them now."

"I need to get to work," I said. "If you're quite finished."

He sighed. "Even a night spent shagging doesn't relax you, brother."

"It wasn't a *night spent shagging*," I muttered. "We just ... fell asleep afterward."

Lewis hooted with glee. "Imagine the paps running with that headline. *Shepperton footballer gets a good night of beauty sleep*." He shook his head.

I shoved at him. "That's not all I did, you prat."

Making my brother laugh was a small moment when I had to recognize why I'd stopped at The Red Lion the night before. Why I'd fallen so easily into bed with Lia. Everything in my life that was wrapped up in my job wasn't simple anymore. Not after a decade of being exactly that.

The nature of my relationship with my parents—that was to say, fairly nonexistent—meant I couldn't show up at the farm where Lewis and I had been raised and offer to help them with something like my brother had done the night before.

But I could stop and see my little brother to share a beer and a laugh.

And in his absence, Lia had offered me a delectable alternative, something to reignite that burn behind my chest, the one that used to fuel me on the pitch.

Lewis held the door open for me. "Hungry? I could see if Maggie'd make some eggs."

"I'm starved. Breakfast would be smart before I go in to talk to Conworth."

He looked over his shoulder. "Ugly match on Saturday."

"Yeah." One-nil against Crystal Palace in a complete and utter slogfest. That was partially why I was sore today, not simply from Lia with the big blue eyes.

Lewis grunted. "Need to do better than that. They're gonna bench your arse for the new French kid. He's bloody fast, isn't he?"

My smile was tight. "I'm aware, Lewis. But thank you for the reminder."

My mobile buzzed, and a text from my manager flashed across the screen, followed by a few I'd missed the evening before.

Conworth: Before you work out, meet me in my office for a chat. You need to do better this weekend.

Everyone in my life wanted me to do better. Do more.

My manager wanted me to be faster.

My brother simply wanted me to try.

A small corner of white caught my attention, a warped

image of serviette appearing behind the bottle of amber liquid on the bar cart. I walked over, smiling when I saw feminine handwriting across the surface.

"Brilliant," I whispered, tucking it into my pocket.

My life wasn't without a heavy load of complications, but just knowing I wasn't the only one who felt what I'd felt, I walked downstairs to my arsehole brother and his empty pub with a wide grin on my face.

Chapter Six

LIA

THE NEXT COUPLE of weeks had a rhythm I hadn't established in the first two weeks on this side of the Atlantic.

My body adjusted, and even though I still needed copious amounts of coffee every morning to wake, I no longer felt like a zombie by dinnertime. At home, the chaos of my days involved a larger coverage of space. Running errands and appointments could easily take me across one end of Seattle to the other. At Oxford, I covered a fairly small area. I found places I liked to eat, places I liked to read, places I liked to study, and places I liked to lie on the grass and stare at the sky like my research topic would magically fall from the fluffy white clouds and plop onto my face.

I didn't really make friends with any impossibly fashionable British girls, like I'd imagined I would, which was apparently quite normal when you were studying abroad for a semester. The girl who lived next door to me, Alyishia—at Oxford for a semester focusing on pre-Raphaelite art—was the closest thing I had to a friendly relationship. We'd traded about seven sentences when we passed each other in the hallway.

I ate a lot of bangers and mash and beef pies because I was *in Great Britain*, and obviously, I would gorge myself on all the meat and carbs I could possibly fit into my skinny jeans. Scones with clotted cream were the other piece I might regret once I finally brought myself to step on a scale, but each time I could continue to close my pants, I thanked my DNA for allowing me to stay slim despite my horrific eating habits while in jolly old England.

I met with Professor Atwood twice a week, and to my utter frustration, she nixed almost every single idea I came up with for my semester project. And among all of that, I hadn't heard a single word from Mr. Excellent One-Night Stand. I annoyed myself with how frequently I checked my phone because I was not that girl. I'd dated casually, and it was fine, no romantic misery attached to anything I'd experienced, but I was not the "omg, is he going to call me soon?" girl.

The most annoying part, though, was what it did to me when I was supposed to be working, supposed to be crafting a research paper on the Brontës to equal one semester's worth of credit, and my annoying brain would drift back to random memories. The way his hand curled around my thigh when he lifted it higher against his side. The way his body caught the light in random glimpses, a bulge in his bicep when he held himself over me, the epic curve of his ass when I slid my hands down his back.

Ladies and gentlemen, it was not the thing to be thinking about when you're meeting with your advisor. My chest felt hot, and I was quite sure my forehead was popping little tiny beads of sex-memory sweat. That was right when Atwood did the thing with my stack of papers that I hated.

Smack.

"You can do better."

The sound of papers hitting with a rude slap on her desk would haunt me for the rest of my life. In the past three weeks, I'd heard that sound so many freaking times. Every time I sat in front of her, waiting for her to review my notes on which angle my research would take, I braced myself for when she looked up over the rim of her glasses, flipped the black and metal clip back around the edge of the papers, and tossed it toward me.

I took a deep breath. "Maybe I can't."

Her eyebrows rose slowly. "Pardon?"

I closed my eyes and fought a wave of utter exhaustion. For weeks, I'd circled around and around—unable to pinpoint which aspect of the Brontës I'd spend the next two months immersing myself in—the result without any success at forward movement.

"Maybe I can't come up with anything good." I huffed loudly, sinking back into the chair. "Maybe I'm just destined to be someone who really, really loves their work, but I'll never pick a thread interesting enough to unspool from the rest of it. Nothing to set me apart."

Atwood narrowed her eyes in consternation because she never, ever slumped, and I meekly adjusted my posture.

"Better, thank you," she murmured. "Now as to the other ..." Judging by the look in her eyes, I braced myself. "What complete and utter horseshit, and if I'd known you'd roll over this easily, I never would've invited you here for Michaelmas."

Oof. I rubbed at my chest because it felt a little bit like she'd jammed the corner of her laptop behind my rib cage or something for how badly that hurt.

When I didn't answer, she prodded a bit more gently. "Why did you say yes to this, Lia?" My mouth opened to answer, and she held up a hand. "No crap answers. This will only work if you're willing to let me push you."

Every sarcastic answer that crowded my throat was a bitch to swallow down, but I managed it. No part of me wanted to dive into the depths with her because whenever someone wanted to excavate why I felt what I felt, I had the overwhelming urge to go skydive out of a rickety-ass plane just to avoid it.

Thoughts, unwelcome and uncomfortable, flitted just beyond reach, and my mentally shaky hands couldn't grasp onto a single one. If it were Claire sitting across from me, or my other two sisters, Molly or Isabel, if it were Finn, or my brother, Logan, or his wife, Paige, I probably could've come up with an answer for them.

This time, there were no narrowed eyes, just patient under- standing on her face as she watched me search for an honest answer.

I shook my head, knitting my fingers together in my lap for a moment. It grounded me just enough to grip one thread as it whirled around in my head.

I don't know what to do with my life, and I've been running from that for years.

The thought was a bit too naked to share. Even thinking it left me feeling unsettled because not once had I ever admitted that to anyone.

"Come now," she said gently. "I see something going on there in your face, Miss Ward."

My hand rubbed my forehead. Was I sweating?

"There is," I answered. "I just, I don't know if it helps with the issue at hand."

Professor Atwood nodded slowly. "All right."

"I mean, it may help. I don't know." Focus, Lia, just freaking focus, I willed myself. I was better than this. I flew across the Atlantic to a foreign country by myself without a single ounce of anxiety medication which, let's be honest, was a giant win. I'd done all this unfamiliar stuff alone, and I'd managed amazingly. Yes, sure, I banged a hot Brit who never called or texted like a hot asshole, not that I'd checked my phone eighty thousand times just in case I missed something coming through, but I'd done really, really well. And just because I didn't know what I was doing with my life, or that I was maybe possibly using continued schooling as an escape from facing that reality didn't mean I was a screwup or anything.

I still had choices.

That stopped me short, like someone clotheslined me with a crowbar across the chest. I had choices.

The Brontës didn't.

"They didn't have choices," I whispered, my thoughts racing and tumbling so fast I could hardly keep up.

Atwood tilted her head. "Take me down that thought with you."

I met her eyes. "They didn't have a choice. The reality they lived in—the death of their mother, that women were still considered the property of their husbands, the modest income of their family, the fact that teaching was truly the only position they could take in order to make money—it was all out of their hands. I mean, we know that Anne enjoyed teaching more than the others, but Charlotte *hated* it. Yet that experience, no matter how powerless or humiliated it made her feel, shaped one of the most iconic feminist characters in classic literature."

"Our dear Jane Eyre," Atwood murmured, her eyes bright and excited as I rambled.

"Their lack of choices—the cage they were forced to live in—shaped everything we cherish about them." My heart raced as I said it, and when Atwood's face spread into a slow smile, a burst of energy spread over my middle.

"And ...?" she prompted.

Right. This was the part of master's classes that felt ridiculously pretentious, when we had to frame everything in "super smart people speak."

I licked my lips. "It was the awareness—the consciousness—of female independence that was impossible for them to recreate in their own lives. They created an accurate reflection of their reality, the social base they knew, but crafted characters that achieved something they had yet to achieve themselves."

Professor Atwood leaned back in her chair, still grinning. "I like it. All three sisters? Or will you focus on one in particular?"

"I'm not sure yet. Can I let you know when we meet next?"

"Of course."

No matter what rhythm my days had found, this was the first moment when I felt like I wasn't insane for doing this semester in London. I felt good. Tired, but good. And the exhaustion was ironic because I was sleeping like the dead every single night.

As I stood to leave, pulling my bag up over my shoulder, Professor Atwood spoke again.

"A suggestion, if you're open to it."

"Always," I told her.

"Have you made your pilgrimage to Mecca yet?"

Her reference to Yorkshire—where the Brontë sisters grew up, where they lived their lives—made me smile. "Ah, no. But I can't wait to go."

"I think between now and when we meet again, you should. Spend a few days there, in fact. Immerse yourself in their world, which was vastly different than if young ladies had grown up here or in London. If you want to start outlining your paper, as you're deciding how to narrow your focus even further, I think Haworth is the best place for you to do so."

I nodded. "Okay. I can do that."

We set up our next meeting, and the ideas for my paper, the thought of a few days away in Haworth had me so excited, I couldn't even wait to book my train tickets until I got back to my place. I found a glossy black bench along a moss-covered brick wall and sat.

God bless the internet and all the spending money I'd saved prior to this trip because, within fifteen minutes, I had a train ticket and a double-bed room at a hotel in Haworth that used to be an old apothecary shop. And it was across the street from the Brontë Parsonage Museum.

"Now this," I murmured, "is not bullshit at all."

It had nothing to do with the scenery I'd see or the size of Haworth, which was a pinprick on the map compared to London. It was the feeling of rightness I had, that I was where I was supposed to be, on the path that made the most sense. Normally, I was the flailing one, hopping around so no one noticed I had no freaking clue what I was doing half the time. If I just kept moving, I could avoid that thought I'd had in Atwood's office.

How do I not know what the purpose of my life is?

That thought. That was what I didn't want to dive into.

And this was the perfect movement. Exactly what I needed.

With a spring in my step, I headed back to my flat because I had three hours to pack and head to the train station.

Just as I was digging the key out for the lock on my door, my phone buzzed in my back pocket.

"Hang on, hang on, dealing with old ass locks here," I muttered, jamming my shoulder into the door.

The phone buzzed again, and I figured it was my sister Isabel because if my family had a pushy texter, it was her. I dumped my bag onto the chair by my small desk and fished my phone out.

Ohhh, hot damn. The excitement at seeing a UK number flash over my screen should've been criminal. *Warning! Reaching critical levels of hope!*

Unknown number: Would you believe me if I told you that I'd been too busy playing football to text you sooner?

Unknown number: It's Jude, by the way. From the pub a couple of weeks back.

Unknown number: Now I've gone and texted three times, which is excessive, but I am sorry it took me this long. I'd love to see you again.

As I read the texts one more time, I tried to smother the smile that bubbled up. But like any self-respecting woman would, I tucked my phone away and packed my bags for my trip.

Jude would get a response, but not just yet.

He may have been spectacular, but his ass waited weeks to message me. Twenty-four hours wouldn't kill him.

After a quick check of the weather showed the same kinda cold, sorta rainy weather, I packed the appropriate amount of layers and waterproof boots, and I hauled my ass to Paddington Station.

It was only mildly difficult to put Jude's texts out of my head as I leaned my forehead against the glass window separating me from the rapidly moving British countryside. As it passed in front of my increasingly heavy eyelids, as the pleasant hum of the train started lulling me to sleep, I couldn't believe how exhausted I was.

Allowing myself to nap was an easy choice as the days I'd held the tired at bay were slowly catching up with me. The four-hour train ride to Haworth passed quickly, though I woke at the train station with a drool spot on my wadded up sweatshirt and a crick in my neck.

From the moment I walked through the center of the small village, I knew this was the perfect place to spend a few days to hone my project. After checking in to The Apothecary Guest House, I freshened up in the bathroom, then took my notepad and slowly wandered the steep cobblestone streets, and I remembered what Claire told me the day I talked to her at Buckingham Palace.

I ran my fingers along the mossy stone walls, damp from the air and musty with history. Closing my eyes, I tried not to think about what anyone was doing at home, what I might be missing, or what might come after this. Instead, I immersed myself. By the time I stumbled back to my hotel room after a dinner, washed my face, and brushed my teeth, my brain was whirring with ideas, and I fell face-first onto the bed. As I drifted off, I had a vague thought I should reply to Jude.

Sleep pulled mightily at me, and his handsome face was the last thing I thought of, which was probably why I had hazy dreams about the way he kissed me, the way he touched me. It explained why I rolled over the next morning and didn't give it a second thought before reaching for my phone.

Wiping the sleep from my eyes, I took a moment and read what he'd said again.

Would you believe me if I said I'd been too busy playing football to text you sooner?

"What a dork," I muttered. And what exactly did I want to say to him?

It wasn't like I wanted to adopt a British boyfriend. My time across the pond was finite. I sat up quickly, propping my back against the headboard, fighting a spinning sensation that rocked my head when I did.

Okay. That was weird.

Once that passed, I chugged some water because I did not have time for head spinning shit on my Brontë immersion week. Water back on the small nightstand and head clear, I fought the impulse to text one of my sisters about how to handle Jude.

Molly, the oldest, was always a solid choice for advice.

Exhibit A- her solid as a rock relationship with Washington Wolves football player, Noah Griffin. They'd been together for closing in on a year now, and if Paige didn't get a wedding to plan soon, hell would reign. Molly was the romantic. She'd swoon all over the place if I told her about Jude.

Isabel, the middle sister, might've been the single one, but she had a zero-bullshit policy when it came to men. Her sensibilities about romance were along the lines of "If I pretend it doesn't exist, maybe it won't find me." But she'd still ring my ears if I didn't text him back and see what happened if I met up with him again.

Claire—while she was the other half of my soul—would tell me to be careful. Yes, she was head over heels in love, but she was also the cautious one. It was so easy to hear her voice. *Just make sure you meet somewhere public. Text us his picture. And don't forget protection!*

A fleeting ache behind my chest blossomed at the thought of my sisters. But part of this whole Oxford thing was being able to get through minor situations like this without them holding my hand. My thumb tapped along the edge of my purple cell phone case.

Me: Apology is accepted, but I certainly hope that's not your best attempt at an excuse. You should go for "my goldfish died" or "I had to vacuum every day."

Me: I wouldn't mind seeing you again either.

I tucked my phone away, refusing to watch for a reply. And it set the tone for the next few days. Jude never responded immediately, but it was always within a few hours. Interspersed with exploring Brontë County, reading books, scrawling an outline in my notebook, and small updates for my family, I found an entirely different pattern to my day than I'd found in Oxford.

Jude: Haworth, eh? I grew up not too terribly far from there, but I don't get home often. It's a beautiful place.

Me: London isn't a terrible backup, though.

Jude: I don't actually live in London. You just caught me on a night in the city.

Me: Where do you live? (Asks the girl who has very hazy geographical knowledge of anything other than the biggest cities in Britain)

Jude: Ha. I live in Shepperton. Takes me less than an hour to drive into central London most of the time.

My thumbs itched to google Shepperton, but I refrained.

The guy hadn't even asked me out again. Between texting with Jude, I found myself wandering the same parts of Haworth over the next couple of days, saving some of my favorite places for the last days—to end on a high note, so to speak. I spent a lot of time outside, reading through *Jane Eyre*, *Wuthering Heights*, and *Agnes Grey*, trying to determine which sister would get my focus. I found quiet spots to sit and stare at the countryside, scribbling furiously in my journal as I put myself in their shoes. I napped ... like three times a day, but whatever.

And it was upon waking from one of those naps that I felt my first unpleasant wave of nausea. Hand pressed to my stomach, I took a few deep breaths until it subsided. Food. I needed food.

I broke off a piece of a granola bar I kept stashed in my purse and heard my phone ding.

Jude: When do you return from your epic adventures?

Me: I have two more days here. I'd like to have a rough outline of my project done before I leave, but someone keeps distracting me.

Jude: Ah, yes. What a prat. Don't worry, I need to go kick a ball for three hours anyway.

Me: Someone punishing you?

Jude: That mouth of yours, American ...

I bit my lip. This was something we'd danced around. I snuggled back under the covers and let the sensation wash over me. By this point, it had been over three weeks since I'd seen him, and based on the amount we'd texted since I'd arrived in Haworth, I'd see him again when I got back, if we could manage it.

Me: Yes, I remember how much you enjoyed it, Brit.

Jude: Immensely. Wish I could've enjoyed it again upon waking up.

Jude: And because I have horrible time management skills, by the time I work up a more polite way to ask, I'd like not to wait another month before I get to see that lovely mouth in person.

Me: I think we could manage that.

My belly fluttered until his words sank in a little.

A month.

It had been a month.

"Holy shit," I whispered. Frantically opening up my calendar app, I scrolled back to the little dot on my calendar of when I'd gotten my last period. Five weeks. I should've gotten my period.

I was late.

The kind of late that was really, really bad.

"Holy shit, holy shit, holy shit, holyyyyyyy shit."

I scrambled from the bed, tossing my phone away from me with fumbling fingers, and speared my hands in my hair when it clattered to the floor.

"I'm just late because of stress," I insisted. To myself. Because I was alone.

In a foreign country.

And possibly pregnant.

From a one-night stand.

My eyes burned. My nose tingled. My hands shook dangerously. This could not be happening.

I mean, it could happen. I remember him using a condom. But with a groan, I knew that my birth control taking had been

... hit or miss ... those first couple of weeks while I adjusted to the time difference.

Claire had been telling me for years that I should set reminders on my phone for my medication. But past advice coming back to haunt me was not what I needed.

What I needed was a freaking pregnancy test. As I leaned down to find my phone where it'd dropped on the floor, I knew I needed to call ... I didn't know. Claire. Isabel. Finn ... no, not Finn, he'd be terrible in this situation. Plus, there was the whole *in medical school and has a new girlfriend* thing. Paige. No. She'd hop on a plane and make me pee on a stick. As I mulled over my options, I noticed that the screen on my phone was on the news app, and before I could navigate away from it, I caught a glimpse of a sports headline, the top portion of someone's very familiar face in a picture.

Hey, Jude, Don't Let Me Down it proclaimed, a nod to the Beatles song. My hand was shaking so badly as I tried to scroll down to see the picture even though I knew—oh my sweet baby Jesus in the manger, *I knew*—by the messy dark hair and the eyes it was him.

My other hand covered my mouth as his face came into full view. In the shot, he was mid-kick, muscular leg swinging toward a ball suspended midair. His face, just as stupidly hot as I remember, was frozen in concentration, his muscular body covered in a blue and white uniform. Maybe if I wasn't freaking the fuck out, I would've thought about how insane it was that the guy I'd been text flirting with all day—the guy I'd slept with after making fun of the sport that employed him—was apparently a professional soccer player.

Football.

Whatever.

The hysterical laughter bubbled up in my throat, unbidden. I thought of his face when I said how boring the game was. I thought of his texts, telling me he'd been too busy playing football to text me sooner. Pretty soon, I was hunched over, wiping tears from my eyes because I couldn't stop the sounds coming from my mouth.

That was when it happened.

The head spinning.

The nausea.

My stomach roiled slowly, unpleasantly, and I barely made it to the bathroom before I puked.

Chapter Seven

LIA

"IT'S FINE. It'll be fine."

I'd said it a thousand times since I hastily packed my shit and hopped back on a train to Oxford. Sorry, Brontës, but I needed to be back in my own flat if I was going to find out I was carrying a little baby soccer player *inside my body*.

I groaned. Also for the thousandth time.

Maybe I'd just had a bad breakfast. Or lunch. Or tea.

My pace picked up as I booked it from the station back to my place. Yes. I liked that train of thought.

And honestly, I had to stick with it because as I approached the building that I would call home for a few months, I knew I absolutely had to convince myself it was true until I was safely ensconced behind locked doors and out of sight.

Have you ever seen someone fumble with a bottle of champagne? The really big expensive ones that would probably kill someone if you used it as a weapon. Molly got one for a party once, some fancy Amazon shindig for work that we were all invited to. She struggled to open it, and because it got jostled, the bubbles were *angry*, looking for a place to go once the pressure was released.

Once she got the cork off, oh, did they explode.

I imagined that happening inside my poor body. I could hardly pay attention to any aspect of my surroundings, wearing veritable blinders the entire time I left Haworth, the entire time I was on the train staring blankly out the window, and the entire time I hoofed it back to my flat.

So much pressure was building in me that the moment that cork came out, holy shit, I was going to erupt like a hormonal Vesuvius. Tears. Snot. Splotchy skin.

Somewhere, in that part of me that hated putting labels on shit like this, I knew exactly what this was.

Panic.

It felt like bottled panic.

Even putting a name to that emotion had my skin vibrating at a dangerous frequency as I took the steps up to my flat. My teeth clenched. My fingers curled into tight balls.

As I hit the top step, my breath sawed in and out of my lungs like I'd just run a freaking marathon. Alishiya was coming out of her apartment with a polite smile on her face. I knew the moment she saw all that angry, bubbling panic because her eyebrows bent in concern.

"Are you all right?"

Tight-lipped, I gave her a, "Mm-hmm," in response because honestly, I couldn't handle anything besides that.

She didn't push, which I would thank her for later. She must not have three sisters and a mama bear mother figure because holy hell, if I was at home right now, they'd be *all up* in my face.

"Shit," I whispered, my voice wavering, my chin wobbling.

What a stupid thought to have in my current predicament. *If I was at home right now.*

The first tear slipped out, and it took every shred of self-control to hold in the sob that wanted to follow it. My hand was shaking so badly that the key clanged in the door. From behind me, Alishiya laid a gentle hand on my shoulder.

"Let me help you," she said, in her lovely Scottish accent. The key taken from my hand, I pressed my fist against my mouth like a fucking cork because all the things had to stay right where they were for just five more seconds.

The door unlocked, and I gave her a grateful look. But honestly, if I tried to talk ... if I opened my mouth even a little ... I'd lose everything I'd held in for the past five and a half hours since I puked up my granola bar.

She smiled. "It'll be all right. Whatever it is."

With a jerky nod, I slid into my apartment and closed the door behind me. For a minute, it served as the only thing keeping me from crumpling down onto the floor. My phone buzzed, and I was slow in pulling it out of my backpack because I had a feeling it was Jude. I'd dropped off our conversation really freaking fast once the whole *I might be pregnant and holy shit, he plays professional soccer* bombshell hit.

I dumped my bag onto the floor and lurched forward to my little couch, fumbling with my purse as I did because I needed one thing.

I needed Claire.

Ignoring the text notifications, I went straight for the Face-Time. We were not even messing around with phone calls. The camera pulled up while I waited for her to pick up, and I winced. I looked like a crazy person.

When the call connected, when I saw her smiling face—identical to mine, but like, not crazy looking—the cork slipped.

Claire's smile disappeared immediately. "What's wrong?"

My chin wobbled.

"Oh my gosh, what's wrong?" Now *her* chin wobbled. "Lia, are you okay? Are you hurt?"

"I ..." I whispered, but my voice was practically inaudible. "I'm not hurt."

"Okay." She sighed. But her face, it was all scrunchy and worried. "Talk to me because my thoughts are going everywhere from brain tumor, to you were robbed, to I don't even know."

I exhaled a laugh, but even that sounded pained.

"Do I need to get on a plane?"

I shook my head. "No, I just ... I need you to be here with me while I do something."

"Okay." Claire looked off camera and shook her head, waving her boyfriend, Bauer, away when he said something. "Hang on, Lee, let me move to the bedroom."

Her camera whirled, and I tried not to focus on the movement, pinching my eyes shut when that didn't work because the last thing I needed to do was puke while on FaceTime. Gross. Hearing the click of a door, I opened my eyes, and Claire was sitting on her bed.

"All right, sorry. What are we doing?"

We.

For my entire life, I'd been part of a *we*. That was the thing about having an identical twin. It's a guaranteed playmate—someone to tell your secrets to, someone to get in trouble with, and someone to hold space for you when you need it. Yes, I loved Molly and Isabel, but Claire turned me into something more.

Slowly blowing out a breath through puffed cheeks, I reached over, unzipped my overnight bag, and grabbed the pregnancy test that I'd picked up from a pharmacy that I passed on the way to the train station in Haworth. I lifted the box up next to my face, and it took a couple of seconds for it to register.

Claire blinked, leaning in toward her phone screen, and I watched her mouth form the words. Her jaw fell open. Her eyes widened.

"Holy shit," she whispered.

Another tear escaped, and I wiped it away using the back of the hand holding the box.

"Oh, Lia."

"Yeah."

Claire licked her lips, rubbing them together before she spoke again. Oh, it was never, ever good when she was being careful about what words she chose. "What happened? Was it ... did you ...?" She blew out a breath of her own and gave me weird, intense eyes. "Did someone hurt you?"

"Oh, my gosh, *no*," I insisted. "No, it's not like that. I-I wanted to. I met him a couple of weeks after I got here."

Claire's entire frame relaxed. "Okay. Good. You know I had to ask. It's not ... it's not like you not to tell me when you slept with someone."

I rubbed my forehead. "I know. But I knew you'd worry if I told you I met a guy in a pub and ..." I waved my hand in a vague gesture.

She mimicked my hand movement. "And ...?"

"Shut up."

Claire grinned. "What's his name?"

Immediately, I shook my head. "I'll give you the recap later. Right now, I just need to know."

She sat up, and I couldn't help but smile at the change in her demeanor. My younger by two minutes twin was going into Mom-mode. "Okay. Are we doing this now?"

"I think so."

I hauled my ass off the couch and into the tiny bathroom. Once the box was ripped open, I exhaled. Hard.

"What?" she asked.

Studying the piece of plastic in my hand, I shrugged. "It's just ... what a weird little contraption, right? You pee on the thing, and it tells you whether you're pregnant with a hot British man's baby."

Claire smiled. "How hot?"

"Really, *really* hot." My answer was so glum, she burst out laughing.

"'Kay, let's do this thing." Her phone must have been propped on something, because suddenly, her laptop was in her lap, and she was typing. One shoulder shrugged. "It does say it's best to wait until the morning when your urine is the strongest.

Or something." The incredulous look I gave her had her holding up her hands. "Fine, fine. We're not waiting. Got it. I'm sure your pee is spectacular right now too."

Using the sink and the knobs on the faucet, I did some propping of my own. Once the angle was good, I ripped open the package and set it carefully on the edge of the sink. "Look away if you don't want to see ass," I warned her before shoving my pants down.

"I'm nervous," she admitted.

"*You* are?"

"Yes! I never thought we'd do our first pregnancy test on FaceTime."

My eyebrows raised slowly. "The fact that you've given our first pregnancy tests any thought at all is freaking me out."

She waved that away. "I know. It's just ... I'm so far away from you."

I kept my face averted from the camera, partially because, well, I was peeing on a stick, and also because if I saw her face when she said that ... I'd lose it.

The cap went into place with a tiny click, and I balanced the test on the ledge of the mirror above the sink.

It felt important to leave the bathroom for my eternal five-minute wait, so I tugged my pants back up and went into the bedroom. And with strategic pillow placement, I propped the phone up next to me in a way where I could convince myself that Claire was cuddling in the twin-size bed with me.

"Remember when Paige and Logan first got married?" she asked. She laid down on her bed too, arranging the phone to mirror my position. "You climbed into the top bunk with me, and we'd lay like this, planning all the pranks you wanted to play on her."

A tear slid down my temple, and my answering laugh was watery. "Yeah. Logan had been both parents for so many years, and I just wanted her to go away so I didn't get too used to her."

"I'm still not used to her," Claire said dryly.

We both laughed at that.

"What's his name?" she whispered.

Before I answered, I filled my lungs, letting them expand fully before I let the oxygen out. "Jude. I met him ... and ..."—I waved my hand—"well, you know that day I was at Buckingham Palace and you asked me if I was bored because I missed home?"

She smiled softly. "Yeah."

"It was that night."

"Ahh." Claire was giving me worried eyes when she spoke again. "Have you seen him since?"

I shook my head. "Just some texting the past few days. He's been busy with work."

"And he was ... is ... nice?"

My shrug was pitiful. "For as much as I talked to him, he seemed like it."

The times I thought about Jude, it wasn't like I was reflecting on his manners.

Oh, how politely *he'd ripped my underwear off!*

"And you used protection?"

"Yup." I rubbed my face.

Claire was quiet.

"I wish I was there, Lee." She sniffed. "This is really hard."

My hands stayed right the hell over my face. "I know."

I wished she was with me too. I'd make her walk the mile into my tiny bathroom. I'd make her check the test against the instructions because she was more patient than I was and she'd actually read them. I'd lay in this bed until she walked out of the bathroom, until she climbed back into bed with me and told me if I was going to have a baby about a decade earlier than I'd ever planned.

"Lia, you have to go look." Her voice was all wobbly, and I pressed my fingers into my eye sockets.

"No, I don't." Why were my palms wet? I licked my lips, and they came away salty.

"Yes, you do." She sounded so gentle. So understanding. If it were me, I would've gone tough love drill sergeant. "You can do this, Lee."

I dropped my hands, and when I pried my eyes open, I saw Claire crying in earnest right along with me.

"I'm scared," I said, my voice hardly above a whisper.

"That's okay. No matter what that thing says, we'll figure it out, okay?"

Before I could think too hard on it—what it would mean, what it wouldn't mean—I snatched the phone and rolled off the bed.

"Read the label first," she said.

I smiled. "I will."

On the back of the box, I skimmed until I saw what I needed to know, reading it out loud to Claire.

"One line is no; two lines is yes."

She nodded. "Okay."

Tossing the box aside, I took a second and looked at the test lying facedown on the metal ledge. It looked eight feet long lying there. In my mind, it grew bigger and bigger until I imagined it squeezing me out of the room.

"You can do it," she said again.

With a hard puff of air out of pursed lips, I snatched the test and flipped it over.

"Holy shit," I whispered.

Two bright ass purple lines.

Claire inhaled. "Two lines?"

My nod was jerky, and I tossed the test onto the ledge, sinking onto the floor of the bathroom with the phone clutched against me.

"Lia," she said firmly, "I can't see you."

"I don't want you to see me," I cried. "Holy shit, Claire, I'm pregnant. I'm *pregnant*!"

"Please let me see you. Not that having the camera smashed up to your boobs isn't great, but I'd really like to see my sister's face right now."

Slowly, I pulled the phone back, resting my hands on my bent knees, but with my head against the wall behind me, I decided that staring up at the ceiling was a better life choice for me.

"What am I supposed to do?"

She was quiet. "I don't know."

"I have to tell Jude," I murmured. "Don't I?"

Claire sighed. "I think that's a difficult question to answer when you don't know what kind of person he is. But if I'm answering in generalities, then yes, I think letting him know is the right thing to do. At least give him the opportunity to support you in whatever way you need."

Finally, I met her eyes. "And what if I don't want to keep it?"

She held my gaze, steady as a rock, unwavering as a mountain. "Then we'll figure that out too. You don't have to decide anything right now, Lia. Not one single thing."

A memory popped up, and I emitted a watery laugh. "Remember when Emmett was born?"

She laughed too. "Of course."

The day our nephew was born was so clear in my mind. But in our strange little family tree, he felt like our little brother. Logan and Paige had been married for a year when she got pregnant, and even though Logan had been the legal guardian to four girls, adding a fifth into the mix felt as natural as breathing. We anticipated the birth of their baby like it was the freaking second coming or something.

Claire and I were thirteen at the time, Isabel fifteen, and Molly was seventeen. The four of us stood in that hospital hallway, ears pressed against the door, waiting for the beautiful wailing sound of what we just *knew* would be another girl. We'd spoil her rotten, the fifth Ward girl, and it was going to be a glorious addition to our girl gang.

Except he didn't emit a wild, loud wail when he was born. He came out clear-eyed and calm. The most peaceful baby that ever existed. When Logan opened the door to let us in, we crowded around Paige—sweat-soaked and wild-haired and holding a tiny little bundle—only to hear the words, "It's a boy."

I looked up at my big brother, and said, "Oh bullshit, it is not."

But the moment I held him, that perfect, scrunched-up, red-faced baby boy, I fell head over heels in love. We all did. He was *our* baby boy, and the most loved child in existence.

"Remember how we used to fight over who got to hold him?"

Claire smiled. "I got so mad at Isabel that one time she tricked me into setting him down. Didn't she tell me that someone caught sight of Justin Bieber in our neighborhood?"

I laughed, feeling strangely calm. Probably denial, but whatever. "What a bitch."

"She had him for hours that day too. Ate dinner one-handed so no one could take him." Claire fell quiet, and her eyes were heavy on me. "Why the trip down memory lane?"

Have you ever felt like someone shoved a ball of yarn down your throat? That was the closest thing it felt like when I tried to swallow.

"I'm twenty-two with a big, loving family, and a healthy savings account."

"That's all very true."

"I'm going to keep it," I said quietly. There was time to figure everything else out. But if anyone could count on their family to help them through something like this, it was us. Each one of them would walk through fire for me. Just like I'd do for them.

Her eyes filled. "Okay."

"But I still have to talk to Jude."

Claire wiped at her face. "Yeah, you probably do."

"And," I said slowly, "I need to tell Logan. And Paige. Oh my gosh, Paige is gonna fly here like, tomorrow, isn't she?"

My sister smiled. "She might."

Fingers drumming on my leg, I made a split-second decision. "Can I ask you a massive, horrible favor where you don't say a word to any of them?"

"Lia," she said in a warning tone. "You have to tell them.

"I will! Just let me talk to Jude first. I can't handle them all freaking out and asking me what I need and what I'm going to do. I won't have answers to any of their questions."

She conceded with a reluctant nod.

"Thank you. I love you."

"I love you too." She sighed. "Do you want to keep talking?"

"No. I should text him and see if he can get together in the next couple of days."

We said our goodbyes shortly after, and I remained sitting on my bathroom floor for a few minutes longer. How did you even properly try to absorb the magnitude of that discovery?

In one moment, all the choices in my life had shifted, like the clicking letters on a train station arrival board.

My life would quite literally never be the same after this.

Neither would Jude's. I didn't even know if he had any other kids. Or a hidden girlfriend. Or maybe he was crazy. Regardless, he should know. If he chose not to step up, then I gave him the option, and the responsibility was on him.

Funny how being abandoned voluntarily by one of your birth parents colored your judgment on stuff like that. With that thought ... my thumbs flew across the screen.

Me: I'm actually open the next two evenings if you are. I'd love to see your neck of the woods.

Jude responded almost immediately.

Jude: What a very American phrase, but tomorrow evening is free in my 'neck of the woods'. If you're good with eating dinner at my place, I can send you the address.

Me: Send away.

Chapter Eight

JUDE

I NEVER USUALLY GAVE MUCH thought to what someone thought of my house. Usually being the operative word. My house-keeper, Mrs. Atkinson (whose first name was Rebecca, but I never dared called her that), tutted at me all day while I hovered around her, cleaning behind where she'd just done.

"Bloody footballer," she muttered, swatting at me with a dusting thing/weapon. "Go kick something and let me do my job."

"She's never been here, and I like this one. I told you that, right?"

She rolled her eyes. Yes. I'd told her.

If fans of Shepperton FC, the mighty Shorthorns, had any idea that their midfielder's only friend was his fifty-five-year-old housekeeper, they'd piss themselves.

"If you're so concerned with what the young lady thinks," Rebecca said with the patience of a saint and the advice of a bloody therapist, "go to the market and get her some flowers or buy her some chocolates."

While she dusted the rest of the family room, I sat on the large gray couch. "You don't think that's too cliché?"

"If a man bought me flowers and chocolates, I'd spend the night flat on my back without blinking."

Groaning, I covered my face. "Mrs. A, have pity."

She cackled. "Get out of here while I finish, young man. You should go do drills in the garden. The way you were handling the ball on Monday was a tragedy. You're slipping in your old age."

"Et tu?" I asked dryly, standing from the couch. "If I'm old, what does that make you?"

"Well-seasoned and incredibly smart." She eyed me over the edge of her glasses. "Is that what you're wearing?"

I glanced down at my white T-shirt and black trousers. "What?"

"You look like you're going to serve her coffee, not romance her." Rebecca set down the dusting wand. "And that reminds me, are you inviting this nice American girl over here for a quickie?"

I whistled. "Awfully judgy of you, Mrs. Atkinson. Maybe that's why she wants to come." I pointed a finger at her. "Plus, you have no idea. She's nice."

"Oh, she's nice if you've invited her to your home." The dusting resumed. "I've seen some of the tarts you've wandered off with over the years."

"Yes, when I was nineteen and stupid and let my first year of playing go to my head. You know I haven't done that in years." My phone rang, and Lewis's number appeared. I sent it to VM but lifted the screen for her to see. "I'm too busy trying not to lose my bloody job to other big-headed nineteen-year-olds to sleep around anymore. Besides, those tarts don't care as much about you when you're old and your money's gone."

"I know how much you make, young man. It's nowhere near gone."

She was right. Even though I was in the last year of my current contract with Shepperton, my payslip had a lot of zeros on it, and I had every reason to believe that I'd get a renewal for at least a year or two, even if it meant they'd transfer me to another interested team. As long as we could stay in the top tier, at least. Our last two wins helped, moving us a bit higher up the table.

I fucking hated disappearing in the middle.

With a glance at my watch, I stood from the couch. "She'll be here shortly. I suppose I better go change my shirt."

"Smart boy." She paused. "You didn't make her take the train from Oxford, did you?"

"No. She said a neighbor let her borrow her car."

"I'll get out of your hair." She patted my face as she passed. "Use your manners, Jude Michael McAllister. Open doors, pull out chairs, and don't attack her as soon as she walks in, all right? You ask her questions and listen to the answers, treat her like a normal human being."

"As opposed to treating her like a non-human?"

"Don't get smart. You know exactly what I mean. Women aren't vessels created simply for your enjoyment because you get paid millions of pounds to kick a ball around."

I felt only slightly defensive when I answered. "I know that."

While Rebecca put away the last of the cleaning supplies and checked on the dinner she'd popped into the oven, I bounded up the stairs to my bedroom to change. Mine was the biggest room in the house, with large windows overlooking the stretch of green grass in the garden. Smack in the middle was a king-size bed decorated in shades of gray. As I tossed the offending T-shirt into the wash basket, I thought for the thousandth time about the best way to tell Lia about what I did.

It was the part I was least looking forward to. The fact she hadn't recognized me, that she thought I was normal, was a huge part of the appeal.

Football to her meant a choice, something you might like or you might not. And if you didn't like it, you simply chose something else.

Football here was embedded in our lives. It was a culture

running in your bloodstream, not just a match that you flipped to if you were bored. And as a nod to that, given I'd have to admit what I did sooner rather than later, I reached into the wardrobe and grabbed one of my bright blue Shepperton shirts. The logo on the chest was small, so it wasn't like I'd be opening the door wearing a full kit with my name on it.

"Jude," Rebecca called. "You have a visitor."

"Oh shit," I whispered, tugging the shirt on. By the time I reached the bottom of the steps, my entire body felt charged with excitement. No, it wasn't ideal for my housekeeper to be the one greeting her at the door, but she was here, and that was what mattered.

Rebecca said something that made Lia laugh, and the sound of it had me smiling.

They stood by the front door, and in the full light of my home, she was even more beautiful than I remembered. Her hair—which had been long and curling down her back the last I'd seen her—was pulled back off her face.

She was wearing something yellow, but to be honest, I didn't really care what she was wearing.

"Don't let him take credit for the dinner, my dear," Rebecca whispered loudly with a hand on Lia's shoulder. "That's my secret recipe, and he's an absolute disaster in the kitchen."

Lia's eyes met mine, the blue of them so deep it was like a gut punch. She smiled. "Duly noted."

"Goodbye, Mrs. Atkinson," I said. "Have a lovely evening."

Rebecca gave me a warning look, and I knew that even in that brief window of time, she found herself just as charmed by Lia as I had been. "It was wonderful meeting you, dear," she said to Lia.

Lia smiled. "You too."

Rebecca left, closing the door quietly behind her. And it was then I noticed Lia's fingers knitted tightly together in front of her and the high color in her cheeks.

She was nervous.

"Come on in," I told her. "Would you like something to drink? I've got red and white, if you want wine."

Lia tucked a loose strand of hair behind her ear. "I actually wouldn't mind some water, if that's okay. Still or sparkling, doesn't matter."

"Of course."

I went to get her a bottle from the fridge, and from the corner of my eye, I saw her wander around the family room, looking at pictures of me and my brother over the years. She stopped at a small white frame and picked it up.

The photo had been taken years ago, after my first game as a top-tier player. I'd changed and showered, so I wasn't in my gear, but Lewis and I were both grinning widely, showing off our Shepperton shirts. There were no smiling parent pictures along the same vein, so she could look all she wanted for more hints of my family, but she'd not find a single one. Life was complicated, and the idea of trying to tiptoe into that conversation with Lia—about my job or my parents—felt just a little bit impossible.

Knowing what I did, it would change the dynamic between us, and suddenly, I found myself wanting to protect this small piece of reality.

I'd tell her. Eventually.

She set the frame down and met me in the kitchen just as I grabbed a second bottle of water for myself.

"Your house is beautiful," she said.

"Thank you."

"My brother was a professional football player in the States."

I choked on my water.

She kept going as if I hadn't. "He won a championship actually. And now he's the defensive coordinator for the same team."

I rubbed at my chest. "What now?"

Lia shook her head. "I could've explained that better. I'm sorry. I'm more nervous than I thought I'd be."

As carefully as I could, I set the water down, my mind spinning with the strange turn of events.

"I'm telling you because I didn't want you to think I was just ... making fun of soccer for the hell of it. I really don't understand it, and that's not an excuse, but my entire life was centered around Logan's job." Her fingers, long and graceful, started picking at the label on the bottle. "Football, American football, is what I watched every single weekend for my entire life. I grew up watching game film with him while I did my homework at night. I grew up knowing defensive schemes and depth charts and what the spread of each game was, and that was my life because he raised me and my sisters."

Her lips, pink and soft, moved with careful precision as she spoke, and I got the sense she'd practiced every word of what she was telling me right now. The light from the garden caught the side of her face and the length of her neck, and all I could do was stare.

In my silence, she kept speaking. "So basically, I'm trying to apologize if I was rude at the bar for what I said. I know I haven't been here long, but y'all are really protective of your football, and I shouldn't have said it was boring." Her eyes searched mine. "Or the thing I said about flopping on the ground. That was rude too."

Maybe I'd invited Lia because I would've cut my arm off to sleep with her again, but with every word, she dug a strange foothold somewhere behind my chest. If what she said was true —and there was no reason it wasn't—I managed to stumble upon a woman who would know precisely what the insanity of my life could be like. She'd understand every facet because even though the sports were different and the culture was different, there were very few people who didn't play who genuinely realized the level of dedication it took to do what I did. She'd appreciate why I'd bleed myself dry for the game.

I walked closer, and she sucked in a breath at my sudden nearness.

My hands reached out, stilling hers where they fidgeted with the bottle. Her fingers were ice cold.

Lia tilted her chin up. She was taller tonight, probably wearing different shoes, and I found that I very much wanted to see how easily I could kiss her from this angle. I wanted to boost her up onto my kitchen counter and step between her legs so I could press as closely as possible.

I barely knew her. Why did I feel like I did?

"Why are you so nervous?" I asked.

"Well, there's the whole *I'm in a stranger's house* thing, and I still don't know for sure you won't murder me and hide my body."

I grinned, coasting my hands up her arms, then dragging them back down again. "So suspicious."

Lia swallowed, eyes huge on my face. "Are you going to do those things?"

"I wasn't planning to, no."

"Good." While she may not have been touching me back, she allowed me to slide my fingers between hers. The drag of my skin on hers, which was far softer, far smoother, felt dirty somehow. Like we were naked, like we were already in bed. Judging by the flush on her cheeks, she felt it too. "You're not like ... secretly married or something, right?"

My smile was slow. "No wife, no girlfriend."

"Do you like animals?"

"Depends on which kind. Dogs, yes. Cats, sometimes, if they're not trying to claw my eyes out. I have a complicated relationship with sheep because I was raised on a sheep farm. I think fish are pointless, and I am out of my mind terrified of horses."

Lia laughed softly. What was she looking for, as those bottomless eyes searched my face? She looked so serious. What a change from the fiery girl at the pub, pushing and pushing my buttons, simply because she sensed that I enjoyed having them pushed.

I liked her. It was a strange realization to have in the wake of knowing how much I wanted her. But I did. I liked her. I liked that she was asking me simple questions, and that she was sweet to my housekeeper. I even liked the flat way she said her vowels in her American accent.

Her fingers curled tightly around mine, like she was afraid I'd pull away.

That was when I heard myself say, "I play professional football."

Lia's lips curled up at the edges. "I know."

I blinked. "Did you know the night we met?"

She shook her head. "You showed up on my news app when I was in Haworth. When I saw your picture, I dropped my phone on the floor."

"Did you now?" I murmured, slowly tugging her closer. Her face showed no shock, no awe, no clamoring to know more. My entire being relaxed.

She nodded, keeping her eyes trained on my lips. "They used your name in Beatles lyrics."

"Journalists think they're so clever." I tugged one hand free of hers, sliding it over the curve of her waist, then her hips. "I'm sorry I didn't tell you."

Lia laid her hand on my chest, spreading her fingers wide. "When would you have? After I commented on the way players flopped to the ground all the time?"

Chuckling, I exerted the smallest bit of pressure on her hips. "Fair enough."

"Th-there's a lot we didn't share with each other."

Her slight stutter was triggered by my fingers sliding up under the hem of her shirt, where endless miles of smooth skin greeted me.

"Any husbands or boyfriends?" I asked.

Lia shook her head.

"Do you like animals?" My nose sank into her hair, and I inhaled deep into my lungs.

"Mm-hmm."

The timer dinged on the oven. There was a perfectly good dinner in there, probably getting burned to a crisp, but we both ignored it.

"Jude?"

My name on her lips did strange things to me. As I hummed in response to that, my lips ghosted over her downy soft temples.

"I ..." Her voice trailed off when I kissed my way down her cheekbones to the corner of her lips. "Holy shit, you're killing me."

Ducking my head, I sucked her lower lip into my mouth, covering her curves with my palm when her hips tilted toward me.

Here. I'd take her right here the first time. In the kitchen, with the dinner burning and the windows open, and the bright, airy space holding the echo of the sounds she'd make.

Then we could talk all bloody night.

Lia moaned when I did the same thing to her upper lip, soothing the plump pinkness of her mouth with my tongue when I pulled away.

"I'm taking my time with you tonight, love." Fuck, I sounded like a madman, like I'd chewed gravel and knives and acid.

"Jude?"

"Mmm?" I nipped at the edge of her jaw, and she sucked in a sharp breath.

Her hand pushed at my chest, and I backed away to look at her face.

Lia licked her lips, hitting me with the full force of her blue eyes. "I'm pregnant."

Chapter Nine

JUDE

It wasn't until I slammed my fifth door of the morning that someone finally called me on my piss-poor attitude.

"All right," Declan growled, shoving me with his meaty paw, "that's enough. If you don't quit slamming all the bloody doors, I'm going to rip your hands off."

I shrugged him off. "I haven't slammed *all* of them."

As our teammates passed us, all headed for the showers or the weight room, I got more than one side-eye.

Declan crossed his arms over his chest and pinned me with his patented *Team Captain stare*. "You made one of the physios cry."

"My knee is fine. He didn't need to go poking and prodding at it without being asked."

"And the new assistant?"

I was clenching my teeth so hard they had to be close to cracking. "I didn't *mean* to hit him in the head with the ball, obviously."

Declan sighed, rubbing the bridge of his nose. "McAllister, you have about ten seconds to tell me what your problem is so you can stop taking it out on the rest of us. We've got enough to deal with right now without you making it worse."

I sank against the wall and stared at the glossy blue and white paint opposite me. I'd spent the best years of my career walking this hallway, staring at those colors and a logo that defined me. No matter what else was happening in my life, I knew who I was the moment I entered this arena.

And today, I didn't recognize any of it. Hardly recognized myself.

He groaned. "This is going to take longer than ten seconds, isn't it?"

"Probably," I admitted with a sideways glance. "You sure you want to hear this? We're not exactly best mates."

"We're not." His massive shoulders shrugged lightly. Declan was big for a goalie and took up so much bloody space, but he still managed to be quick enough. "But we've got a young team this year, and they look up to you. You're the one with your name in the lights, the one who gets to stand in the corner, arms spread wide, listening to the screaming fans when you score. They want to be you, but they'd also take your spot away from you in a heartbeat if you fuck it up for yourself."

The look I gave him was dry, but after five years of playing with him, I knew Dec's style of encouragement pretty well.

"My point is, if you've got something bleeding into your performance, you better figure it out. Because the second you take it onto the pitch, you've got a problem. And you are too valuable to this team for that to happen. I never thought it was something I'd need to worry about prior to today."

"It was one bad practice after a pretty ... life-altering evening."

"Tell me."

I cut him a look. "Can you pretend to have manners for two seconds?"

His steady gaze was what I got in answer, rather than a *please* tacked onto his gruffly spoken command.

Someone on the coaching staff passed us with a murmured greeting, and after he passed, I gestured to an empty pressroom so we could have some privacy. Declan preceded me in, sprawling out in a black desk chair.

"Oh, bleeding hell, he's shutting doors and everything," Declan murmured. "That bad?"

Bracing my back against the door, I stared blankly at the opposite wall for a minute. What I saw there was Lia's face, drained of all color, when I responded to her bombshell with ... well ... not very much tact.

"A few weeks ago," I started slowly, "I was in London to meet with my agent and stopped at my brother's pub. Met a girl." Closing my eyes, I tried to imagine again how easy it had been between us that night. How easy it had been those first few moments she was at my place. "American, studying at Oxford for Michaelmas. Had no idea who I was."

"You sure?"

I nodded. It was a fair question, and one I'd asked myself more than once since Lia stormed out of my house the night before. "It was one night. She left her number, and we messaged a few times but couldn't find time to meet up again until last night."

Declan's chest expanded on a deep inhale. He knew something was coming. Something was always hanging in the balance when guys in our positions slept around indiscriminately. We'd seen various types of fallout for years. Men cheating on wives, or girlfriends with groupies or prostitutes, the women going to the paps with their sordid tales.

"She came over last night for dinner, and we made no plans beyond that. Everything was fine—better than fine—at first. Then she told me she was pregnant."

That brought his chin up slightly, his eyes carefully assessing. "And what did you say?"

"I …" My throat worked on a hard swallow. "I asked her why she was telling me."

Declan pursed his mouth.

I held up a hand. "I know, not my best moment, but clearly,

I wasn't expecting her to say that. We used protection. I'm not stupid."

"It might not have beeen particularly well-delivered, but it's a fair question in our position. People lie about all sorts of things for money."

What a diplomatic answer. Which was why I winced when I told him what I told him next.

"I don't think that's why she blew up at me," I said, scratching the back of my neck.

"She doesn't like money?"

"More like, I don't believe she needs it." My hand dropped from my neck. "Know the name Logan Ward? American football."

His head tilted. "Sounds familiar, but I can't place it."

"Won a championship with the Washington Wolves about ten years back, give or take. Now he's the defensive coach."

Declan nodded. "And?"

"Lia, that's her name, is Logan's younger sister."

Understanding dawned. "Please tell me you didn't know that before you said what you said." The loaded silence answered for me, and Declan cursed under his breath. "McAllister, you arsehole."

"I didn't know anything about him, about their family, when she dropped this bomb on me. So no, I shouldn't have said what I said, but it's not like I ever expected her to say *that*. I met her once, spent half a dozen hours around her, and most of those were spent sleeping." It felt like the weight of the entire building was pushing my shoulders down. Kids, a family, a wife were all things I'd thought about in the abstract. Always coming below the rest of the priorities I had in front of me.

When I win a league cup and hoist it up in my hands ... then I'd think about settling down.

When I prove I didn't waste my life on something frivolous and shallow, like my parents always believed ... then I'd focus on my own private life.

When ...

When ...

When ...

A dozen things came before it because it wasn't something I missed. I didn't lay awake at night wishing for someone beside me. I laid awake at night thinking about how I could keep my life and my career going in the right direction.

Staying away from women who only wanted me for my money, for my job was easy.

"When she said she was pregnant, all I could see was head-lines and solicitors and DNA tests and soap opera bullshit I never signed up for. And how bloody angry I'd be if we came to the end of it, and she lied because I was a better target."

Declan studied me quietly. This was part of how he worked, though. He listened well, and he listened to what we didn't say. Those were the best listeners, weren't they? They were the ones who heard all the important things in the spaces of silence.

"It's not like I had time to think through exactly what it meant that she was raised in the world of sports. That the man who raised her was an elite athlete. All I thought—at the time she told me about her brother—was she understands this crazy. And right on the heels of that, she tells me she's preggers. It being mine, Declan, it didn't even register at first."

He grimaced. "And her reaction?"

I exhaled. "She told me to get fucked, started crying, then stormed off. The way she slammed my front door gave my performance today a run for my money."

"So you both have a temper then."

"Apparently."

Declan leaned forward, bracing his elbows on his thighs, hands clasped together, and pinned me with a serious look. "Do you think she's lying about it being yours?"

Pinching the bridge of my nose, I closed my eyes tightly and conjured an image of her face.

Nerves first, as I tried to kiss her.

Resolve next, as she pushed me away to say the words. Disbelief. The widening of her eyes.

Hurt. The pinch of her brows.

Then rage. I'd seen fireworks explode with less glittering anger than I saw behind Lia's blue, blue eyes.

In the span of only a few moments, I saw so many different sides to her—this woman who was still a stranger for all intents and purposes. A stranger in a country that wasn't her own, by herself.

I dropped my hand and looked at Declan. "No. I don't think she's lying."

"Then fix it, you git." He stood. "See what she needs and take care of it."

I must've had a blank look on my face because he rolled his eyes.

"Does she need to see a doctor? Does she have the vitamins she needs? Is she living in a safe place? Does she want to keep it? Bloody hell, McAllister, you're thirty-one years old. Grow a pair, call her, and make it right."

He slapped me on the back and shoved me sideways, so he could leave the room.

I pulled out my mobile.

Me: I'm sorry. I was an arse. I'm done with practice, and I'd love to chat if you have a minute.

My phone started ringing in my hand, Lia's name appearing in large letters across the screen. My heart leaped into my throat as I answered.

"Hello?"

She was quiet.

"Lia?"

"Yeah. I'm here."

I sank against the wall again. "I need to apologize for how I reacted last night. I was a total arse."

"Yes, you were." She sighed heavily. "But ... I shouldn't have stormed off either. I guess the insinuation that I was lying didn't ... sit well with me." Before I could open my mouth, she interrupted. "And I know, I know why you're cautious. But that's why I told you about Logan first. I'd never ever take advantage of someone because of what they do."

"I know," I told her. "The truth is, Lia, we don't know each other. At all."

"We're kinda going about this backward, huh?"

I smiled. "A bit."

"Can we, I don't know, meet for coffee? Or tea?"

"That sounds like a very smart, adult decision for us to make."

Lia laughed, and the sound of it, after the past twenty-four hours, finally felt like I was doing something right. It was okay to have my priorities shift, no matter how the conversation went with her or how she wanted to handle it.

"I'm open tomorrow, if you are."

"Why don't we meet somewhere in London? Bit of a happy medium for both of us."

"You can do that without being ... I don't know ... mobbed?"

It was my turn to laugh. "Yes. In Shepperton, I get recognized far more often than I do when I'm in London. Sometimes a fan will approach, but it's not common."

"That's kinda how it was for my brother too," she said. "We actually had a pretty normal life growing up, considering what he did."

She was an anomaly, and I found that I quite liked it.

Not only that, but I still had to wrap my head around the fact she was pregnant, and it was mine.

Suddenly, I wanted to tell her that. Offer some olive branch to this woman who I didn't exactly know very well.

"I can't get over it," I admitted quietly. "To be honest, Lia, I've never given it much thought. Having kids."

She exhaled audibly. "I know what you mean. I'm only

twenty-two, Jude. This wasn't in the cards for me for a very long time."

I closed my eyes. Young, especially compared to me, hardly past the cusp of truly feeling like an adult.

"Lia," I said, "we'll figure this out together, yeah?"

Through the speaker, she sniffed quietly. "Yeah."

Chapter Ten

LIA

THE THINGS I knew about Jude Michael McAllister could fit on my pinky finger. At least, for the time being.

You're going to be a baby daddy- take two was already off to a better start as I sat across a tiny table in a tiny cafe, watching him wolf down that English breakfast thing I loved.

Add that to the list of things I knew:

-Jude could eat an entire meal in four bites.

-He looked great in a black knit hat.

-He took his tea with one sugar.

And so far on take two, he hadn't accused me of trying to pass off another man's baby as his.

"Are you not hungry?" he asked, eyeing my plate. "Do you feel all right?"

It was a graveyard of the poor croissant that I'd picked at, and the scone that had gotten similar treatment.

Which was a sad thing, because carbs were my jam in pregnancy.

I sat back and gave him an appraising look. "I feel okay. Morning sickness tends to hit me in the afternoon, but it's only happened a couple of times. When it did, I kinda thought maybe I hadn't eaten enough or wasn't drinking enough water."

He nodded.

The owner of the cafe ducked under the counter and swept away some of the trash from our table. "Will you loves be needing anything else?"

"I'm fine, thank you," I said, smiling up at her.

"Thanks, Sheila," Jude told her. "Maybe just a bit of privacy while we chat, if you don't mind."

He slid her some cash, and she patted him gently on the shoulder before dashing off to flip the closed sign on the door. "I'm just going to pop over to the market for a few things. Be back in a tick."

As she slid out of the door and jogged down the steps, I watched her tuck the cash Jude had given her into the cup of a vagrant sleeping curled around his dog at the end of the block.

"She's nice."

Jude nodded. "She gave my brother, Lewis, his first kitchen job years ago."

"Is that your only sibling?" I thought of the picture in the flat, the man who looked so much like Jude.

"It is. The pub where we met, I helped him buy it after I started playing. He wanted a place to call his own."

My eyebrows popped up. "That's a generous gift."

Jude shot me a rueful smile, showing just the slightest hint of a dimple in his scruff-covered jaw. "It was. We grew up on a sheep farm, actually. And neither of us particularly warmed to that life, so I thought I'd help him take a different path." He took a sip of his tea. "What about you? Brothers or sisters?" At my immediate, wide smile, Jude laughed. "Is that a loaded question?"

"No. Well, maybe." I set my chin on my hand and took a deep breath. "Claire is my twin sister. Isabel is two years older than us. Molly is two years older than Isabel. Logan, who is actually my half-brother, is the one who raised us from the time I was ten. And his son Emmett, with his wife Paige, is technically my nephew, but he also feels like my brother, because I'm closer in age to him than I am to Logan."

Jude's jaw was all but unhinged by the time I finished. "That's not a family, that's a bloody army."

I laughed. "It's ... chaos. I love it."

"Do they know?" he asked quietly.

The laughter dried up in my throat, an ache welling immediately behind my chest, like he'd turned on a faucet with his words. "Just Claire. I wanted to talk to you first."

"I'm so sorry I reacted the way I did, Lia." He leaned forward and pinned me with those green eyes. So green that I felt that same swirly feeling in my belly that I did when I met him. When he started kissing me in his kitchen before his stupid mouth and my stupid temper ruined the moment. "It's not an excuse, but it was one of those moments where—because I'd never even given it much thought, having kids, you know—my reaction caught even me off guard. If that makes sense," he added.

"It does. I think I suffered from the same problem." I covered my hot cheeks. "I've never told anyone to get fucked in my entire life."

He laughed, a large, booming sound born from somewhere deep in his broad chest. Oh, that sound set off a series of sparks that should have worried me. Lack of chemistry was not our problem.

It was part of why I reacted the way I did in his kitchen, I came to realize later. The flame between us had simmered the entire time I was separate from Jude. All it took was being in the same room, and my skin went incendiary. It's a terribly helpless feeling, if you think about it. When someone has the power to make you feel that way simply by existing, it's deeply unsettling at first. And my reaction to it—that tidal wave crashing over my head—was to draw my weapons as quickly as he'd drawn his.

He folded his big hands on the table. "What do you want to do next, Lia? Where can I help?"

What I wanted to do next was ask him not to say my name like that, all British and hot. Despite all odds, and some patchy birth control taking, he'd impregnated me with his super sperm, so hearing my name on his lips made me feel like warm putty.

"I guess ... I guess I need to know if you want to help. If you *want* to be in this with me."

It was the last thing I wanted to ask, but parental abandonment issues were a bit of a hot spot for me. For all my sisters.

Our dad, much older than our mom, died of a heart attack when we were young. I hardly remembered him; other than pictures I'd seen. But our mom decided one day that being a single parent of four after her golden meal ticket was gone just wasn't something she wanted anymore. Brooke had dumped us on Logan's front porch, and in truth, it was the best thing she could have done for me and my sisters. Logan, and later, his wife, Paige, gave us the family we had now. They were my people—the small army, as Jude had put it—who would always have my back.

And just like me, they'd never allow for a child—my child— to be treated as a prop for someone's vanity.

So, if Jude didn't want to play Daddy, he better speak the hell up now before this kid came out.

"I do want to be in this," he said. "I reckon I've got time to wrap my head around it, eh?"

I gave him a smile. "Yeah."

Neither of us brought up the fact that my life was on the opposite side of the world. Or that we'd need legal agreements up the wazoo, due to the nature of his job. That someday, we'd need custody agreements and child support discussions.

All the thoughts made my stomach seize up uncomfortably.

With two hands, I mentally shoved all that shit down.

"Do you need to see a doctor?" he asked.

I blinked. "I don't know, actually. I did some googling, but I can't tell if I qualify for the NHS free coverage since I'm only visiting for a semester."

"I'll make a call."

His calm assurance was enough to steady my stomach and bubbling nerves at all the unknowns. And when we said our goodbyes outside of Sheila's cafe, he walked me back to the Tube station with a promise that someone would contact me.

It set the precedent, a small step in the right direction of how the next couple of weeks unfolded. I didn't see him because his game schedule was packed (apparently they had like ... forty different cup tournaments they played in outside of regular league play. Don't even ask me because I was still trying to understand).

Me: Okay, I'll concede that penalty shootouts are exciting. WAY better than a tie. You have to admit those are stupid.

Me: Nice goal, BTW. I like how you faked out the goalie.

Jude: Those are the rules, love. That's why the points matter.

Me: Yeah, what's up with that too? You can like, get DEMOTED. Y'all are savage.

Jude: That's what makes it exciting. I'll convert you yet.

Jude: How was the appointment with the doctor?

Me: Good. It's too early to hear the heartbeat or do an ultrasound or anything, so we just went over good eating and talked about morning sickness and stuff. She took all my vitals. My blood pressure was a little high, though.

Jude: Was it? Is that normal for you?

Me: Well, I was afraid to touch anything because the office was so FREAKING fancy, and also, I'm pretty sure I saw Victoria Beckham in there. Or her doppelganger. Did you send me to the nicest doctor in England or something?

Jude: I asked our team doctor for a rec. They said they'd send me the bill, yeah?

Me: No one asked me for a single penny. Or a pound. Whatever.

Me: I do have money, though. I don't expect you to pay for everything.

Jude: Sorry, had to go into training and then meet with my manager.

Me: Running into a meeting with my professor. She's about to rip my outline to shreds.

Jude: No worries. Maybe we can connect next week?

Me: My turn to apologize. This week has been crazy. I was right about the outline.

Jude: What does that mean? You start over?

Me: No, I just need to dig deeper.

Jude: Will I understand your answer if I ask what you're diving deeper into?

Me: Charlotte Brontë's educational and employment history and how it influenced the conceptual presence of female independence in her work.

Jude: Right then.

Me: Basically, she hated her job and wrote about it because she hated that other women were forced into the same situations.

Jude: Makes sense.

Me: Why are there no commercial breaks in soccer? Football. Whatever. It's not good for people who need to pee all the time.

Me: I waited as long as I could and then missed your goal. THERE SHOULD BE COMMERCIALS.

Jude: Why do you think American corporations don't push football? They can't make as much money off us because we actually let people play the game.

Me: Okay, okay, I walked into that one.

Claire: IF YOU DON'T TELL OUR FAMILY SOON, I'M GONNA LOSE MY MIND, LIA. I almost slipped today with Isabel. We were working out and I swear, if she hadn't been at work and easily distracted, she would've pushed me on it.

Me: I know. Don't yell at me.

Me: Logan and Paige will want to make me come home. And I want to finish the semester.

Claire: Le sigh. I get it. BUT COME ON. You're asking a lot of me here. I did tell Bauer, though. *hides face*

Me: I figured you would. You're a terrible liar.

Me: I'll tell them soon.

Claire: Define soon.

Me: SOON. Go make out with Bauer or something.

Claire: How are you feeling? Is Jude being nice?

Me: Tired, but good. I puked in an Oxford trash can the other day, and you should've seen the faces of the people who passed me. One called me a "drunk American" under her breath. LOL.

Me: And yes. We've just been texting this week and last. He's BUSY. Did you know football players can play 3+ matches in a week here? That's friggin' nuts!

Claire: OMG, ARE YOU CONVERTED NOW?

Me: I'm just ... learning. But it's not as bad as I thought. It's kinda hypnotizing to watch. Plus ... Have you SEEN their thighs??

Claire: No, but you sure have.

Me: DAMN RIGHT. <3

Isabel: Claire said something weird today about you not being able to do kickboxing class when you come home. Then she made her weird 'I'm hiding something' face.

Isabel: WHAT THE HELL IS GOING ON.

Me: I'll call soon! Sorry, it's been crazy here. Love you. Mwah.

Isabel: Don't think I don't know what you're doing. Can I still come and visit before you leave? I need a reason to take a vacation.

Me: Yes. Talk soon. <3

Paige: WHY AREN'T YOU ANSWERING YOUR CALLS, DUDE

Me: YOU ALWAYS CALL WHEN I'M BUSY. Does everyone in our family have their phone on caps lock or something?

Paige: Sorry. I miss you. I miss your voice. When are you coming home? Haven't you gotten enough knowledge yet?

Me: You have three other sisters to pester. And Emmett. Go bug them.

Paige: I love you too, L.

Me: <3

Jude: Care to come to a match this weekend?

Me: Like ... in person? In the stands with all the crazy screaming fans?

Jude: That's the general idea. I could give you a pass if you'd rather sit in a box.

Me: No way. I love the crazy screaming fans. I never wanted Logan's box passes either. Box seats are for pansies.

Jude: That a girl. I'll put the tickets under your name at the window by the main entrance. Make sure you wear blue and white; otherwise, they'll make you switch seats because they'll think you're a Bethnal Green fan. Trust me, you don't want that. They're wankers.

Me: You cannot be serious.

Jude: I would never joke about it. They don't mix home and away fans.

Me: Y'all are crazy.

Jude: I'll see you afterward.

Me: <3

Me: SHIT, sorry, didn't mean to send you a heart. I do that with my sisters and Paige and ... sorry. Awkward.

Jude: No worries.

Jude: <3 (It took me a really long time to figure out how you did that)

Chapter Eleven

JUDE

"YOU SEEMED FRUSTRATED OUT THERE, Jude. What did you want more of today that you weren't getting?"

What I wanted was to smack the microphone out of my face, but I smiled at the journo. "A bit more of everything, I suppose. We were outplayed, and there's no pretty way to say that. They passed better, defended better, scored more. Makes it hard to win."

"Do you think Shepperton can pull themselves together once the break is done? Or do you need to see some changes on the roster when the transfer window opens? There's talk that management is eyeing some younger talent heading into the rest of the season."

I kept that smile pasted on my face until it hurt. "I think we've got a great team right now. We've just got to communicate better when it counts. If the management makes some changes this winter, then I trust they'll do what's best for the club." I nodded, then started edging toward the door of the room. "Thanks."

He wanted to ask more, it was obvious, but honestly, I wasn't much in the mood for talking.

It was a shit game in shit weather, and all I wanted to do was take a hot shower.

Everything had set up perfectly in the eighty-ninth minute when I got the ball and had a free stretch to run.

But instead of a win, instead of a draw, we went in the wrong direction. That Bethnal Green keeper was a lucky bastard because the one finger he'd gotten on the ball was enough to keep us from a draw. They got three points and moved ahead of Arsenal on the table. We stayed where we were. Like a bloody car that couldn't get out of neutral.

I left the press room and hooked a right toward the showers. One of my newer teammates, an acquisition from Paris St Germain, murmured something in French as he passed. It sounded an awful lot like he was calling me a name that I never would've dared to repeat in front of Mrs. Atkinson. Declan exited another press area and lifted his chin.

"You looked like shit today, McAllister."

I gave him a look. "How in the bloody hell they decided you should be captain is beyond me."

"Because I'm not going to tiptoe around your ego to make you feel better." He crossed his arms over his chest. "I can admit where I fucked up today. Can you?" When I didn't answer, he lowered his voice. "You had someone right behind you who could've taken the ball, could've come at the goal from the side, and instead, you went for the glory shot. It's not always your job to save the day just because you're trying to prove you can still play."

"I'll remember that the next time I get a perfect shot," I said dryly.

"If you get the shot, then take it. But that wasn't it. You were too far away from the goal, you didn't have the right angle, and you were running too fast to bend it the way you would've needed. But if you'd passed to Sebastien, he would've had it."

Pride had me wanting to defend myself, and I fairly choked

on the words as I swallowed them back down. "Is that why he's calling me names?"

"Probably." His eyes never wavered. "Pull your head out of your arse, Jude. I mean it."

His words rang in my head while I showered and changed. None of my teammates talked to me, all murmuring quietly after the dejection of another loss when we really needed a win.

In the quiet of the locker room, the heavy weight of a loss felt like all the balls I'd kept juggled in the air were falling one by one.

Maybe it was like this for other players, but I'd never ask. For me, losing felt like unleashing a screaming banshee that tailed behind me until our next game. All I could hear were the things my parents had warned me about when I was an eighteen-year-old, giving up my life to play in Germany.

Why can't you just be content with a normal life?

Why can't you be proud of the work we do and help us contribute in a way that means something?

It's vain. Frivolous.

Playing games doesn't keep the world turning.

Every single time we lost, every single time someone hinted that I wasn't valuable anymore, I felt like my parents were watching, nodding their heads because they were right all along.

I sighed. Most games, I never even thought about looking up in the stands, even on the odd game that Lewis came to, because it was simply another reminder of how my family didn't understand me, didn't see exactly what I had accomplished in my life. Those empty seats in my mind lit every fire underneath me. And today, they hadn't all been empty.

Not once, in all my years of playing, had I walked out of a loss with someone waiting for me. There was no telling how she'd react or try to handle me, so I braced myself for whatever it might be. I braced myself to see how she'd react, this girl I was supposed to be getting to know.

When I left the room, I stopped short in the doorway,

because across the hallway was Lia, waiting for me with a smile and beautifully flushed face.

"Hi." I sounded like an idiot.

Her smile spread even further. "That was so freaking fun."

My head tilted. "We lost."

"I know, but ... oh man, you know how long it's been since I've been at a game? Any game?" She laid a hand on her chest. "There is nothing like the energy in the stands. And holy shit, you were not kidding about the fans. I heard curse words I didn't even know existed."

What a balm she was to all the frayed, edgy parts of me left-over from the game. Not because she was trying to soothe me, but because she saw the beauty in it, even with the loss.

We fell in step as I walked us toward the exit to the car park. Her shoulder brushed mine.

I stopped. "You're soaked."

"It was raining out there," she whispered, like she was telling me a secret.

My face felt hot. "Obviously. But that can't be good for you."

She waved that off. "Dude, I'm from Seattle. Rain don't scare me."

As Lia started walking, I couldn't help but marvel. Her hair was a frizzy mess, barely contained on top of her head, she'd sat through that disastrous 1-0 defeat in the cold, bone-soaking rain, and she was acting like I'd handed her a winning lottery ticket.

"Who *are* you?" I asked.

Her smile was sweet. "Isn't that what you're trying to figure out? Who I am while I'm trying to figure out who you are." She shrugged, as if it was so simple.

And maybe it was.

Maybe I was the one complicating it.

Everything in my life was complicated, though, except her. And that was the strangest part of all. I didn't exactly know where I stood with her, but suddenly, it felt desperately impor-tant for her to be the one thing I should do right.

My team lost, probably because I was being a selfish arsehole.

But this was something I could do.

"Are you hungry?" I asked her.

"Yes." Lia clasped her hands in front of her. "I'm not saying I'd murder someone for some fries right now, but I'd seriously hurt them."

"Chips."

"Hmm?"

I set my hand on her back, steering her back toward the exit. "They're called chips, love. And if you're okay with coming back to my place for a do-over, I will make you the best bloody sandwich of your entire life."

Lia stopped walking and pointed a finger at me. "Do we need ground rules for being alone in a house together?"

"I don't know. Do we?"

Clearly, she'd expected me to give her an actual answer. Lia blinked a few times.

I laughed. "Tell you what, if we make a promise to each other that tonight, clothes stay on ... would that make you feel like we're being responsible?"

She started walking, a tiny smile on her lips. "Just for tonight, we promise that?"

"For a start."

Lia nodded. "I like it. Let's make our own rules, McAllister. After you make me an epic sandwich."

Close to an hour later, she was curled up on the corner of my couch, chin resting on her tucked-up knees, watching me with expectant eyes.

Before I set the plate down, I pointed at her. "No judgment until you try it."

"I promise," she answered solemnly.

Lia had changed into one of my Shepperton hoodies while her shirt was in the dryer, and it positively dwarfed her slim frame. She made a show of shoving the sleeves up while I set the plate in her lap.

Her hands froze. "What the hell is that?"

"You said you wouldn't judge."

"There's bread covering my fries." She blinked. "Why is there bread covering my fries?"

"Chips." I handed her a napkin. "This is a chip butty. Buttered bread and chips."

"Oh my gosh, *why?*"

"You promised." I plopped next to her on the couch. "And I'd hate to think you'd lie to me, now that we're making our own rules."

She grumbled something unintelligible under her breath that had me smiling. It felt good to smile over something so simple. When was the last time I'd done that? I smiled all the time about scoring goals and winning games, but that was it.

Doing something so simple for someone and having it bring me joy was such a novel sensation.

Lia gave me a side-eye as she lifted the sandwich.

She took a bite and chewed.

Her eyes fell closed.

Her entire body sagged.

And then she moaned.

I had to shift on the couch because the last time I heard that sound, I was fairly certain my hand had been between her legs.

"Ohmygawd," she said. Another bite. "Why is thi so goob?"

I laughed. "Are you going to share?"

Her eyes narrowed. "You'd get in the way of a pregnant woman and her cravings?"

My arm found its way along the back of the couch, my fingers draped just to the outside of her shoulder, and the length of her hair tickled my arm. "No," I murmured. "I reckon I wouldn't as long as you look that happy."

Lia finished chewing another bite, swallowed delicately

before she set the plate down. "Are you giving me flirty eyes, Jude McAllister?"

"You tell me," I murmured.

Instead of answering, she took another bite, lips curled in a smile.

My fingers tugged lightly on her hair. "I don't quite know what to do with you, Lia Ward, and that's the truth."

Her cheeks flushed a lovely soft pink, and I took the moment of quiet to snatch the rest of her chip butty off the plate.

"Oh, you ass!" She laughed, leaning forward to grab it. I was too quick, though, devouring the rest of the sandwich with one massive bite. Before she could resume her original position, I tugged on her arm as I fell backward on the couch.

Quite naturally, she landed tucked against my side with my arm curled around her shoulder. Her head fit perfectly into the crook of my neck, and I inhaled a deep lungful of her clean, wonderful scent. There was no change to Lia's body, it was far too early for that, and maybe this type of thing was the worst bloody idea I'd ever had, but it felt right.

"We went from hypothetical flirty eyes to cuddling very quickly," she said, finger tracing circles on my chest.

"That we did." I closed my eyes. When was the last time I'd felt this bone-deep sense of rightness anywhere other than the pitch? I was always moving, always going, always driving myself forward to fix or do or work.

Rarely did I get quiet moments of peace. The thought of ending this particular one seemed like a crime.

I barely knew her. She didn't know me any better. Yet we'd agreed we could make our own rules. And why shouldn't we?

I wasn't going to ignore how singularly perfect it felt, doing something as simple as lying on the couch with her. Admitting that, though, seemed too fast. Like she could travel along with the strange thread of my thoughts, Lia set her chin on my chest and pinned me with those eyes. Did she even realize what a weapon they were? What damage they were capable of?

My free hand traced the line of her jaw, the edge of my thumb lightly glancing along the bottom edge of her lip. What would she do if I tugged her closer and sipped at those perfectly soft, perfectly pink lips? In the growing warmth I could see on her cheeks, I had my answer. In the reaction of my body, I had clear proof of my desire. And it would be easy, wouldn't it?

But this ... I'd let her edge her toe over the line if she wanted to cross it.

That was when she inhaled shakily and set her face back down on my chest.

Right then.

I closed my eyes and willed the lower half of my body to get the fuck on board.

Voice light and easy, I tried my very best to play it off. "My body is far too tired to move you off me, though, if that's all right with you."

She sighed, her rib cage expanding underneath my palm and spread fingers.

In that sigh, I felt her hesitation to ask any further questions, and truth be told, I wasn't sure I'd know how to answer.

"I could take a nap." With that, her finger stopped its movement, and when I glanced down, I saw the fan of her long, black lashes fall closed.

Settling further into that sense of rightness, paired with a refusal to look too far into what we were doing, I allowed myself to do the same.

Chapter Twelve

LIA

HAVE you ever woken up with deja vu?

I've done this before.

Not the sleeping on Jude's couch part. My back ached, and his couldn't be any better, but there we were.

Sprawled on top of his insane body, as the sun crept into the sky, I once again woke up with all my important bits touching all of his.

My leg hitched up over the top of his thigh, like I'd unconsciously tried to hump him in my sleep.

My hand had crept underneath the hem of his shirt, and I couldn't help but smile at the placement of my fingers. Apparently, embedded underneath the skin of my fingertips was a homing beacon for his happy trail because that line of hair and the soft, warm, heavily muscled skin around it had my toes curling from how badly I wanted to explore.

All of him, from the top of his dark-haired head down to his very big and very proportionate feet, was like a freaking jungle gym, and it was hard not to want to play on all the parts when I woke up like this.

Making tiny movements so as not to wake him, I turned my nose further into his chest and inhaled deeply. Was it a pregnancy hormone thing? That he smelled like crack and Christmas and cinnamon rolls and everything good that I wanted to hoard to my greedy little chest. The feeling that came with his scent, clean and masculine, was something I wanted to cling to with both hands.

It made me realize just how much I missed the easy affection of my family. The hugs. The playful shoving. Wrestling with Emmett. Someone sitting behind me and braiding my hair while we talked in Logan and Paige's kitchen. There had never been a time in my life when I'd gone so long without someone to clutch me tight in a hug or rub my back while I talked.

Just as I had the night before, I set my chin on his chest and studied his face.

It was stupid how handsome he was.

It was also stupid how much I wanted to wake him up and ride him until his eyes rolled back in his head. Maybe not *stupid* because we'd said we'd make our own rules for how this was going to play out, but the impulse certainly came with complications.

A subpar, clinical word for that little, teeny baby inside me (roughly the size of a raspberry, according to Sir Google). Sometimes, if my brain started racing too far ahead into the future—to all the unanswered questions waiting patiently for me to answer—my hands started shaking, and I felt very much like I was standing over a dark pit where I couldn't see what waited for me at the bottom.

It might've been a feather bed made of unicorns and sparkles, and I'd land with a gentle bounce.

Or it was something scarier, something bigger that I didn't want to face, and every single time, I backed away from the edge of that pit with a speed that should've scared me.

What if I wasn't good at this?

Oh, that whispered thought was enough to send a slow trickle of ice down my spine.

Would the slight vibration in my limbs wake him?

Could I distract him if it did?

Lurid images danced behind my closed eyes of all the ways I could do that, but I shoved them back. In my clearer moments, when I didn't feel like I was avoiding some big shadowy unknown, I knew better than to dive headfirst into the physical chemistry I felt with Jude. Like the night before when all he did was touch the lower edge of my lips.

Had that reduced me to a throbbing, achy mess? Yes.

Did it solve any of our problems? Nope. (My inner hormone queen who wanted to climb him like a tree pouted very much at that.)

With a resolve I didn't know I had, I carefully extracted my hand out from underneath his shirt, bidding a fond farewell to his happy trail. Jude didn't stir, which was a good thing. If he'd woken, voice all low and rough and calling me *love*, I would've stripped in five seconds flat.

But he was out.

As I eased my way toward the other side of the couch so I could get up, I remembered Logan being the same way after game day. Especially a loss.

The mental toll was massive on my brother, and I wondered if Jude was the same way. Not all athletes were. They could leave their wins and losses and mistakes on the confines of the field. The leaders weren't like that, though.

As I tiptoed into the kitchen, Logan weighing on my brain, I realized how much of my discomfort stemmed from not just missing family but something else entirely. I was withholding the truth from them because it was easier. Somehow, without all their eyes on me, I felt I could skate seamlessly through the hard.

I found my phone in my purse, battery dangerously low considering I hadn't plugged it in the night before, and I saw a text from Claire that had me smiling.

Claire: If you think I didn't notice that your Find my Friends location stayed in Shepperton last night,

you're friggin' crazy. ARE YOU SLEEPING WITH HIM AGAIN? The stupid happy in love side of me is dying for details.

Claire: Also, I'm gonna give you a deadline for telling everyone because I saw Finn and almost slipped again and HAVE I MENTIONED I'M BAD AT LYING.

Me: Not sleeping with him, though we did sleep last night. Just sleep. They lost their match and he had that "I'm a big tough athlete and I bear the mental burden of the team's poor performance" face (you know the one) and the cuddling that happened after was not planned, trust me. He made me a french fry sandwich, and it just … happened.

Claire: I do know that face. Good morning.

Me: It's late there, why are you up??? Good morning. I miss you.

Claire: I miss you too. Working on some curriculum stuff for a new reading program at the youth center, and I didn't want to stop. I'm off tomorrow and can sleep. Did you really just sleep? (I'm giving you the serious eyes)

Me: Yes. Fully clothed cuddling. He wanted to kiss me, though.

Claire: And you resisted? I'm impressed. I DO know that face, and it's potent. Bauer had that face after he fell in one of his last competitions. I shocked myself a bit with what I was willing to do to make it go away when we got home. There were props involved.

Me: OMG STOP. Don't want to know.

Claire: Lia, seriously, when are you going to tell them? You've known you're pregnant for weeks. Don't be afraid of their reactions, okay? They love you. Everyone here just wants what's best for you. And don't be afraid of what comes next. That's what family is for. We'll help you.

Sitting at Jude's table, I stared at my phone and marveled over the fact that she could see through me, even this far away. There was comfort in that consistency, even if it still terrified me to try to figure out what came next.

"Good morning," Jude grumbled, walking into the kitchen with a slight smile on his face. "Coffee? Tea?"

"Coffee would be great."

He paused in the act of opening a cupboard. "You're okay to drink it?"

I nodded. "A cup or two won't hurt anything."

"Right."

He measured the grounds and added water to a very normal-looking coffee maker, the kind I used in my apartment back in Seattle.

My old apartment, I mentally corrected. The one that wasn't waiting for me when I came back. That pit opened up again, and I kicked it closed in my mind.

"You were smiling awfully big for someone who hasn't had caffeine yet," he said.

"I was texting Claire."

"That's your twin sister, right?" he asked.

"Yeah." When I sighed, he chuckled under his breath. "I miss her," I admitted.

"That'll happen."

While I watched him move around his kitchen with such

ease, I tucked my knees up against my chest and thought of all the things I didn't know about Jude.

"I haven't even told my family yet."

Jude gave me a surprised look. "Why not?"

"Claire knows," I amended. "But I think I'm running out of time on the rest of them."

Before he said anything, he reached into a small cupboard and took out a small container, then two white plates. On the plate, he put a scone and set it on the table in front of me. Out of the fridge, he produced a container of jam, then clotted cream.

"They'll want to know everything," I explained. "How I feel and what I want and what's going to happen ..." My voice trailed off.

"What happens next is on you and me, yeah?" He took a seat across from me, sliding the cream and jam in my direction. "If we're making our own rules and all."

"Yeah."

His eyebrows lifted. "You don't sound sure of that."

"I am." I inhaled. "But a big family that's also an opinionated family, and not just big and opinionated, but we've always walked through big life stuff together, you know? They'll have *thoughts*. And I'll know all of them in less than five minutes of dropping the proverbial bomb."

"Ahh," he answered carefully.

For a moment, I waited to see if he'd elaborate, but he simply stayed quiet.

"Is your family like that?" I asked casually.

"No." He nudged the plate closer, my cue to stuff my face with more carbs. Like I needed encouragement there. "Compliments of Mrs. Atkinson," he explained. "I try not to eat too many of them during the season, but I figure this is a good morning to indulge a bit."

There was an undercurrent to his words, and a warmth in his

tone as he said them, but in the wake of my messages from Claire, I wasn't sure I was ready to explore what that was. Making our own rules was great and all, but I still didn't know what the hell Jude and I really *were*. And for now, I was okay with that. So was he.

But even knowing that, Claire was right. I was afraid to tell my family because it meant I had to face all the questions when none of the questions had answers.

About me, me and the baby, me and Jude and the baby, and me and Jude. Separate categories with lots and lots of unanswered questions.

As I broke open the scone and spread the cream over the surface, followed by the jam, I thought about how rarely I needed to explain the dynamic of my family to someone who had no backstory.

"I'm going to tell them today."

He watched me carefully. "All right."

"Have you told your family yet?"

"No."

I waited for him to elaborate. But again, it was just ... that one word. There was no emotion in it, just like there was no change in his eyes or mouth. Huh.

The bite I took of the scone was indecently big, as was the moan that came out of my mouth as I chewed. His crooked grin in response was a whole lot of things. Endearing. Human. Sexy AF. I managed to swallow. "Holy shit, did she bake these?"

"I reckon she did, but she'll never admit it if she didn't."

"If I could bake a scone like this, I'd tell everyone I've ever met in my *entire life*. Don't ever fire her."

Jude was so amused, eyes warm and dancing like I'd not seen them since that first night.

"Whu?" I asked, mouth full of happiness. His gaze, well ... it was more loaded than my scone. And I had a lot of cream on that baby.

"I can't remember the last time I gained so much pleasure from something so small."

As I swallowed, I imagined that my cheeks were bright ass red. This guy had me flustered and quite easily. Normally, I was the fluster-er. With men. Or maybe, compared to Jude, they'd all been boys. There was no way for me to run circles around this man or outmaneuver him to get what I wanted.

And honestly, all I wanted was more stretches of time like the one we'd just had—uncomplicated snuggling, a little flirting, and a side of baked goods. I broke off a corner of the scone and held it out to him, pulling my fingers back when he tried to reach for it.

Feeding him something delicious when I felt like it. That was one of my new rules.

Understanding lit his eyes with something steamy that I felt right between my thighs.

Jude opened his mouth, and I set the scone in. Before I could retract my hand, he gripped my wrist and held it in place, sucking lightly at the tips of my fingers.

Now that I felt in entirely different areas of my body. If I wasn't nipping out through my shirt, it would be a freaking miracle.

"Delicious," he murmured.

The way he licked his lips as we both settled back in our seats had me feeling all squirmy and restless, and judging by the smirk on his face, he knew it.

"I have to go to the facility in a bit," he told me.

I nodded. I knew the drill, so it wasn't surprising. "Meetings?"

"Not today. I need some work done on my hamstring, and I'm sure my manager wants to make my ears bleed, reminding me why I'm old and slow and can't score goals anymore."

He sounded so deliciously grumpy when he said it that I smiled.

"Oh, that's funny?" he asked.

I swear, I tried to wipe the grin off my face. It was so tempting to climb on his lap and show him exactly how not-old and not-slow he was, and all the different ways he could score, but I also knew this was a bruise for every elite athlete.

"No." I wiped scone crumbs off the side of my mouth. "Should I clear out when you do?"

Jude shrugged. "No rush on my end, unless you need to get your friend's car back to Oxford."

I shook my head. "She doesn't need it until this weekend. I may work here while you're gone, if that's okay with you? Maybe get the phone call out of the way too."

What a seemingly insignificant thing I was asking. But it wasn't, and I think we both knew it. Allowing me into his space with no supervision was a big freaking deal.

He stood, taking a moment to tower over where I sat in that chair. Jude lifted his hand, brushing an errant crumb from the corner of my lips. "Whatever you need, it's yours."

Well, okay then. If he was trying to make me want to mount him like a bucking bronco, he was doing an excellent job.

That smirk, that warmth, it returned, and I think he knew exactly what was going on in my head.

Maybe we had a thousand unanswered questions between us, but whether we wanted each other was not one of them.

"I need to change and go," he said.

I nodded. Good. I needed him to change and go too because now that my belly was full of carbs and coffee was hitting my system, I was feeling all sorts of feelings that I shouldn't be feeling.

All of them complicated.

And I think he knew that too. He asked quietly, "Do you want me to be a part of the call with your family?"

Did I? *Let me contemplate that for all of about one one-hundredth of a second ...*

Absolutely not.

Logan would have a heart attack on the spot. Paige would find a way to become the first human to physically burst through a FaceTime call and appear next to me, simply so she could castrate Jude. Just ... nope.

And he did not need to know any of that yet. *I* didn't need any of that yet.

"No, that's okay. I think it'll be easier if I do it myself."

"Are you sure?"

"No," I answered.

Jude smiled. "You have ten minutes to change your mind because after that, I'll likely be gone until around four."

"I won't change my mind."

Having him there would definitely make it harder. And telling them was already going to be hard enough.

Chapter Thirteen

LIA

ANY STRONG OFFENSIVE scheme had certain key components, and when it came to me telling my family the news, I was going to approach this exactly like it was coming straight out of a football playbook.

A good offense created smart mismatches, pitting your best offensive player with their weakest defensive player. Maybe I couldn't do exactly that with Logan and Paige, but I could bring in my staunchest ally: Claire.

She was on her way to their house, ready to sit with them while I delivered the news and jump in if I needed backup.

It was also imperative if I had any intention of maintaining control, that I only tell Logan and Paige. At least for the first phone call. Molly and Isabel loved me, but I couldn't gauge how they'd react, so for the time being, I couldn't risk my offense being outmanned and overpowered.

In my head, I could imagine our scheduled phone call at seven in the morning Seattle time (three in the afternoon my time) as a play mapped out on Logan's whiteboard in his office. Xs and Os and arrows, signifying who would run which way, who would run the post route, who would run the fade, and if it was a pass play or a run.

For today, I was the quarterback, and my family was in the strange position of being lined up in front of me, blocking some invisible goal line. I didn't even know for sure what I wanted from the phone call, other than like, I didn't want to end up bursting into tears.

No crying = success.

As the hands on the clock slowly circled closer to three, I felt a nervous tightening in my belly. Maybe I should've waited until Jude could be a part of it and fortify my O-line, if I was taking this sports metaphor even further.

Maybe it was because I'd spent the day in the quiet of his beautiful home, that the slow creeping of time felt particularly ... well, *slow*. No one was around to distract me, and no matter how hard I tried, I couldn't focus on the work I was supposed to do.

My laptop had sat untouched on his kitchen table all day, and I'd moved from the couch to the teak furniture in his private garden a few times, managing some disjointed scrawling in my notebook. I read a few pages of the book on Charlotte that I'd brought from my flat, but the words bled together, and I found myself reading the same page for a solid hour.

It was that frustration that had me wandering slowly around Jude's home. Was it low-key stalking? Yes.

But come on, I was having his child, so I didn't think it was too strange to peek around a bit when he left me unattended in his private space.

All the rooms were immaculate, and it seemed like as much of a reflection on his personality as it did on the fact he had a full-time housekeeper. Who, he'd assured me, had the day off and wouldn't randomly stop by.

The house was updated but still held the charm of almost all the buildings in England. It was in the slope of the ceiling in the guest bedroom decorated in sedate blues and whites, in the curling wood detail of the crown molding and the wavy spots of the glass in the windows overlooking that beautifully landscaped garden. Jude's garden was separated from his neighbors by tall ivy-covered brick walls, and it gave the space a magical, old-world feeling that I liked very much.

I spent the most time in his bedroom, which was just as clean as the rest of the house, but there was an astonishing lack of personal details anywhere to be found. I stopped in front of the large dresser and slid open the drawers, finding everything neatly folded. In the bottom drawer were a few faded photos underneath a dingy gray shirt with a farm logo on it, probably his parents' place—based on what he'd told me. My eyes narrowed when I saw something soft and white and fluffy peeking out from underneath the shirt. I tugged it out, smiling when I held the small little sheep in my hand. It was made of some sort of soft wool, and the tiny pink nose and black circle eyes were quite cute.

I found myself clutching it to my chest like a talisman.

"Do you think the sheep is cute?" I whispered to little Raspberry. "Maybe we'll do sheep in your nursery."

When I left the room, I couldn't stop my brain from whirring with nervous speculation of how this phone call was going to go.

My phone buzzed.

Claire: I'll be there in ten minutes. How do you want to do this?

I took a deep breath and went down to the kitchen, where I'd decided to do the FaceTime call on my laptop, so I could see their faces more clearly. Unconsciously, my hand drifted to the nonexistent bump of my belly.

My little raspberry baby was still hiding, invisible to the naked eye, except for maybe the tiniest tightness on the waistband of my pants. A thought zipped into my head, completely unwanted, where I wondered if our mom—Brooke—had shown much, or if she'd been one of those pregnant women who suddenly looked like they'd shoved a basketball under their shirt.

And it was just another question I couldn't answer. I'd maybe seen one picture of her pregnant with me and Claire. Revisiting those parts of our past wasn't exactly high on the priority list. All I remembered of the picture was a giant bump covered by the black lace of some fancy dress she'd worn for a black-tie event she'd attended with our father.

The heel of my hand—still clutching the small sheep—pressed on the sudden spike in pressure on my chest, and I forced that image out of my head. Claire. I needed to answer Claire. How *did* I want to do this?

Me: Quickly and painlessly.

Claire: I know. But I meant more like, do you want me to mentally prep them?

I sat at the table and flipped open my MacBook. My hand shook a little when I pulled up the FaceTime.

Me: Just let them know that I'm okay, but I need to talk to them about something and I wanted you there for support.

Claire: You've got it.

Claire: It'll be okay. I promise.

Claire: Heading in. I LOVE YOU, LEE.

"I think I'm gonna puke," I whispered. With a quick glance at the clock, I wondered if I could shove another scone down before this circus kicked off. Pinching my eyes shut, I resisted because no matter how delicious it was, the scone would not solve anything. And that was the truth with Jude, as well. Having him with me to do this wouldn't make the words any easier to get out. Not to mention that, despite what he might believe, I wasn't worried about their disappointment. I was worried about their worry.

They'd want me home immediately.

They'd want to wrap me in their arms and help me carry the load, and the worst thing I could ask of my big, chaotic, opinionated family was to stay away.

When the bridge of my nose started tingling, it was the first warning sign that my entire playbook for this call was going to go to shit. I clenched my jaw together and took a deep breath.

"Stupid hormones," I said in a voice that wavered dangerously. And they were stupid. In my mind, I imagined my emotions like an angry ocean—white-capped waves that had stayed off in the distance until this very moment. My hand went to my belly again, and I felt calmer. It would be fine. We would be fine.

Claire: They're worried, but okay. I'm calling now.

Before I could second-guess it, I stood, darted to the cupboard, and snatched the bag of scones, shoving a piece of one in my mouth before I took my seat again. I set the sheep just beyond the laptop, where I could see the smiling black mouth. The ringing began as I swallowed my scone, and I clicked the touchpad to answer the call. At the sight of Logan and Paige, huddled close at the table where we'd eaten a million meals, I almost lost my grip.

"HI! We miss you. Are you okay?" Paige asked. Logan wrapped an arm around her shoulder and studied the screen with so much intensity that I almost laughed.

"Hi." I exhaled. "It's good to see your faces."

They exchanged a quick look. "You doing okay, kid?" Logan asked.

"I'm eating a scone in England. How can I not be okay?" I lifted the baked good in question, and Paige gave me a tiny smile, but they were not fooled by my answer.

Claire popped her head in behind Logan's shoulder. "I'm sitting over here, but I can hear you just fine."

"Why is your sister here for this?" Logan asked.

Right. Okay then.

"Logan," Claire said, "don't interrogate her. I'm here because she asked me to be."

His face gentled, which took a lot because my big brother had never been described as gentle. Ever. He was a bruiser, an iron-willed coach. The only piece of his life that received softness was us.

"You look good," Paige interjected. "I miss looking at your face."

"You could always look at Claire and pretend it's me." At my joke, her bottom lip wobbled, and her big blue eyes welled. I sighed. "Oh, Paige, don't cry, please."

She waved her hands in front of her face. "Sorry. I didn't expect it to be so hard to have one of you move away."

"I didn't *move* away. And Molly travels for work all the time."

"I'm a big ole hypocrite, I know." Emotions under control, Paige tucked errant strands of her red hair behind her ears and gave Logan another loaded look. "I think we're just worried. You've called, but anytime we want to see you, you find a reason you can't. So when you have your sister show up, and you're in an unfamiliar place"—she gestured to the background—"I think you can understand why we're a little caught off guard."

I sat back in my chair and rubbed my face. "I know."

"Where are you?" Logan asked.

From their vantage point, all they could see was the French doors that led from Jude's kitchen to his beautiful garden, a far cry from my tiny student's flat, which they'd seen pictures of.

"I'm at a ... friend's place."

Paige visibly fortified herself. "Lia, your brother and I love

121

you, and no matter what it is, you need to tell us. We will still love you."

"I know you will." My hand went back to the lil raspberry again. Could it sense my nerves? I let out a slow breath to calm my racing heart.

Paige took the reins again. "And if you're scared to tell us, like ... you found someone we weren't expecting and maybe you think we'll be disappointed, we won't be. I'd love another daughter, and if that's who you love, then I will be the best girl mom in the whole world."

My head tilted. "What?"

I heard Claire clear her throat, but I couldn't tell if she was laughing or redirecting.

Logan pinched the bridge of his nose. "Paige, just let her talk."

She looked at him. "I just want her to know we love her."

"She *knows*. How about you let her tell us."

"What are you talking about?" I asked.

Claire popped her head in the camera again. "Paige thinks you're coming out. That you're trying to tell them you have a girlfriend."

"Oh." My heart warmed impossibly at how she'd prepped for any and all news. "I'm happy to hear that you'd love me regardless, but I'm not trying to tell you I'm gay."

She swallowed, eyes searching my face. "Okay. Whatever it is ... we're your family."

Lips pursed, I blew out a breath, and ripped off the Band-Aid. "I'm trying to tell you I'm pregnant."

Silence.

For four solid seconds, there was nothing but wide eyes and silence.

"Holy shit," Paige whispered.

"You're what?" Logan asked. "How?"

I raised my eyebrows. Claire choked on a laugh.

His cheeks reddened. "Forget I said that. "

Paige blinked rapidly. "Okay. Okay. I'm ... who? Who? What happened? And when?"

Logan's chest expanded on a deep breath, and I could practically see him shift gears, see the helplessness written all over his face. "Are you okay?"

I nodded. "I'm good. And Paige, I'm just about ... nine weeks along."

Paige pulled out her phone and started tapping on the screen. "So that was ... pretty much right when you got there."

"Y-yes."

Logan's eyes flipped to my sister. "You knew?"

"Yeah. I was on the phone with her when she took the test a few weeks ago."

He nodded slowly. "That's why you were acting so weird when I asked about her."

Claire laughed. "You know I'm the worst liar."

Paige kept her eyes on her phone, which was when my worry started to grow again. Every second I couldn't see her eyes, it got worse. "Apparently, you're a good secret keeper, though," Paige said evenly.

Logan sighed.

"I asked her to," I said. "I wanted to tell you myself."

"Great," Paige answered. "Now you've told us, and I've got flights up right now. How soon can you pack?"

"I'm not booking a flight home, Paige."

Her hands froze. Logan's eyes closed, but I saw his hand curl tightly around her shoulder.

Paige's face finally lifted, and her eyes were bright with tears. "You're staying?"

"There's no reason I can't finish out the semester."

"You're pregnant, Lia, and in a foreign country and alone. There. That's three reasons to come home." A tear spilled over her cheek. "You don't have any of us there with you. Have you been sick? I got so sick with Emmett; it was awful. Don't you remember? And I can't i-imagine you in that tiny flat all alone, with no one to bring you crackers and hold your hair like you girls used to when I was pregnant, a-and"—she stopped, hiccupping around a sob—"I hate the thought you're doing this alone when you don't have to."

My own eyes watered, and I curled my fingers into a fist, the sharp edges of my nails providing just enough pain to keep my emotions at bay. "I was only sick for a couple of weeks, but it's better now. I feel okay, Paige, I promise. Just tired. I'm taking my vitamins and eating well and drinking a lot of water." I leaned in, fighting the urge to wrap her in my arms because it was hard seeing the toughest woman I knew this way, out of worry for me. "And I'm not alone."

Logan's jaw clenched. "What's his name? Does he have a job? Is he …" He cleared his throat. "Is he treating you well?"

"His name is Jude McAllister, he's thirty-one, and yes. A very good job, actually. He's the one who set up the doctor, and I'm at his place right now while he's at work. We're ... getting to know each other."

Logan's brow furrowed. "What was the name again?"

"J-Jude McAllister."

His eyes narrowed.

Heeeeeere we go, I thought.

"Why does that name sound familiar?"

Paige glanced at her husband, swiping at her cheeks. "Does it?" Before I could stop her, her fingers started flying across the screen again. The moment she saw it, I knew. Her eyes got huge, and her jaw dropped somewhere to the vicinity of her belly button. "Holy effing *shit*, Lia, is this him?"

"*That* Jude McAllister?" Logan yelled. "The footballer Jude McAllister?"

I nodded weakly.

They both stared dumbly at the phone screen, and I could only imagine what headlines and images had popped up.

I mean, Paige could hardly argue with the *why* of it. He looked (and played) like David Beckham and Tom Brady's DNA were combined in a lab somewhere. And Logan definitely couldn't argue about his ability to financially help with the baby. The Brits were generous with their football players, that was for sure.

Logan dropped his head into his hands. It took a second, but he let out a groan. "I swear, you girls have an athlete radar, and it's going to be the death of me. Couldn't one of you end up with a lawyer or a teacher or a dog trainer or something?"

Claire's hand appeared on the camera, giving our brother a condescending pat on the back. "Bit hypocritical coming from you, don't you think?"

"No!" he shouted, lifting his head. "Because I know exactly what goes into this life. The drinking and the drugs and the parties and the women. Do you know how hard it is to be an elite athlete and not succumb to all that bullshit?"

It was Paige's turn to be in the comforter role. She gave me a small smile, even as she wrapped an arm around Logan. "You managed it, though. And we know a lot of guys who do. Maybe Jude is one of them." When Logan turned to her, she cupped the side of his face. "And even if he had a past, we can't hold that against him as long as he's doing right by Lia."

"Thank you," I said quietly. My heart was still hammering, but mainly because I hadn't anticipated this part being the largest hurdle. "Logan, look at me." It took a second, and I could tell my big brother was struggling with this just as much as his wife had but was far more reticent to show it. "I need you to try not to worry, okay?"

"Impossible," he answered, voice a gruff, tortured whisper. "I worry about you four every single day as it is, and not because I don't trust you. It's part of the deal when you love someone so much that you'd die for them. The worst thing you can imagine is them hurting and you can't do anything about it." He shook his head, and that was when I lost the battle.

Playbook was out the window.

I sniffed as the first tear fell. Even with the quick movement of my hand to make it go away, he caught it.

Logan's eyes held mine. "I don't know this guy, and I hope he is doing whatever you need him to do, but the second he doesn't, he has to answer to me, because that is my *job*. The moment you were born—you, Claire, Molly, Isabel, and Emmett—it became the most important responsibility of my life to make sure you're taken care of and loved the way you should be. I won't apologize for that."

"I don't want you to," I told him. There was no disguising the tears in my voice, all thick and wobbly. "It took me so long to tell you guys because I knew it would kill you to be so far away from me."

"We love you, Lia," Paige said.

"I love you too." I exhaled heavily. "It will be okay. I promise."

"But you're coming home at the end of the semester, right?" she asked.

My mouth opened, but no sound came out. I didn't know. Did I want to be an ocean away from Jude when his child was born? Was that even fair?

"That's the plan," I managed, but her eyes narrowed because she heard the pause all the same.

"What about a job?" Logan asked. "You won't have your master's yet, will you? You'll need a semester off if you're due in the spring."

"I don't know." My voice sounded about as big as a church mouse. "I-I haven't thought about it."

Claire appeared behind Logan. "We have plenty of time to figure that out."

That was why I wanted Claire there. Because she could probably sense my inner freak-out building.

Paige smiled. "Can we talk next week maybe?"

I nodded. "I promise."

"You look tired, baby," she murmured. "Why don't you go take a nap while you have some peace and quiet, okay?"

I was tired. I was so, so fucking tired.

The nerves had powered me through the entire day, and in one fifteen-minute phone call, I felt like every ounce of energy had been sucked into a black hole at my feet. "Okay."

"We love you," she said.

"Love you guys too."

Claire waved, and Logan gave me a tiny smile, but I could tell what it cost him. My big brother would lose a lot of sleep over this.

Once the call disconnected, I sank back in the chair, heaving out a giant sigh of relief.

The rest of the scone beckoned, as did the giant bed I'd seen upstairs, the one covered in plush pillows.

If Jude had a problem with me trying out all the sleeping surfaces in his house, he wouldn't have left me here, a veritable Goldilocks, trying to find the one that fit just right.

Cute little sheep in hand, I walked up the stairs, finished the scone, and smiled as I passed the guest room where I'd laid to read earlier. The doorway to his room, with its big masculine bed and sturdy wood frame, looked just about right. I'd set the timer on my phone and be back downstairs before he got home, I promised myself, as I crawled onto the perfectly firm mattress.

I groaned in bliss, pressing my face into a pillow that smelled like him.

My eyes fell shut, and with the phone call behind me and the smell of Jude surrounding me, I fell fast asleep.

Chapter Fourteen

JUDE

EVERYONE HAD LEFT THE PITCH, dispersed to various meetings or treatments, so before I went home, I found myself standing in the middle of the endless stretch of green by myself.

It was hard to remember moments when this job wasn't complicated and didn't come with a metric ton of entanglements. All day, I'd faced various aspects of exactly how I was slipping from my long-held perch. The physio working on my hamstrings commented on all manner of issues she'd noticed in my play the day earlier. Declan cornered me in the weight room and had a chat with me about my attitude. But honestly, what kind of attitude did he expect when we were playing like shit and all eyes turned to someone new to fix our problems?

He'd struggle too if someone asked him to step down as the captain.

My manager sat across from me, the barrier of his desk impossibly wide as he discussed exactly why I was looking old and slow and distracted, and I was slowly whittling down all my chances at being in the starter position. With our upcoming match at Aston Villa, we had a chance—and a very good one— to earn three points and move higher. Behind me were players younger, faster, and in his words, had the focus that I *used* to be famous for.

Complications.

A hopeless mess that I wasn't even sure how to go about untangling.

The only thing that felt clear was the grass beneath me, the white lines lining the space, and the ball that sat in front of me. Digging my toe underneath it, I bounced it on the top of my foot once, twice, three times, and when the fourth bounce hit the grass, I pulled back my left leg and drilled it as hard as I could toward the goal.

It hit the back of the unguarded net, and the sound of the ball rattling the woven fabric of the net made me smile. Thought fairly innocuous to some, it was one of my favorite sounds in the entire world. Buried in that sound was my legacy.

And as much as I didn't want to admit it, that legacy was fading to everyone except me.

I walked off the pitch, nodding to the security guard stationed at the tunnel, and made my way to my car. The drive from the facility back to my house was less than twenty minutes, and as I got farther away, the knots surrounding my day loosened around my chest. It was the first time in a very long time—maybe ever—since I'd headed home with the knowledge that someone was waiting for me.

Someone I wanted to see, someone I wanted to spend time with, and not only because of the baby.

I was still wrapping my brain around the future, and how the addition of a child inevitably altered it. Lia wasn't just in my future, some concept I couldn't quite grasp. She was flesh and blood, and right in front of me as somehow the least complicated part of my life.

Her easy acceptance of what I needed to do today and the way she was able to face the reality of my life without flinching were attractive options to be presented with. I smiled as I pulled my car next to hers, thinking of how happy that scone had made her. Her ability to find pleasure in those small moments was something I could learn from her. I used to be able to.

Like the sound of a ball hitting the back of the net, normally drowned out by the roaring of the crowds. They were intertwined, to be sure, but maybe the lesson I needed to learn by this sudden veering my life had taken was to appreciate the building blocks when I was faced with them, instead of stepping my full weight on top in order to get to the next one.

The crowds wouldn't be there without the ball in the net.

I wouldn't either.

Unlocking the front door, I called out her name, wondering if coming home to her on this day was another building block. The house was quiet with Lia nowhere to be seen on the main floor. Tapping my thumb against my thigh, I thought of where she might have gone. It was a bit of a walk to any shops or restaurants, but doable. My phone showed no texts from her, and I was a bit later coming home than I'd anticipated.

From upstairs, I heard a creak, and I smiled. It came from my bed. I knew that sound. It was the sound my bedframe made any time I shifted. I took the stairs quietly, avoiding the spots that made noise. Approaching my room, I decided not to worry so much about what step might come next, what step should come next. I'd simply enjoy whatever place we found ourselves in, whatever place Lia wanted us in.

The rules would be made to our specifications, and I found that I quite liked that. No one could tell us how we should be doing this, whatever this thing was between her and I. This was the one part of my life that felt smooth, felt instinctual in an entirely different way than I was used to.

And lying in the middle of my bed, curled on her side underneath the quilt that Rebecca insisted on putting on my bed, I could understand why. Everything inside me felt drawn to Lia, tugged toward her like she'd yanked her fist inside my chest and refused to let go. No part of me could define why it made so much sense to me to climb quietly onto the bed next to her, so I didn't even try. That morning, she'd been open to the easy affection between us, and for a moment, I'd thought she'd curl her clever fingers around my trousers like she had that first night and pull me closer. It was in her eyes to do exactly that, but she'd resisted.

She was the stronger of the two of us, that much was clear. Because seeing her laid out on my bed like that, nothing inside me wanted to act along the same lines. The sleek line of her back, the silky fall of her hair down her back, and the perfectly round curve of her arse was the perfect gift to come home to.

She shifted when I carefully curled myself around her, sliding my arm around her waist and intertwining my fingers over top of hers. Of all the places she could have napped, she chose my bed, and as I held my breath to see if that shifting meant she was waking up, I knew she'd done so for a reason.

The hand not laying on hers brushed against something soft, and I lifted my head, eyes widening when I pulled the tiny sheep—made by my mum—from underneath the pillow.

"What the bloody hell? Where did you come from?" I murmured. His pink nose wasn't as bright as it used to be. The gray wool of his body faded with age. I didn't even know why I still had it because almost every single remnant of my childhood was tucked away—out of sight, out of mind.

Lia's fingers tightened around mine when I spoke, and her breathing shifted from slow and steady to shallow, rapid, excited.

The sheep was tossed off the bed, and I heard her chuckle under her breath.

"Poor little sheep," she whispered.

"He'll fucking survive." I buried my nose in her hair and inhaled deeply. Her back curved sinuously, and that arse pushed back against me.

I used to my other hand to push her hair out of the way, dropping kisses against her neck when I heard her whisper my name. Pausing, I made sure it wasn't an entreaty to stop, and that was when she turned, eyes drowsy with sleep and cheeks flushed with desire. Immediately, she cupped my face, sliding her hands up into my hair.

"I was dreaming about this," she murmured, and the husky tone of her voice had me shifting my hips restlessly.

"Were you now?"

"Mm-hmm." She licked her lips. "You woke me up like this. Differently, but like this."

I tilted her chin up with my thumb and ducked my head down so I could nibble along the line of her neck. Her fingernails dug into my scalp.

"Different how, love?" I spoke into her skin.

"W-with your hands." She arched her back again when the edge of my teeth found her jaw. "You'd taken off my pants without waking me."

"Trousers," I corrected with a grin. Her fingers tightened in my hair, and I hissed at the bite of pain. I sucked on her neck, hard, and she let out a surprised gasp.

"If you mark me, Jude …" she warned.

I lifted my head and met her gaze. "You'll what?"

Lia's lips curled in a devious smile. "Return the favor."

Given the way she'd yanked on my hair and the length of her nails, I didn't doubt it. I ducked my head again, sucking the soft lobe of her ear into my mouth. She whimpered. "Would you mark up my back? My arse? Would you use those lovely nails and stake your claim?"

"Yes," Lia gasped. "You'd love that, wouldn't you?"

I licked up the side of her cheek, and her thighs split around my legs, making room instantly.

In answer, I gripped her chin and took her mouth in a ferocious kiss. Our tongues tangled instantly, my head tilting so I could deepen it further. The familiarity of kissing her was a stark contrast to our first night, where the novelty of her was what made it so bloody sexy. And in that familiarity, I found a haven that I hadn't anticipated, a distraction when I'd least expected it. My hands dug into the flesh of her arse underneath her leggings, and I had to keep myself from tearing at her clothes.

Enjoy the small moments, I reminded myself, regardless of what came next.

We kissed like that, hands gripping over our clothes in a way that I hadn't in years. She held me so tightly, her arms around my neck and fingers in my hair. Lia sucked my tongue into her mouth, and I fought the urge to grip her hands and anchor them above her head, sink myself into her like I had before, just to see if I'd imagined how good it had been.

"What else happened in this dream of yours, my naughty girl?" I whispered, pulling my mouth away from hers, keeping just out of reach when she tried to kiss me again.

Her hand slipped up the back of my shirt, and the tips of those nails dug into my flesh, making me grin. Her eyes glinted, and as the sleep cleared from them, I saw a question emerge even before she voiced it.

"Are we making a new rule?" she whispered. The doubt was tempered by the fact she couldn't keep from touching me. From my back, her hand inched around, where she used that wicked fingertip to trace the squares of my abdomen just above the button to my trousers. "Because I wouldn't mind knowing what we're doing here."

I knew what she was asking.

But quite badly, I realized I didn't want to lose the ease of this relationship we'd stumbled into by way of a weak condom and her spotty memory at taking a few pills. Without those two things, I might never have seen Lia again, and at the moment, with her lithe body laid out like an offering, that felt like a fucking tragedy.

So I chose the wider path, the one more easily trod.

I glanced down meaningfully. "*You* are roughly three centimeters away from making me very happy, it seems. And I"—my hand did some sneaking of my own, up the line of her

soft stomach and to the warm, overflowing cups of her lace bra
—"am about to conduct an experiment."

Her lips curled up. "What experiment is that?"

"Size checks are now mandatory, I'm afraid." I gently lifted
the hem of her shirt and placed a kiss above her belly button.
She hissed when I tugged the cups down and continued my delicious journey.

"C-careful," she whispered. "They're tender."

"I can be gentle."

"Can you?" Her hands moved down, pulling open my
trousers and gripping me with unexpected strength, my back
bowing in unanticipated pleasure. "Because I'm still learning
that particular talent."

I laughed into her skin.

Lia whispered just next to my ear, lifting the hairs along the
back of my neck when it was paired with what she was doing to
me with that clever, clever hand. "My size check is happy to
report consistently above average sizes."

With a tortured groan, I snagged her lips once again. Each
kiss built upon the last, each time her tongue tangled around
mine, frantic energy powered our hands, mine seeking the same
intention she seemed to have for me.

"Yes." She sighed as my fingers slid to their preferred destination. "Oh, oh, I like this rule."

"Just this, love," I told her. My breath hitched. I took her
mouth again, deeper this time, and she tilted her head.

Lia arched her hips into my palm while I emitted harsh puffs
of air against her soft, soft lips.

She found her release just before I did, in the bend of her
back and the way she pinched her eyes shut, the utter relief in
the sigh she allowed me to taste from her mouth.

Relief.

To me, Lia felt like sweet relief.

By the time I groaned into her neck, and I fell like a great
weight on top of her, I felt like I was in high school again. Our

clothes were hardly even undone, yet the satisfaction spreading like warm caramel through my veins was absolutely brilliant.

For so long, the oblivion found in nameless women, the chasing of yet another goal, another benchmark that only meant something to me did nothing to ease the disquiet clawing at the inside of my rib cage.

But now, here, was peace. And I found that I didn't want to skip a moment of it.

Chapter Fifteen

LIA

Molly: Can you tell your little strawberry that I am the favorite aunt? I feel like subliminal messaging is important right now, and I don't like the leg-up that Claire will get because of the twin thing.

Me: It is a strawberry right now. Good sleuthing.

Me: What about Isabel?

Molly: Isabel doesn't threaten me because I have a MUCH more maternal nature than she does. She'll be like... the cool scary aunt. Not the favorite aunt. It's an entirely different category.

Molly: PLUS, Isabel is visiting you in a few weeks. She'll get to plant her own subliminal messages before I get a chance.

Molly: I NEED YOUR HELP IN THIS, OKAY?

Me: I'll get right on that after I meet with Atwood. About to listen to her eviscerate my first draft.

Me: Are you home now? Didn't you just film something in ... Georgia? Somewhere south?

Molly: Tennessee. We did a piece on the Titans. If Noah got transferred there, I wouldn't be sad to live in Nashville. DON'T TELL LOGAN I SAID THAT.

Molly: He'd probably be more heartbroken to lose Noah from the Wolves than to have me move.

Lia: Oh, please. He would not.

Molly: I know. But he knows it's a reality we may have to face someday. Contracts expire. Athletes change teams.

Molly: Good luck in your meeting!!

MY FINGERS ITCHED to ask Molly about dating an athlete. Yes, we'd grown up with Logan, and yes, I knew all the ins and outs of his life, but that was my brother. Now I found myself in an entirely different position. Most nights, I was in Oxford in my cute little flat and my cute little bed, working on my paper in various places around the city. As I'd learned, the city limits housed ten different libraries, and each had a distinct mood. The Old Library at Oxford Union was my favorite, though. Something about the curved ceilings, lined with beams, the floral-shaped windows that allowed the light to stream in, and the pre-Raphaelite murals adorning the walls, I always felt just a little bit more connected to my material. Less distracted by ... well, by my entire existence.

Even the little strawberry seemed more well-behaved when I was in that building.

When I was curled up in the green leather chair that I'd claimed, I somehow managed not to think about the little piece of ever-changing fruit with its milestones and new body parts that slowly took shape.

I managed not to think about Jude and how we'd somehow slipped into a relationship with no label, the byproduct of whatever arbitrary rules we decided were acceptable. Chemistry had the wheel of that particular decision, considering it was hard for us to keep our hands off each other when we were alone. We hadn't slept together again, not since that first night, but everything else we'd done seemed to make that a friggin' technicality at this point.

But I still wasn't sure how to balance it among everything else.

Or if I should even try. It was completely possible I was borrowing trouble at this point to try to force Jude to put a definition on what we were doing. Or what we weren't.

As I approached Atwood's office, it made me think about Charlotte Brontë, as I often did. *Conventionality is not morality*, she'd written in *Jane Eyre*, and it seemed like an especially appropriate quote for my situation with Jude.

Was it conventional? Hell to the no.

Very little about it was done "normally." But what was normal anyway? My brain started spinning around that question, and I found myself pausing outside Atwood's door long enough that she finally popped her head out.

"Are you coming in? Or are we meeting in the hallway now?"

I blinked. "Sorry. My brain is all …" I waved a hand around my head.

She smiled. "I was a bit foggy in the early parts of both of my pregnancies, so I can relate to the ..." She did some hand waving of her own. "One evening, I found myself quite parched, and when I started pouring water out of our pitcher, I realized—too late, mind you—that I was pouring it onto a dinner plate, rather than into a cup."

I laughed.

"What were you thinking about?" she asked. "Anything you want to talk through?"

Sinking into the chair opposite her desk, I let the thread of that thought snowball for a moment before I answered. "I was thinking about what Charlotte said about conventionality. How the definition of normal or right changes with every generation. Look at me, for example. In their time, I would've been absolutely ruined if I'd found myself in this position. I would've been forced to marry the man who ruined me, no matter the circumstances that led to it. And if I hadn't married him, I—and by extension, my family—would have been ruined in polite society. No choices would've been offered to me."

"True." Atwood sighed, a soft smile on her face. "And what made you think about that?"

I shrugged. "Everything, I guess. Even now, people would say the way we're doing things, the father and I, isn't conventional. They'd equate that to *right* or *wrong*. Similarly, how many people thought the Brontë sisters were wrong for writing their books? They had to publish them under male pseudonyms to even have a shot at making money from what they did. Society would judge them, define them, and cast them into a set category because their choices defied convention."

"And you worry that people will define you because of your choices?"

"No." I shifted in the chair. "Or I don't think that's what I'm doing. We don't wear our choices like a scarlet letter. People only know my choices if I choose to share them."

She hummed. In front of her was the same navy-blue teacup that she always drank out of, and she paused to take a sip. "That's quite true."

"We don't need to talk about it." My fingers, knit tightly

together in my lap, covered the small bump underneath my black sweater, and I saw her eyes drift there. "Really. I just ... I do that sometimes. Anytime I don't know exactly what I'm doing, or should be doing, I think about them. About the sisters. And how few choices they had, simply because of when they were born, you know?"

As I spoke, I fought a feeling of defensiveness when no one had even called for a discussion on my choices. Professor Atwood removed her glasses and set them on the surface of her desk.

"Lia, I know we need to discuss your first draft—and we shall—but for a moment, would you allow an old lady to give a piece of advice?"

I gave her a look. She wasn't a day over forty-five. Old, my ass. "You're not old, but yes."

She smiled. "It's natural in this field to fixate quite strongly on the past. We're paid to do so, aren't we?"

Slowly, I nodded, not entirely sure where she was going with this.

"I know that you're still sussing out what you'd like to do with your degree once you finish, but no matter what you decide, I'd give you one word of caution." She turned the edge of her teacup to line it up with the edge of her desk, and when the angle was right, she glanced back up at me. "Be careful that you don't anchor your thoughts so firmly on the past that it's hard for you to deal with your future, especially if part of that future is unclear."

"That's not what I'm doing." But my fingers tightened over my belly, my chest felt a little tight at the gentle delivery of her words. "Isn't it a good sign that I think of them often? That I'm constantly trying to correlate our societal dilemmas with what they went through?"

"Of course that's good."

"Then why do I feel like you're chastising me?" Oh, my gawd, were my eyes getting blurry? Was I crying in her office?

"Lia," she said gently, "I'm not chastising you. But I do see in you something that I used to struggle with myself, and I don't want you to only plant your thoughts on the past when you should be able to look straight to your future."

My future. My future was one giant foggy question mark.

And there was time to wave those clouds away.

I stood, and I saw the regret in her eyes. "I have to go," I told her.

"We still need to talk about your draft." Her chin lifted. "I apologize if I overstepped."

"I, uh, I can email you about your openings next week." I slid my backpack straps over my shoulders. "Besides, I have a doctor's appointment in London."

In three hours, but she hardly needed to know that.

She raised her eyebrows. "You're going to London for that? They couldn't get you into a doctor here?"

Atwood still had no idea who the father was, and explaining that he paid for the friggin' fanciest doctor in the universe to stick a gel-covered wand up my hoo-hah did not sound like a fun time, given what she'd just said to me.

"Yeah, it's a long story." I tucked my hair behind my ear. "Thank you for your advice."

She smiled gently. "I hope your appointment goes well."

She knew, probably just as well I did, that we were both being fake AF with our polite goodbyes. I wasn't feeling all that thankful over what she said. I felt attacked. I felt ... vulnerable.

The Tube ride to London felt too long.

And it felt too short.

Jude was meeting me at the doctor's office for this appointment because we were going to try to listen for the heartbeat, and for some reason, it was the first time in a long time when I didn't know if I wanted to face him.

If I was fixating on the past to avoid my own future, wouldn't I be doing that with my own past? I had a laundry list of items to choose from, if that were the case.

-Father dying when I was young: check.

-Mother bailing when it wasn't so super fun to be a parent anymore: check.

-Brother becoming Dad, which made for a very confusing family tree when we had school assignments: check.

But none of those were even remotely things I wanted to fixate on. Because they were done. Over. Nothing about them could be changed.

I got off, minded the gap and all that jazz, and let the ebb and flow of the crowd leaving the station guide me up onto the street. The trees were devoid of leaves by this point in the fall, and it felt appropriately barren.

There was no lush, pretty scenery to distract me from what Atwood said, and even the grandeur of the buildings didn't adequately hold my attention.

Always looking for a distraction.

The thought drew me up short, only a block away from the doctor.

Were Jude and I both guilty of what she'd said?

I rubbed my belly, wondering if the little strawberry could sense my unease. "Sorry, lil fruit," I murmured. "I'll try to slow the mental anguish."

Rounding the corner, I spied Jude's tall form against one of the white colonial columns propping up the ornate entryway to the office. He was wearing a black knit hat and aviator glasses that covered half his face. All that was visible was his dark scruff along his jaw and the stern line of his mouth.

Maybe what we were doing was a distraction and nothing more, this refusal to address what was waiting for us, but when he looked up and saw me, I could not help the way I reacted to that slow, sensual curve of his mouth.

I knew what that mouth was capable of.

"Hello," he murmured, sliding a hand over my hip when I approached. Quite naturally, my hands slid up the marble-hard planes of his chest, and I lifted my chin. He took the hint, smart boy that he was. Jude gave me a soft kiss but didn't deepen it. "Good meeting with your advisor?"

A buzzing sound went off in my head, like a game show contestant had hit the wrong button.

Not the topic I wanted to touch on.

"Fine," I told him. "You're early."

He grinned. "I wanted to scope out the building and see if you were exaggerating about how posh it was."

Lifting one eyebrow, I pinched his nipple, smiling in satisfaction when he yelped.

"And you weren't," he finished.

What I thought about saying next was not what came out of my mouth. What I thought about saying was, Of course, I wasn't exaggerating. But what came out of my mouth was, "Have you told your parents about the baby yet?"

Jude froze. Hell, so did I.

Maybe Atwood's advice made me so uncomfortable because she was right. It was a thought I didn't want to dwell on too much.

Jude gently turned our positions, so my back was against the column, his arm caging me in, an effective barrier from any prying eyes on the quiet, tree-lined street.

"Not yet," he admitted. His hand snuck under the back of my shirt, and he traced the bumps on my spine. "Soon."

I opened my mouth, this time not even sure what I was going to say, and he leaned in, sucking my bottom lip into his mouth.

"H-how was work?" I asked, tilting my mouth away.

He kissed down my neck. "I hardly want to talk about work when I could be doing this."

My fingers curled into the material of his shirt, and even as I recognized what he was doing—serving up a delicious distraction—I wasn't able to find the strength to resist it.

Not conventional.

Maybe not even wise.

But I tilted my head and yanked him closer, earning me a grunt of satisfaction when my tongue slid wetly against his. One of his palms spread wide over my stomach, and I felt a warm glow somewhere in the vicinity of my heart.

Wise, conventional, whatever word someone else might suggest ... I decided they were all overrated, and I lost myself in his kiss.

Chapter Sixteen

JUDE

By the time we were back at my house and Lia had curled up in her favorite corner of my couch, I'd sort of stopped hearing that little *whomp-whomp-whomp* sound in my head.

Sort of.

I scrolled the screen of my phone.

"Did you know the average heartbeat is up to a hundred and sixty beats per minute?"

Lia glanced at me, a bemused smile on her face. "I did not."

"His was fast."

Whomp, whomp, whomp. Like a horse galloping on hard dirt.

Now the smile spread on her face. "His? I thought it was my job to get a feel for the sex."

"Awfully sexist of you." I lifted my phone screen and tried to pretend I wasn't a little embarrassed that I'd been the first to admit which gender I thought the baby was. "Sir Google says that boy heartbeats average a bit higher, so you can sod off."

She laughed. "There are so many girls in my family, it's just weird to imagine having a boy."

Weird was not the adjective I would've used.

Everything laid out in my head like a road map, all the ways I'd be able to do right by him when my parents hadn't done right by me. And maybe everyone did that to a certain extent when faced with impending parenthood. The mistakes of our own families felt like blinking beacons, bright and obnoxious. And not just obvious but easily avoided.

My parents, from simple, hardworking stock, couldn't imagine anything other than the life they'd both been raised in. My father was a farmer because his father had been a farmer. He dug his hands in the dirt, day in and day out, because it was what McAllister men did.

Until me.

And Lewis.

Though they accepted the life he lived because my brother still worked his fingers to the bone in his pub. He wiped down dirty counters and cleared tables, if need be. He poured drinks and stayed until the middle of the night if required. To them, it wasn't farming the ground for our food, but it was honorable because it was service. But to them, I was nothing more than a show pony who could kick a ball into a very large, very easily found target. My success, in their mind, was rooted in vanity and excess, a failing on their part that I wasn't more content in the life that they'd raised me.

To them, I didn't serve anyone except myself. No matter that the entire world understood the unifying effects of sport, and the passion and joy and camaraderie of cheering on the same team. The entire world except my bloody family, it seemed.

To them, it was frivolous, this thing I loved and had dedicated my life to.

My son—or daughter—would never feel like that.

Whatever passion they were born with, whatever thing lit them up inside, I'd move heaven and hell to help them hone that into a life. I'd never make them feel like less for loving something different than I did. The opposite actually. If they wanted to paint or draw or write or spin pirouettes or design clothes, I'd tear my hands to blood and bone if I could carve out a place in the world for them to do the thing they loved.

And I could feel that building up inside me with a zealot's fire as I watched Lia flip channels on the telly in my home.

Everything else might be going wrong in my life, branching off into directions that felt crooked and dangerously flimsy, except her.

"A girl is fine by me too," I murmured, sliding a hand up her leg, where it draped over my lap.

Lia rolled her eyes. "I'd hope so."

"It was fast, though, wasn't it?" I asked. "The heartbeat."

Funny, if I laid my hand over my chest, I got the strangest feeling I'd feel it pounding in that same rhythm. *Whomp, whomp, whomp.*

She hummed, moving her own hand over her stomach. When the doctor rolled the wand over it as Lia lay flat on the table, it was hardly detectable. "It was amazing." The graceful length of her fingers spread wide over her stomach, and she smiled softly. "I wish I could feel it."

There was no doubt in my mind she'd be a wonderful mother. If pressed, I might not even be able to articulate why, or not well, at least.

We'd talked about so little, she and I. And the things she did seem to want to talk about were the subjects I wanted to avoid like a kick to the balls. It was instinct, I supposed. The same way I could stand in front of a keeper for a penalty kick and know in my gut that he'd go left, so I should kick right. I knew she'd be the best kind of mum. Fierce and fearless and intelligent.

In Lia's lap was her notebook and a dog-eared copy of *Jane Eyre* that was always in her bag.

"How did your meeting go?"

She sighed, moving the notebook and novel to the side so she could burrow further into the couch. "I kinda ... argued with her. Or she argued with me. I don't even know."

I tilted my head. "What about?"

Lia's eyes, that deep midnight blue, hit me like a punch to the chest when she looked up at me. She'd looked at me for a lot of reasons, out of lust and out of fear and in anger, but this was something different. There was a hesitation that I couldn't make out.

My hand squeezed her leg. "What is it?"

"She said something, and it made me feel a little defensive, I guess."

Gently, I tapped her leg, so she stretched out. Taking a foot in hand, I dug my thumbs into the arch and listened to her groan, an indecent sound that shouldn't have been so sexy, considering I was rubbing her feet, yet it was.

"Was it your paper? I thought you were happy with your first draft?" For ten days, she buried herself on her computer, working on ... something important. The world of academia was hardly my comfort zone, but I was still trying to understand what it was she did. What she wanted to do.

"No, it wasn't my paper. She's still reviewing it, I think." Her back arched when I dug into a spot on her foot. "Oh, holy shit, that feels amazing."

At Lia's age, I'd been just taking the premier league by storm, one year after my transfer from the German team where I got my start. But maybe to her, that paper was the same type of thrill as hoisting a cup over my head was for me.

"What are you going to do with that fancy paper?" I asked. Groggily, she lifted her head, and I stifled a laugh at her expression. It reminded me of when my head was clenched tight between her thighs and she'd just about torn the hair from my head as she came to a screaming release a couple of days earlier. "When you finish, I mean. Take the Brontë world by storm, as it were?"

"If you want me to answer"—she hissed in a breath when I moved to the other foot—"you have to stop doing that." I held my hands up, and she exhaled heavily. "I don't know, really."

My eyebrows lifted. "Meaning ...?"

"Meaning," she drawled, "I don't know what I want to do with my degree just yet."

"Aren't you close to graduating?"

"Yup."

"With your master's degree."

She tapped a finger to her nose. "You got it."

The look I gave her was incredulous. "How do you *not* know?"

"Okay, judgy, a lot of people in this world go on and get their doctorate while they decide if they want to write or research or teach. It's not that uncommon." She sat up and folded her arms over that marvelous chest of hers. "I don't think there's anything wrong with not knowing."

Maybe not wrong, but I tried to wipe the look off my face of total and complete lack of comprehension. How did one not know? She'd devoted years of her life at uni studying this subject.

I chose my words carefully—pregnant woman and all. "It certainly seems like you have a lot of options."

"I do." Her chin was pointed at a mulish angle, and it was surprisingly sexy, as was the defiance in her tone.

"And once you decide which one, you'll be incredible. Prove you were right in wanting what you want."

Lia's brows lowered over those eyes of hers, confusion clear. "Prove to who?"

I shrugged. "Everyone."

She hummed.

"What?"

"Nothing," she answered lightly.

"Bollocks. That's not a nothing tone. Don't try to read anything into it." My entire career was based around proving a point. Every day that I showed up to work my arse off, it was to prove a point. Every time I scored. Every time I left a piece of myself on the pitch, it was the prove a point. "Come to my match on Saturday?" I asked her.

She smiled. "Of course. Is your family coming to this one? I'd love to meet them."

To match her smile with one of my own was difficult, but I tried. "I'll ring and ask. It's hard for them to leave the farm."

Lia sat up and swung her leg over my lap until she'd settled nicely on top of me. My hands slid up her back while her fingers played with the ends of my hair. "It's a big game, though, right?"

"Very." Adding three points now, with how the rest of the table was shaking out, would be a bloody relief.

"Chelsea's good, though, right?" She peeked at me under her lashes.

I smiled. "Someone's been doing her homework."

"A little. But with their best striker injured, don't you have a better chance of beating them?"

With a groan, I tugged her closer. "Keep talking, I could get off listening to you like this."

Lia laughed. "I just mean, wouldn't your parents want to be at a big game?"

And that killed it.

I kept my face even. "Depends on what needs to be done this time of year at the farm. November usually means rotating the crops for grazing, deworming, that sort of thing."

She hummed. "And you had to do that growing up?"

"Unfortunately."

"I like the idea of farmer Jude."

I didn't. I hated it, which was why I left. But still, I found myself smiling at the look on her face. "Do you now?"

She nodded, ducking her head down to kiss either side of my lips. What did my heartbeat sound like when she did that? Was it racing and whooshing and filling the room with the indistinct drumming?

I turned my head to suck at her lips, but she pulled back.

"Are we playing now, love?"

"Maybe," she murmured. "I keep thinking about you tossing me onto a bale of hay and having your way with me."

"Oh please, we can do better than that." My hand came up

and gripped her chin so she couldn't evade me. With the edge of my thumb, I pressed down on the center of her luscious mouth, hissing in a breath when she sucked it between her lips. "That kind of mood, eh?"

She grinned—wickedly, in fact— and my thumb fell away. Underneath her, my body was aching and tight, heavy with wanting her.

"I think it's my turn in the driver's seat." She whipped her shirt over her head, hands diving down to the button on my trousers when it fell onto the floor.

I surged up and took her mouth in a deep kiss, my hands gripping the curve of her hips while she writhed on top of me, chasing the sharp edge of relief that way.

"Thatta girl," I said against her lips when her movements sped up, her face flushed a pretty pink. "Show me what feels good to you."

Slipping my hand between us, I hardly had to do much, and Lia cried out, her chest heaving, her body shuddering in a way that made me crave her dangerously. Never before had I ever wanted a single woman long enough that I was willing to follow the path of how we could make each other feel for a long period. The possible complications had never been worth it.

But as I cupped the back of her head and tilted her at the perfect angle for a searching, searing kiss, something that again, had my heart thrashing dangerously, I knew she'd be the one to make me want to risk it. Risk anything.

Lia pulled away, pupils dilated and lips red from our kisses. "Your turn."

"Is it?"

She slid back until she was on her knees in front of me. My fingers slid between the silk of her hair. This woman, smart and sexy, didn't need me to prove myself to her. She simply wanted.

Nothing about this was empty or transactional. For the first time in my life, it felt meaningful. I almost pulled her up off the floor because I wanted to be with her in this, but that thought was fleeting, erased by the feel of her mouth and the cool strength in her fingers.

I laid my head back on the couch and shut my eyes, tightening my grip on her hair as she helped me chase the same feeling she'd just had.

Helpless and open was how I felt when I finally shouted her name into the quiet of the room. And my hands shook when I tugged her back up onto my lap.

Suddenly, proving my worth to anyone but Lia felt like a fool's errand.

Chapter Seventeen

LIA

FOR MY SECOND MATCH, I was far more prepared. This time, I had a Shepperton Shorthorns sweatshirt over my thermal leggings, Jude's jersey on underneath as a second layer, a poncho in my small purse in case it rained, a blue-and-white-striped winter hat emblazoned with Shepperton FC along the folded edge with a giant blue poof sticking off the top, and on my cheek was this friggin' adorable little temporary tattoo that I'd found in a shop down the road from the stadium, the horned logo in bright blue and white.

I walked to my seat, the energy in the building like the best shot of pure, unfettered electricity. Nothing was like the excitement of a live sports event. I'd take it over any concert, any play, any show in the entire world.

A small block of empty seats was located around the one I knew was mine, but the moment I saw the tall man in a solid blue shirt, I knew immediately it was Lewis. He had the same dark hair, the same straight nose, the same broad shoulders. But where Jude's build was muscular, Lewis was husky—the kind of guy who looked like he gave the very best kind of hugs.

I slid down the aisle, smiling at the four old men who stood to allow me to pass.

Lewis glanced in my direction and moved to do the same.

"No worries," I told him, "I'm right here." I pointed at the seat just to his right.

His face lifted in shock. "Ahh. Right then."

I held out my hand. "Lia. I take it Jude didn't tell you I'd be joining your family today."

With a rueful smile, he gave mine a brisk, hard shake. "No, but that doesn't surprise me. My brother is hardly forthcoming about the details of his personal life."

Because he said it with a warm tone and obvious love in his eyes, I didn't feel a surge of defensiveness for the man not here to defend himself.

"Are your parents coming?"

Lewis's smile faded just slightly at the edges. "I expect not."

Song erupted around us, and I whipped out my phone to take a video. Lewis watched me with an unveiled curiosity. Once I stopped recording, I shot a text off to Molly, knowing she'd get a kick out of it.

Each star player had a little song, and the fans—en masse—knew when to start singing them. Jude had one too, but I hadn't been able to remember the words once the match was over.

"Our fans in the States don't do stuff like that," I shouted over the din, hooking my thumb over my shoulder. "I think it's so cool!"

He nodded. "It's different here. Football transcends sport, if that makes sense." Lewis leaned in because I could hardly hear him. "For good and for bad, in fact. Some of the songs are bloody ruthless. One of the players on another team has a song about his wife because she started some drama passing stories to the papers. Didn't sit well with the fans."

"No way!" I laughed. "That's savage."

I tried to imagine that happening to Logan because Paige had been famous in her own right as a model when they first got married. He would've lost his mind if the fans had created a song about her.

"Jude told me a little about you right after you met," Lewis admitted, once the raucous song came to a close. "But I didn't know you were still ... seeing each other."

Given the jovial atmosphere, the electric happiness that the mood of the stadium gave me, I tried really, really hard not to let that bother me. I was twelve weeks pregnant with his child, and his brother knew nothing about me. Forced to pause our conversation because of a family of Shepperton fans passing in front of us, I took a moment to breathe out my disappointment in a few gulping breaths.

It was fine.

I'd kept Jude more than a little occupied the past few weeks, and if I was completely honest with myself, anytime his family came up, he changed the subject. He distracted me. And the last time I'd brought them up, I was the one who climbed onto his lap and rode him like a jockey rides a racehorse.

A grimace crossed my face before I could stop it.

I thought about what Atwood had told me, about my tendency to focus on the past to avoid an unknown future. I thought about how Jude had reacted to my lack of clarity of what I wanted to do with my degree once I'd finished it. And I thought about how easily he and I fell into the palpable chemistry between us to avoid the reality of our separate situations.

Hell, my reaction to my meeting with Atwood left me feeling so unsettled that I'd gotten my pregnant ass down on my knees in front of him. In fact, if he'd pushed the door open, I probably would've crossed that invisible barrier we had around having sex again. I would've willingly allowed him to sweep away all the icky feelings she'd planted with that one seed of a thought.

Lewis saw the look on my face, and I tried to erase it with a smile, but he held up his hands. "I'm sorry, that came out rude, didn't it?"

"No, it's fine, really. I've been with Jude a lot, and I've never seen him talk to you, so I should've guessed."

He smiled again, but this time, it held an edge of discomfort. Great. Excellent first impression.

I laid a hand on his arm. "Sometimes I forget not everyone is like my family. I have four sisters, and we talk constantly. Don't worry about it."

Lewis studied me again, and I felt a little bit like an animal in a zoo exhibit. *And to your left, ladies and gentlemen, we have the exotic American female.* The teams walked out of the tunnel, players holding hands with children of various ages, each wearing matching jerseys to the teams.

"Okay," I said to Lewis. "What's up with the little kids?"

He grinned. "They do it for a few reasons, but primarily, it's used to raise money. Parents can pay to have their kids walk out on the pitch with one of the players, but it also helps foster a sense of ... sportsmanship, I suppose. No one can rain down curses or throw cups at the opposing players when they walk out together with innocent British youth, eh?"

"Ahh. See, back home, we'd never take away our ability to be merciless with the away team. I think our heads would implode."

"How very American of you," he teased.

"I'm pretty sure your brother said the very same thing to me the night we met."

He took a slow drink from his cup, only glancing at me once before he seemed to come to a decision. "You're not like anyone I've ever seen Jude spend time with."

So many questions popped into my head.

About the kinds of women he was with in the past, about the number of women, and if anyone had crossed the impenetrable moat that seemed to surround their family. And like the secure, confident woman I was, I did not ask a single one of those questions.

I simply smiled. "Is that so?"

Lewis nodded, leaning closer so I could hear him while the team captains shook hands in the middle of the pitch. "Don't get me wrong, my brother hasn't dated anyone of consequence in years. And even when he did, back when he was first in the league, it was exactly the kind of woman he shouldn't have been with. They fawned over him, and it just ... it didn't help keep his feet on the ground. And Jude struggles as it is to do anything else with life beyond football, so people like that make it worse."

Groupies. Every sport had them. Every celebrity faced them at some point. I'm sure my brother had too. But according to him and Paige, he never wanted anything to do with that life-style. It was a house of glass built on the edge of an unsteady cliff.

"Athletes are just normal people who do abnormal jobs." I grinned at Lewis. "It's one of the things my brother drilled into our heads growing up. And the more people who elevate that athlete to a god-like status, the more they believe it."

"That's right." He nudged me with his shoulder. "I'm glad he has you, Lia Ward."

I wasn't able to answer because the ball went into motion, and for the next ninety minutes (plus stoppage time, which ... I was still trying to understand), we yelled and screamed and clapped and stayed on our feet while Jude and Shepperton FC absolutely left their hearts out on the field. As the clock kept moving forward, and Lewis explained that the whistle could blow any time once stoppage was met, I found myself breathless with the rhythm of the game.

It wasn't boring.

It was beautiful.

The stamina of the players, the way they passed with preci-sion and ruthless accuracy, and the strength they were able to hone in their movements, I almost cried when Jude snagged the ball from a Chelsea player and took off toward the opposite end of the field. He kicked it in front of him as he ran, passed to one of his teammates to the left, who handled the ball with his feet so deftly, I almost lost sight of it.

It shot back toward Jude as he charged the waiting goalie,

whose arms were outstretched in anticipation of what might come next.

Jude's right foot drew back, and he caught the ball just as it flew in front of him. It arced, perfectly, beautifully, impossibly into the top corner of the net, and the crowds erupted.

Lewis swept me up in a giant bear hug as we screamed, and the little old lady next to me wrapped her arm around my waist while she did the same.

The whistle blew, and the high of the win felt like I'd done drugs or something.

All my senses were heightened, my skin buzzed, and my heart pounded.

And for the first time all match, I saw Jude look up in the direction of our seats. His hair was a mess, and his jersey was filthy, but his smile was blinding.

I waved frantically, and he lifted a fist in the air.

"Want to go with me to meet him when he's done? Maybe we could grab a bite to eat at your pub?"

Lewis smiled, face flushed red from the celebrations. "If you two want to popover later, I'd love to say hi, but I have to get back. Tell him congrats for me, will you?"

He gave me a brief hug and followed the crowds out of the stadium.

When I looked back down at the players on the field, Jude was staring back up at us, but his smile wasn't quite as wide as before.

Maybe he and I were kidding ourselves in our constant search for distractions, but I slid my hand over my stomach and vowed that I'd do what I could to move us forward. No more focusing on the past.

Chapter Eighteen

JUDE

It was the moment when she screamed at the telly that I had my first real moment of pause when it came to Lia Ward.

"Oh, you fucking moron," she bellowed, hand speared in her hair as she paced my living room. "Of course, they were going to blitz. Block! Come on, get him, get him, get him!"

With a wince, I watched the Washington Wolves quarterback get viciously sacked. Lia groaned, sinking back on the couch with a deep breath.

"All right?" I asked cautiously. Normally, I might have slid a hand up her back to rub in soothing circles, something I'd learned that she liked. Any physical affection made Lia purr like a bloody cat, actually. But as this was my first experience seeing her watch American football, I felt a bit skittish. Mainly because she swatted my hand away the last time I tried to calm her down.

"No, I'm not all right." She tossed her hands in the air at the next play. "What is he *doing*? Why would you do another pass play? They're killing us on the line." She pulled her phone out, frantically tapping out a text. "Idiot. What an idiot."

"Texting the coach your suggestions?" I teased.

"Yes."

My eyebrows popped up. "I was joking, love."

She glanced over at me. "So was I. It's my sister Isabel."

"Ahh. Does she concur with your game analysis?"

"Yeah, the head coach is an idiot. He should've been fired last year. I don't know why Allie hasn't stepped in."

My head tilted. "Who's Allie?"

"Paige—Logan's wife—it's her best friend. Allie owns the Wolves."

"Goodness," I murmured, "I had no idea I'd impregnated sports royalty."

Lia smacked me in the stomach, and I grinned.

"And Isabel is the one visiting in a couple of weeks."

Before she answered, she watched with a frown as the Wolves offense failed to get a first down. "Yeah. You'll love Isabel, mainly because you won't be intimidated by her."

"Are most people?"

"Oh, yeah." Lia laughed. "She manages a boxing studio back in Seattle, and I swear, you take one look at her, and you just know ... this chick could kick my ass without breaking a sweat. She's tough, and smart, and funny. She's the best big sister because I always knew no one would mess with us when Isabel was around."

Her family was so different than mine. Listening to her talk about them, I felt a bit like I was a voyeur trying to understand what normal family dynamics were through the very extraordinary group she'd been born into.

"And she's also watching at home, screaming at the screen like a maniac?"

"Yes," she answered immediately. "Paige and Claire are at the game, but they're also probably screaming like maniacs. It's a family trait."

"Sounds like it."

"But"—she held up a finger—"I actually have messaged Logan during the game with ideas."

"You have not."

"He ignores me." She narrowed her eyes as she thought. "Usually. There was one time he said he saw my message during a commercial break and ran the defensive scheme I suggested."

"You are *joking.*"

Her eyes got big. "I would *never* joke about that. The running back was kicking their ass. Logan needed the inside linebacker to blitz the gap."

I threw my head back with a good belly laugh. I couldn't help myself.

It was enough to have Lia's tense shoulders relaxing for the first time since the game started. Shepperton had the day off, we'd played midweek, and she begged for control of the telly on Sunday night so we could watch her beloved Wolves---the team her brother played for and now coached. The camera panned to him as the defense took the field for a new series.

"Defensive coordinator Logan Ward has made quite an impact on this team's defense since he took over the clipboard," the announcer said.

His counterpart hummed. "Indeed. They've consistently ranked in the top three for sacks and takeaways, and this season so far, they're the top scoring defense in the league. That's largely in part to the addition of Noah Griffin to the roster last year, and how he's stepped up under Ward's coaching."

Lia smiled.

"That's your sister Molly's boyfriend, right?" I asked.

She nodded. "He used to be our next-door neighbor when we were younger. Molly had the most obnoxious crush on him, so it was total kismet that they ended up working together at Washington."

It was interesting, sitting with her while she watched her loved ones play the sport they loved. My parents had never come to a single one of my matches since I became a professional player. My brother came a couple of times a year, but I'd never see him afterward. No one had ever waited to tell me how excited they were for our win or console me after a loss. Never had anyone tell me they'd screamed like a maniac in the stands. Not until Lia.

"What's it like?" I found myself asking.

When she turned to me with a question in her lovely eyes, I wanted to retract the words immediately.

"What?"

It felt as though I'd rolled over, exposing a soft underbelly that I'd never inspected before. My throat felt dry, and I couldn't quite conjure a flippant response with her looking at me like she was.

"To watch your family do what they love like this." I gestured weakly at the screen. "Across the ocean, they still hold enough weight in the world that you can sit here on my couch and watch them do this incredible job."

Suddenly, I found myself holding my breath that she wouldn't brush off my question. I hoped she'd give it proper thought because I wanted to know, quite desperately, what most families must've felt.

"It's ..." She paused, clearly searching for the right words. "It's weird sometimes. Mainly because it's so normal for me to have my brother on camera. I'll admit that I don't think too existentially about it, but other times, like right now ... I'm sitting with you while they talk about my brother and my future-brother-in-law, and honestly, I could cry from how proud I am to call them my family." She smiled. "I was like, twelve when Logan won the Super Bowl, and oh, man, I was so obnoxious when I went back to school. I didn't appreciate the magnitude of it then like I do now, but knowing that people I love have had such an effect on a game on this scale is pretty fucking cool."

If I'd been anyone else, less emotionally stunted, less ... British, I probably would've teared up at her words. I tried not to think about when Lia needed to go back to Seattle when her semester was done, but moments like that made it difficult to ignore because I'd miss her. I'd miss having her around and hated the thought of it, almost as much as I hated the idea of how completely inept I was at trying to have any sort of healthy relationship. Maybe if that was all she'd said, I could've turned back to the game and marveled at how nice it must be to have a family like that. But then she spoke again.

And when she did, she sealed her fate.

She smiled at me, completely unaware of what was happening behind my rib cage, what vulnerable emotions were daring to escape from between the skin and bones. "I guess it'll be that way with me and the little nectarine, huh? We'll be wearing our Sheppertons kits and screaming like maniacs for you next season. We'll be the loudest cheering section you've ever heard."

"Will you?" I said roughly.

Her eyebrows bent in over her eyes. "Of course." Gently, she took my hand and laid it on top of the small bump under her black and red Wolves shirt. "This ... this makes us a family, Jude. We'll always have your back."

What was she doing to me?

Why did the fabric of my carefully constructed world feel like it'd been ripped in two?

Lia's beautiful face softened at whatever she saw in mine, and instead of commenting on it, she turned, muting the game. She cupped my face with her hand and slowly leaned forward, placing a soft, heartbreaking kiss on my lips.

"No rules," she whispered. "Just ... whatever we want this to be."

My body caught up before my brain did. My hands slid up her arms and into her silky hair, where I could tilt her head and take our kiss into a different depth. Somewhere darker, some-where delicious.

She sighed into my mouth, and I pushed her backward onto the couch, prowling over her and caging her head with my arms while we kissed.

I pulled back, and she blinked slowly.

"*My* bed," I said. "No couch, no bloody single bed, no

worrying about anything except what I'm about to make you feel."

Lia smiled. "An excellent idea."

I stood off the couch and held my hand out to her. "Shall we?"

Chapter Nineteen

LIA

When the strength of his fingers curled around mine as I took his hand, I almost stopped.

Not because I wasn't sure about crossing this particular barrier—my hormones were screaming at me to bang the bejeezus out of him—but because I was afraid that ascending that staircase would kill the electric mood.

Weeks ago, I'd stopped trying to figure out what shifted things between us. Sometimes it was a look that lasted just a fraction of a moment longer than was polite. Sometimes, he slid his hand up my back, and I wanted to shove my hand down the front of his pants. Sometimes he breathed, and I wanted to shove his hand down the front of mine.

It was easy, was what I was trying to say. And when those moments happened, we acted on them. We rarely took the time to relocate.

But I was so, so wrong. Because instead of trailing him like a horny lil puppy on a leash, Jude tugged on my hand so that I preceded him up the steps to his bedroom.

"Did you know," he asked lightly, hands curling around my hips as I took the first step, "your arse is abso-bloody-lutely perfect?"

I almost tripped on the second step. "Is it?"

He exhaled a laugh, and I found myself smiling. Yes, I knew I had a good ass. Genetics were strong in the Ward family, and we might have gotten a healthy share of family dysfunction, but we'd also gotten high cheekbones, big blue eyes, long legs, and a great frickin' ass.

After my breathy question, he crowded behind me, burying his nose into my hair and inhaling greedily.

"I could fucking inhale you," he murmured.

"Sounds painful." Was my voice shaking? I think it was. My hands were. My heart was. Every inch of me had a slight vibration that spoke to his potency. My legs could hardly hold me up when I felt him behind me, big, so, so big and so ready.

Yes, we'd touched each other and yes, we'd perfected the art of non-sex sex over the past couple of months, but I was also so, so ready to feel him again.

Jude slid his hands up, gripping the hem of my shirt and tugging. I paused, because I was not trying to fall on any stairs right before the big show. He tossed the shirt behind us and fastened his mouth on the base of my neck and sucked.

"Holy shit," I groaned, my hand tightening on the banister when he deftly unfastened my bra as I neared the landing on the second floor. His tongue, wet and hot, dragged down the line of my neck, and his clever hands cupped my breasts underneath the loosened cups. They were so sensitive that I hissed slowly, each gentle swipe of his thumb directly tied to the apex between my legs that was lighting up like a friggin' neon sign.

"Are you ready? Just like this?"

Oh please, if he thought I couldn't orgasm from his voice alone, he was kidding himself. I cleared the top step and whirled, snaking my arms around his neck and attacking his mouth.

The kiss was a strange thing, if you thought about it.

Some were sweet and short and dry, the established motion of lips as a point of connection between two people who knew each other well. And some were in an entirely different category. They transcended the kindling of passion. They transcended the fueling of lust.

This kiss, as he pushed me against the wall and ground himself against me, was one of those transcendent kisses.

This kiss was Jude fucking me.

This kiss was Jude making love to me.

The lines blurred entirely between the two.

I felt his heart in that kiss just like I felt my own. It was in the slick slide of our tongues, the serpentine motion he'd established, rolling his hips as my leg hitched up along his skin. And it was in the strange anticipation I felt to fall backward on his bed, in his home, with his arms wrapped tight around me.

We stumbled from the hallway through the open doorway, and he bent at the knees to boost me up into his arms. I leaned my head back, and he licked across the tops of my breasts, still partially covered by the bra we hadn't quite freed me of.

The moment before he laid me on the bed, everything slowed. He lifted his head and speared me with a look so full of the things he normally managed to hide.

He wanted so much more from this, maybe more than I'd ever realized.

I thought of his expression down on the couch, when I'd told him we were a family now, and I felt only the briefest moment questioning whether this was a good idea or even smart.

Jude was so deep under my skin, and that brief flash of vulnerability buried him even deeper. I wasn't sure I could pull him out, even if I wanted to.

His knee braced on the bed, and with the utmost care, he lowered us until my back hit the mattress. That he'd managed it so gently was a testament to his unbelievable strength. Again, he kissed me, and my back arched up because I missed that slide of his skin against mine. Quickly, he broke the kiss to tug his shirt off, and when his chest and stomach were bared to me, I couldn't help the happy sigh.

Jude grinned, and if I'd been standing, that grin would've made me weak in the knees.

While he worked on his pants, I pushed mine down, only leaving my black lace underwear when he raised an imperious eyebrow. "Let me, love."

I held my hands up. "Bossy."

Before me, he stood completely naked, and why wouldn't he? He looked like a Greek god, carved to perfection. With one finger crooked behind the center bow on my bra, he slowly pulled it down, watching the skin uncovered inch by slow, torturous inch until I laid there in only a small scrap of black lace. That came off next—again, with only two calloused fingers pulling it down my legs.

"Beautiful," he whispered. Jude planted his fists on the bed and prowled up over me like a great big cat, stopping only to drop a gentle kiss on the curve of my belly.

Inexplicably, tears pricked hot in my eyes at that kiss.

No, whatever this moment was between us, it wasn't stupid, and it wasn't a bad idea.

I'd go to my grave remembering him like this. That was the thought in my head when he took my mouth in another searing kiss.

That was the thought in my heart when he brought me up over the crest for the first time with his hand. Then he whispered into my ear that my pleasure was perfect, that I was the most beautiful thing he'd ever seen in his life, and he couldn't wait to feel me again. How he'd dreamed of it night after night.

Part of me wanted to reverse our positions, so I could sit up over him and watch as he got his pleasure. Where I could—eyes wide open—see the moment on his face when he let go of all control.

But when he gripped my thigh tight in one strong hand and

pushed inside, I lost my breath. I lost any idea that wasn't this one.

Jude moved so slowly at first that I almost screamed at him, almost raked my nails down his back, almost exploded again from unspent frustration.

He whispered things into my skin that weren't clear, things I couldn't make out behind the rushing and roaring in my ears. I arched up, my hands stretching up over my head until I'd braced my palms flat against the headboard. He lifted his head and stared down into my face for one breathless beat.

Jude looked stupefied. He looked confused. He looked like someone had knocked him flat with a two-by-four.

But instead of making some pleasure-loaded confession, I saw the moment he was ready to stop prolonging whatever tight-rope he was walking. His jaw clenched, a muscle popping behind the dark scruff on his face, and oh, oh, he began to move.

By the time I was flung past the second peak, I was practically sobbing, his back slick with sweat and his eyes boring into mine with an intensity that might have scared me if I didn't feel so amazing.

I arched into one particularly brutal snap of his hips, and he yelled my name.

He was, without a doubt, the most beautiful thing I'd ever seen.

Jude slumped over me after a few more slow movements, and I curled my arms around him, tightened my thighs around his hips, and kissed his shoulder.

"Whoa," I whispered, my heart pounding in a jittering, jangling beat behind my ribs.

He lifted his head and grinned again, and it was such a dopey grin that I burst out laughing.

Jude laughed too, rubbing his hand up and down my back.

After we cleaned up, I snuggled underneath the covers next

to him, and the sigh of relief that came from deep within his chest made me smile again.

It was no wonder that sex became an addiction for some. The sense of power, the relaxed euphoria that I felt lying next to him was unparalleled. The ultimate high that I hadn't even known existed.

"Stay the night?" he asked.

I turned slightly, laying my head on his shoulder. "I don't know, my small bed in my small flat sounds so appealing right now."

He tickled my side, and I laughed into his skin.

Jude was quiet for the next few minutes, doing nothing more than running his fingers through the ends of my tangled hair. When he spoke, I could feel the rumble of his voice underneath my ear.

"Care to take a little holiday this week?"

I grinned happily. "Yeah. You can get away?"

"I can, yeah. We have international break next weekend. No matches."

Propping my chin on his chest, I rubbed my fingertips along the scruff on his jaw. "Where should we go? There's a lot I haven't seen yet."

"You had to leave Haworth early, yeah?"

"Yeah. *Someone's* unborn child made me pukey, then I saw that same someone on the cover of a newspaper and cut my trip short to come home and take a pregnancy test."

He exhaled. "I wish I would've handled all that better."

I kissed his chest. "I know you do. But I think we're in an okay place now, right?"

Jude cupped the side of my face and drew me up for a soft kiss. "Aye, we are."

When I pulled back, I grinned at him. "So, you're taking me back to Brontë country?"

"If you'd like. You can make me smart, tell me all the things I need to know about these famous ladies."

"Okay." Was it possible to want to mount him again already? Because the man had hardly had any recovery time, but when he started planning trips for me to go back to my literary idols' hometown because he remembered I had to cut my time short, it made me feel all sorts of things. Sexy things.

"What's that look in your eyes?"

I bit my bottom lip and watched his gaze track the movement. "Take a guess."

His hands moved low down my back, one palm slowly covering my bare bottom. "You must have a lot of faith in my abilities. I'm old, love."

My own hand started exploring. "You feel pretty *spry* right now."

When he laughed, a sexy, quiet, exhale of a laugh, I pushed on his chest, swung my leg over his lap, and did exactly what I'd imagined earlier.

Chapter Twenty

JUDE

BY THE LAST handful of hours in Haworth, I'd become addicted to a certain look in Lia's eyes. I'd discovered certain things triggered it.

- Scones (good scones, at least. She ate a dodgy one at our first cafe stop and spit it out into her napkin)

- Ancient school buildings where famous literary icons taught the youth of the village

- Orgasms

These were not listed in order of priority, of course, because during the two nights we spent exploring Haworth Village together, I saw that look numerous times. We entered the church building, and she grabbed my hand, squeezing it so tightly I thought my fingers might fall off. When we walked through the Parsonage Museum, the home that the Brontës' lived in, I heard her sniff quietly. In alarm, I'd tugged her round to make sure she was okay, but she had such a blinding smile on her face, I found myself smiling in return.

"Happy tears," she whispered. "Thank you for bringing me back."

I kissed her there, soft and quick, and I remember feeling like it was such a normal thing to do.

•

A quick kiss in the middle of a normal day.

The way she walked close to me as we strolled through the park on our way back to our hotel room to pack and head back to London.

Our fingers brushing against each other's when we sat and ate a quiet lunch tucked into a small cafe.

For those three days and two nights, with her curled up against me in our rented cottage in the village, everything felt remarkably normal. We didn't rush what we saw or at the places we ate or when leaving the bed in the mornings.

When she worked on her laptop, notes strewn across the sturdy wood table on the stone floor, I worked out in the small garden in the back. There were no major distractions for either of us.

Maybe this was what the rest of the world experienced on a day-to-day basis. But for me, it was bloody foreign. Enjoyable, but still strange. And conversely, it was exactly the kind of thing my parents always told me I was sacrificing to do what I did.

Don't you want a normal life with a family? A woman who loves you and children to raise? What kind of life do you think you'll have chasing a ball around for millions of pounds every year?

It was something my mum had asked me back when I was getting my first offers in the premier league. My dad had given up by that point. He knew my success in the German Bundesliga had cemented my path. It was only a matter of time before I came back home and dominated on one of the strongest tiers of play in the entire world.

As we packed our bags and locked up, I watched Lia with a dawning sense of accomplishment. The look in her eyes, with the exception of the scones, were all from things I'd been able to bring to her.

I'd accomplished something that my family never thought I'd be able to.

A good woman, smart and sexy and funny, and children to raise. And still, I was a premier player.

Lia wrestled her dark hair up into a bun on top of her head and faced me while my mind raced. "What's going on up there?"

I blinked. "What now?"

She tapped her temple. "You look very deep in thought." She approached, sliding her hands up my chest. Quite naturally, my own settled onto her hips. As I pulled her closer, her eyes softened. "It's sexy."

I hummed, dropping a kiss onto the curve of her newly exposed neck. "Nothing interesting."

Lia sighed, melting fully into my embrace. For a few moments, we stood like that, and I tried to remember how long it had been, before her, that someone had simply hugged me for the pleasure of it.

Maybe that was why I was so addicted to touching her whenever she was in reach. Because I could and because it felt fucking great. I wasn't reading between the lines of those touches, and neither was she. I'd found someone—something—quite remarkable, even if it was quite by accident.

It was in that quiet embrace, and recognizing the power of it, that I had an idea.

"What do you say to a small detour on the way back?"

Lia's face spread into an excited grin. "I say yes."

My girl was always up for an adventure. Excited to attend a losing match, simply because the atmosphere was electric, unafraid to stand for hours in the rain to experience it. As I watched that look in her eye again, at the thought of experiencing something new, I desperately wanted to get this right. I wanted to be the parent I'd never had. I wanted my child to know love and support with this beautiful woman to teach him or her about excitement and adventure and loyalty, and hopefully me to teach them about hard work and grit and the beauty of achieving your goals by doing something you loved.

Shortly, we were back in my car and driving down the roads of West Yorkshire under a cloudy November sky. As we approached Stocksbridge, the steel mill looming off in the distance, I couldn't believe she hadn't asked me a single question about where we were going. Lia relaxed in her seat, taking in the sights with a soft smile on her face.

"I always wonder if people get this excited when they drive around my state, you know?"

"What do you mean?" I made a turn away from town and toward the farm where I'd grown up, the roads growing smaller, the houses farther apart in the green countryside.

"This is all normal to you, you know? But every stone house I see, every perfect little green hedge, or rolling hill, it's nothing like what I see back home, and I just want to soak it all up. I wonder if people drive around Seattle and feel like that."

I glanced at her with amusement. "I'd reckon so. You have mountains in Washington, yeah?"

"Oh, yeah."

"Then I'm guessing they all gawk out the windows just like you are, love."

She smacked me in the stomach, and I laughed. It was a good momentary distraction because as I took the final turn, my parents' house rose up just over the next hill. It looked exactly the same. Mentally, I had to do some calculations to remember exactly when I'd been back last. Typically, we gathered at Lewis' house or pub so we were both on neutral ground.

The house was all weathered rock and dark-framed windows, probably the same ones that needed to be replaced the last time I'd been there. Five years was what I figured. Wooden fencing stretched along emerald plots of grass, and a few fat sheep grazed near the house. The barn had been painted, a fresh coat of white covered the planks of wood. I could hear the goats, a new addition since I'd been out last, and tried to muster a smile when Lia exclaimed when they crowded the fence as soon as she got out of the car.

"Oh, how cute are you guys?" she said, laughing when one particularly brash one jumped over the group to try to find food in her hand. "Goodness. I wish I'd come prepared." She held up a hand to shade her eyes and glanced at the sprawling land surrounding the house. "Where are we?"

A quiet voice interrupted before I could answer. "J-Jude?"

My mum was standing in the door that led to the kitchen, a bright red towel clutched in her hands as she stared at me like she'd seen a bloody ghost. Her hair was still dark, streaked liberally with gray along her temples, something she'd never felt the need to hide.

I came next to Lia and set my hand on her back. She glanced at me with a million and a half questions in her eyes. I smiled down at her, then looked back to the house. "Hello, Mum."

"Ohhhhh," Lia breathed. She cut me a glance. "You could've warned me," she whispered under her breath.

"Surprise," I whispered back.

Lia lifted her chin and smoothed a hand over her hair. Given we had made no plans other than to drive back home, she'd dressed for comfort with a massive hoodie over jeans and tall brown boots. Looking at her, there was absolutely no indication she was pregnant. She looked young and pretty.

"What are you doing here?" Mum asked, eyes traveling from me to Lia and back again.

I curled a hand around Lia's shoulders. "We just took a holiday in Haworth for a few days. Thought we'd drop by to say hello on our way back home."

Her hand came up, and I noticed the tremor in it as she laid it on her chest. "Right. Your father is out in the backfields. He won't be back for about thirty minutes yet."

I nodded, just as Lia cleared her throat sharply.

Right.

"This is Lia Ward, Mum."

Lia smiled, moving forward to hold her hand out. "It's so nice to meet you, Mrs. McAllister."

"You're American."

The smile on Lia's face deepened, a dimple appearing in her cheek. "Your son said that in almost the same tone the night we met."

My mom didn't smile back. Probably because she wasn't terribly happy to see us.

They didn't do surprises well. Any change to their routine, to their schedule, was absolutely out of the question.

Lia's smile faded slowly. "Umm, what kind of farming do you do? Jude hasn't told me too much."

She hummed. "Of course, he hasn't. We have sheep and goats. We sell milk and cheese, the wool from the sheep, and the meat, of course. But we've started doing tours as well. That's where my husband is. He's got a school group here for a tour."

My head reared back. "You do? Dad hates people stomping around his farm."

"There's good money in agritourism, Jude." She glanced at Lia briefly. "We can't all make millions of pounds a year playing games."

Lia's mouth fell open before she snapped it shut.

I may not have reacted on the outside, but the arrow buried deep, even if she hadn't intended it that way. That was the thing about my parents. In their discomfort of what I did, the success I'd found, they managed a razor-sharp level of disdain that I wasn't even sure they were aware of.

"Quite true, Mum." I lifted my chin. "You could cash the checks I've sent you, though, if he hates doing tours so much."

"We're perfectly capable of supporting ourselves, Jude." She did some chin lifting of her own. "Riding on your coattails is best reserved for others."

Lia, as I expected, didn't let that barb slide. She smiled again, but I could see how it cost her. "I certainly hope that wasn't aimed at me, considering I've just met you and you know nothing about me."

My mum's cheeks flushed a rosy pink. "No, not you. I apologize if it sounded like it. Past experiences have taught us that almost everyone who meets him wants something from him, is all."

"Well," I said slowly, "I suppose you'll be pleased to know that Lia had absolutely no idea who I was when we met. Called football—what was it again, love?—boring?"

Lia blinked. "Umm, yeah. Somewhere along those lines. I just ... I didn't understand the game like I do now."

"She's here studying at Oxford for Michaelmas," I told my mum, who was regarding Lia with guarded curiosity in her eyes. "Getting her master's degree in English Literature."

That softened her just the slightest. My mum always loved to read.

Lia glanced between my mum and I. "I specialize in the Brontës. That's why Jude took me to Haworth," she said, looking up at me with a strained smile.

"I was always fond of the parsonage museum myself," my mum said.

I glanced over at her. "You've been there?"

"I do travel some places, Jude," she answered crisply.

It was that tight reply, the defensive snap in her voice that pushed me just slightly over the edge of propriety. "Right. Just not anywhere you might see me do my job, right? And certainly not if I ask you to."

Lia tightened her fingers around mine, eyes focused on the ground.

My mum lifted her chin. "You gave us no notice, Jude. Just like always, you expect the world to stop revolving simply because you've asked it to. But people have lives and jobs that don't bend to your whim."

"I wasn't asking you to bend to my whim, Mum."

"Weren't you?" She shook her head sadly. "You messaged your father at midnight the night before your match without so much as a *please, it would mean something to me if you came.*"

With my free hand, I gestured to Lia. "I wanted you to meet

her, Mum. That's why I wanted you to come to the match. Didn't Lewis tell you?"

"I haven't connected with your brother in a couple of weeks. We've been busy, and so is he. Doing our jobs."

Lia lifted her head, giving me an unfathomable look.

I swallowed, wondering why I'd expected this to go any differently. "And who am I to understand real work, is that right?"

"I didn't say that."

"You didn't have to," I tossed back.

My mum exhaled, looking tired and older than I remembered. "Why did you come like this, Jude? What did you think would happen?"

It was on the tip of my tongue to tell her Lia was pregnant, that her first grandchild was on the way, and I'd never, ever make it feel the way they made me feel. But even five minutes with her, and everything went to shit. I might know exactly how to hit the self-destruct button on my relationship with my family, but even I wasn't so stupid.

"Fuck if I know, Mum. Thought you could meet someone important to me and not have it explode at our feet, but I guess that was hoping for a bit too much, wasn't it?"

Her chin wobbled, but she didn't so much as blink.

"Tell Dad I said hello."

Lia held fast when I tried to turn toward the car, and I gave her a questioning look, but her eyes were fastened on my mum.

"It was nice to meet you, Mrs. McAllister," she said. Lia refused to budge until my mom's shocked gaze came back to her face. "And I hope we can meet again soon under better circumstances. I'd love to hear more about what you do here."

My mum let out a shaky breath and nodded. "Nice to meet you too, dear."

Then instead of waiting for me to take the lead, Lia pivoted, all but dragging me back to the car, where she let go of my hand in order to climb back in.

She didn't say a word until we'd driven down the dirt lane that led away from the farm, and when she did, I found myself bracing for a verbal tirade.

"Well," she said softly, "that explains a lot, doesn't it?"

I exhaled a laugh. "Yeah. I suppose."

"At least when I get Isabel from the airport next week, I can tell her I've met your mother now."

Pressing my foot on the accelerator I tried to ignore Lia's strained tone, and the worried wrinkle in her brow. I tried to ignore the fact she didn't hold my hand on the drive back. Or that when I dropped her off in Oxford, the kiss she gave me was subdued.

"Thank you for the lovely getaway," she whispered, smoothing her hands along the collar of my shirt.

"Are you cross with me?" I asked, unable to stand the feeling that I'd just wedged a chasm between us.

"Not cross, no," she said. "I'm ... sad for you, I think. I don't know exactly what I feel."

That helped a bit but not entirely.

The one thing I seemed to do right suddenly felt precarious. I kissed her again, ignoring the way a couple of arseholes whistled as they passed.

She pulled away with a breathless laugh.

"Talk soon, yeah?" I asked.

Lia nodded. "Yeah."

But as I drove away, I couldn't shake the feeling that I'd just laid the groundwork for my own demise.

Chapter Twenty-One

LIA

ISABEL and I made it three days of blissful sister coexistence after she arrived.

At Heathrow, there was screaming and crying and hugging and soul-deep happiness that one of my people was finally here with me.

There was the requisite touristy stuff and jet lag recovery the first few days. We ate the bangers and mash and did bus tours, and she drank beer (I only snuck one sip because I really, really missed the occasional beer).

"Can we go in there? I think I need a Union Jack T-shirt."

"You do know that we'll pass about a hundred different stores exactly like this one."

She grinned. "Indulge the tourist, please. If this is what will keep me awake until tonight, then you're going to help me find a T-shirt."

I held up my hands. "Fair enough."

She was quicker than me, partially because her legs were longer, but also... not pregnant people were faster than pregnant people.

"Your bump is adorable," she commented, flicking me a quick glance as she slid hangers down the rack.

I ran my hand over it. "I feel good. My energy picked back up around eleven weeks, but I swear, if I keep eating this many scones, I'm going to gain a thousand pounds."

Isabel smiled as she held a shirt up to look at it. I could tell in her face she wasn't sure what to say next.

"What is it?"

She carefully hung the shirt back up. "Nothing."

I held up a white T-shirt covered in a black and white rendering of Queen Elizabeth with a red and blue lightning slash running down her face ala David Bowie.

Isabel grinned and motioned for it. "Perfect."

We wandered a little bit after she got the shirt. Since Isabel wasn't a student, I couldn't take her inside the Rad Cam (the Radcliffe Camera, also known as one of Oxford's most famous buildings), but I could show her my favorite place to sit and work. We worked our way through Oxford that way during the first couple of days, finding small nooks to sit where she could caffeinate, I could eat, and I'd get tiny snippets of what I was missing back home.

"What about Emmett?" I asked. "How's he doing? He's never around when I talk to anyone."

Isabel smiled. "The little prince is fine. I already told him he's going to be dethroned as the favorite when you give birth."

"You did not."

"Hell yeah, I did. Kid needs to be prepared."

I rolled my eyes. "You have the tact of a semi-truck, Isabel. He's nine. No one will be replacing anyone."

She glanced at me over the rim of her cappuccino. "You'll be living there, though, right? When you go home?"

My fingers plucked at the scone, and I took my time slathering cream and jam on it. It wasn't the first probing question I'd gotten from my big sister, but it was just the most obvious.

"I guess," I said. "I hadn't really thought about it."

Isabel hummed. The subject dropped. For another day at least.

On day four of her trip, we made our way into London where she'd booked another hotel for a few nights, and at her insistence, I packed a bag to stay with her, working on my paper while she slept in until late morning. We were just around the corner from Hyde Park, a beautiful tree-lined street in a quiet neighborhood, and when she stopped to take some pictures of an overflowing flower cart on a street corner, she poked me again.

"Have you thought of any names?"

My hand went straight to my belly. I found myself doing that more in the past few weeks. It was an interesting sort of reassurance. Yup, the bump was still there, as if I couldn't tell from the aching back and ravenous appetite and massive boobs.

"Not really," I answered.

We waved goodbye to the woman selling the flowers and pulled our hoods up to turn the corner toward Hyde Park.

"Isabel is always a classic choice for a girl," she said about a block later.

I nudged her with my shoulder, laughing under my breath. "If it's a girl, there's no shortage of family names I could use."

"True." For a while, I thought she was going to drop that subject too. We crossed the street and entered the park through the black wrought-iron gates. "I thought there'd be snow," she commented as she crouched to take a picture of one of the first fountains we passed.

"It's kinda like Seattle." I tucked my hands into my coat and shivered. "It can get cold enough for snow, but it's just not common. Lots of rain, lots of clouds, but honestly, I don't mind it."

She stood and gazed over the park. Now that her jet lag had dissipated, the dark circles under her eyes were gone. I didn't know why I studied her as if I'd expected her to change in the months since I'd last seen her. Maybe because *I'd* changed so drastically. But she was the same Isabel, tall and striking. Her hair, darker than the rest of ours, was braided down her back, and she had her head covered with a black cap. Even dressed casually, something about her was intimidating and drew the eye when she passed.

"You look good," I told her when we started walking again.

"So do you."

"I look pregnant, Isabel. You have to say that."

"I don't *have* to say shit, Lia. If I was worried about how you looked, I'd ask you about whether you were eating healthy or getting enough exercise." She softened her response with a teasing smile. "Your looks are not one of the things I'm worried about."

I stopped walking. "What's that supposed to mean?"

Iz muttered something under her breath that I couldn't hear.

"I didn't hear you."

"You weren't supposed to hear me." She pointed at a restaurant up around a curve in the path. "Need anything?"

I shook my head. "No, I'm okay for now. But if you need to use the toilet, let's go in and grab some tea or something."

"Where's our next stop? I can wait."

"Kensington Palace," I told her. "It's on the other side of the park."

"Sweet. Maybe I'll catch a glimpse of William, and I can tell him about the poster Molly used to have on her wall."

I snorted. "I forgot about that. I told Jude that if I'd come a couple of years earlier and met Harry when he was single, he would've been shit outta luck."

She smiled but didn't say anything. She'd asked a few questions about Jude, about his job, and about football overseas in general. But I got the sense that my sister was treading very, very carefully. Which was unlike her.

As we curved around the meandering paths, stopping at bridges for pictures, I waffled on how much I wanted to push Isabel on her comment. When you came from a big family, your relationships with each sibling were unique. Claire and I were twins, so ... that was a gimme for reading minds and feeling all the same feels and doing weird prolonged eye contact when I knew exactly what she wanted to tell me without her saying a word. Molly was the warm, friendly sister. As cheerleaders went, she was the one you wanted in your corner. She was the sister I could count on to listen to me cry without judgment, the one who'd wrap me up in a hug and tell me everything was going to be okay.

Isabel ... she was actually a lot like our brother, Logan.

If I burst into tears right now, she'd probably get a panic-stricken look on her face, and I'd get an awkward pat on the back. But on the flip side, she'd dole out pragmatic, no-bullshit advice anytime we needed it. And if anyone, and I mean *anyone*, threatened the people she loved, she was an absolute savage.

And I knew, as we walked and looked at buildings and fountains and bridges and made small talk, that that was the reason I hadn't told her about what happened at Jude's parents' farm.

She'd hate him for putting me in that position—arguably one of the most awkward I'd ever been in—and I didn't want Isabel to hate him. I wanted her to like him because if she did, she'd smooth the way for the rest of my family to like him too.

Yes, my time in London was drawing to a close, and Jude knew I was going back to Seattle for the birth, but what about later? What about when I finished with school?

We approached Kensington Palace from the front, and Isabel grinned the entire time she snapped pictures. "It's so fucking pretty I could puke."

I shook my head. "Such a way with words. But you curse like a Brit, so you'll fit in just fine at the match tomorrow."

"Yeah, about that ..." She turned her camera and snapped a quick selfie of us with the palace in the background. "Tell me more about him."

"What do you want to know?"

We got in line to go into the palace and huddled together

when the wind picked up. "I mean, what's his deal? You get this
googly-eyed look on your face when you talk about him, and I
know you'd slept there the last time I called, so don't even
pretend you didn't."

I ducked my face into the collar of my coat to warm my
cheeks. And to avoid figuring out how to answer the question.

"We're ... I don't know exactly."

Isabel rolled her eyes but softened it with a teasing grin.
"What are we, sixteen? You're having a baby with him, Lia."

"I know that." I exhaled. "There's something there. And we
waited to sleep together again. It's not like I told him about the
baby, and we hopped back in bed. But we get along. We're
getting to know each other, and we like each other. Does there
need to be some big label on it?"

She studied me with a careful expression on her beautiful
face. "Not necessarily. But you're also going home soon. You're
done with your paper, right?"

I nodded. "Just making some finishing touches on the end.
But ... Atwood's notes on my draft were lighter than I expected,
so I think I'll finish early."

"Just be careful." She tucked her arm through mine as the
line moved. "I just don't want to see you get hurt, okay? Being a
single parent is hard enough without adding drama with the hot
baby daddy footballer."

I wanted to laugh but didn't. For the first time in a long time,
I thought about our mother. Briefly, at the beginning of my
pregnancy, I kept looping around the idea that I might be bad at
being a mom simply because I was born to someone bad at
being a mom. But the distraction of Jude and our relationship
had kept those questions at bay.

"You don't think being a bad parent is like, in the gene pool,
right?" I asked. I tried to say it sarcastically, but instead, my
voice sounded reed-thin and wispy, easily carried away by the
cold wind. And not like Isabel could know it, but I thought
about Jude's parents too. How hard his mom had been on him. I

mean, yeah, stopping by that way wasn't his best idea, but she could hardly hide her disdain.

My hand went to my belly. Little peach could make facial expressions now, I'd read. How weird, right? Nothing to see, muted voices and jumbled movements, and as Isabel and I stood there, they might be smiling.

"Uhh, no." She gave me a weird look. "Are you being serious? Lia—"

I held up my hand. "I was kidding. I just meant, you know, sleeping with him when we haven't even talked about like, custody or any of that."

I wasn't actually kidding, but I refused to ruin this day of exploring London with my sister. Impulsively, I leaned in and gave her a tight, bruising squeeze.

"I'm glad it was you who came to visit."

She pulled back and turned away before I could see her face. She cleared her throat a little, and her eyes were red when she faced me again. "Damn straight. I'm going to be the favorite aunt."

I laughed. "That's what Molly said."

Iz rolled her eyes. "Please. I've got this one in the bag."

We moved closer to the entrance. "Ready for your first football match tomorrow?"

"Oh, my Lord," she teased, "he's even got you calling it football, not soccer. He must have a magic penis."

I shoved her. "Ugh, who invited you here?"

Isabel laughed. "Yes, I'm very ready for my first match. I probably shouldn't tell him I was rooting for Liverpool last week when they played, huh?"

"Probably not." I eyed her. "Why?"

"Amy is a huge fan. She always has the TVs at the gym turned to the matches when Liverpool plays."

I grinned, thinking of Isabel's boss. "Is she still going to sell the gym?"

Isabel's shoulders slumped. "Yes. I'm so sad. She's like my

Yoda, you know? And who knows who she'll sell it to. They could be an asshole or a misogynist or a terrible gym owner. They could fire me because maybe they don't want a manager, and then I'll be destitute and angry because I love my job and don't want to work anywhere else."

I grinned, looping an arm over her shoulders as we turned into the grand, soaring entryway of Kensington Palace to have our bags checked. "Maybe none of those things will happen, and she'll sell it to some hot, mysterious man who'll sweep you off your feet."

Isabel rolled her eyes. "I'd quit before that happened."

"Cheer up, Iz. You don't need to worry about any of that right now." I hooked my purse back over my shoulder when the security guard handed it back with a smile. "Today, we see palaces, and tomorrow, we watch the Shorthorns beat Tottenham."

The security guard snorted.

"What?"

He held his hands up. "You're dreaming, dear. Shepperton is going to get bloody wrecked tomorrow."

"Geez," Isabel muttered. "I thought the British were supposed to be nice."

He winked, tipping his hat at us. "Cheers."

We entered the palace smiling, and I kept my fingers crossed that the mood would carry us over into the next day.

Chapter Twenty-Two

JUDE

WHAT's the saying about hindsight? Well, mine was twenty-bleedin'-twenty, because I should've known that everything would go to shit when we got kicked from pillar to post by Tottenham. Yeah, we scored two goals, but that only did so much when they scored five.

Their bloody captain, who I had no problem with when he wasn't running my team into the ground, got in my face more than once, calling me old man and slow. He might have been teasing because the fucker grinned like a clown when he said it, but all I could do for ninety minutes plus stoppage was imagine punching him right in the bloody mouth.

Losing was always hard in our league. Especially when your team hovered only a few spots above relegation. Each loss, each time you failed to add points added a sense of urgency to the time spent on the pitch.

We were fine. For now.

But in a few weeks or another month or two, it could be an entirely different story.

Losing was even harder, though, when your manager pulls you into his office and says, "I'm probably going to bench you next week, Jude, and I want you to know it now before anyone else does."

It took everything in me not to explode. "I can play better," I promised.

"You've been telling me that for weeks, McAllister. I've got guys younger and faster and hungrier, and that makes them better options for me when I'm trying to win more games."

I clenched my jaw, practically heard the crack of my molars from the effort it took me to keep the words crowding my throat from coming out. It hurt to breathe through them, breathe through the bruise to my pride, if I was honest.

There wasn't much worse for a footballer than to feel useless or like a hindrance to their team. And after a wet, sloppy loss on a muddy rain-soaked field, useless was an apt word for how I felt.

Ineffective.

And if I was honest, I couldn't stop the word worthless when it whispered through my subconscious. If I wasn't this ... if I couldn't do this, what was I? What good was I to anyone without this part of my identity?

All the things I used to define myself came straight from the game I played. My drive. My passion. My work ethic. None of those things were in question, which was what made it even worse. Those things were in my control, but the reason Coach wanted to bench me, that was nothing I could grasp onto.

I nodded stiffly and left his office without another word.

I showered. Changed. Packed my bag. No one said anything to me in the locker room, and I was glad for it.

I was supposed to get my head on well enough to go meet Lia and her sister visiting from the States. Lia and I hadn't even seen each other since I dropped her off in front of her flat after the disaster at the farm and all for good reason.

She was finishing her paper and didn't want to stop while the work was good.

I was training my arse off to prepare for a brutal stretch of

Liverpool and then Tottenham, both games serving us brutal losses.

Fucking red birds and fucking roosters.

All of that to set up the fact that when I walked out of the locker room, I was in a foul fucking mood when my brother sent me a text.

Lewis: Sorry about the match. Can you swing round after you're done? I'm assuming Lia is with you. I've got something for both of you.

Me: I'll ask her. Her sister is visiting from the States, and I don't know if they've got plans for us after this.

Lewis: It would mean a lot.

I dropped my head back and let out a slow breath. That moment right there was when I should've canceled all of it.

Should've called Lia to reschedule meeting her sister until the next day.

Should've told Lewis to sod off because I was in a horrid mood.

But that useless feeling would've only intensified, and I knew it. The only thing worthwhile I'd done in the past few months was Lia. Just that one thing.

I took a deep breath, smoothed a hand down my weary, old, slow face, and turned the corner where I knew the two women would be waiting for me.

They were leaning up against the wall taking selfies of the Tottenham logo in the background, and I took a moment to study them. Lia's sister was taller than her with sharper cheekbones and a sharper jawline. Her hair was darker, and when she smiled, it didn't spread as widely as Lia's. But the similarities were stunning, and I could only imagine what the four sisters must look like all together.

Isabel saw me first, and the look she gave me reminded me of a flock guard dog that my parents used to have. In one split second, she assessed me with unguarded caginess. *Are you a friend or a foe?* That was what I saw in her eyes, with her arm around her younger sister.

Lia looked over, and the brilliant smile on her face swept away just a bit of my awful day.

"Hi," she said. "Rough game. I'm sorry."

If Isabel hadn't been there, I would've wrapped my arms around her to take whatever comfort she may have given me, but I couldn't shake the feeling that like the guard dog on my parents farm, she'd rip my arm off if I made the wrong move.

I attempted a smile. "Can't win them all, right?" Lia gave me a curious look, then slipped her arm around my waist. I sighed, kissing the top of her head. I'd missed her smell, missed the feel of her next to me over the past couple of weeks. My hand found her belly. "My how you've grown."

She pinched my side. "Thanks for pointing it out." She turned, gesturing behind her. "This is my sister, Isabel. Isabel, this is Jude McAllister."

I held out my hand, which she shook firmly. "Welcome to England, Isabel. I'm sorry we couldn't have given you a better match today."

Her smile was small, but her eyes had lost that initial wariness. "Can't win them all, like you said. Besides, it was a good match for the Spurs fans, right?"

I rubbed the spot on my chest over my heart. "I hope you're not describing yourself. I can't take it."

She laughed. "No. I'm a fan of sports, honestly. Any time I can see someone compete doing something they love, that's what I'm a fan of."

"A testament to your upbringing, no doubt. Unsurprising that you'd elevate the athlete over the team."

Isabel hummed, sharing a look with her sister. "Athletes are just normal people ..."

"Who do abnormal jobs," finished Lia.

I raised an eyebrow.

Lia grinned. "Something drilled into our heads growing up so we didn't place athletes on a pedestal. Because when they mess up, and they will, you know they have bad days just like the rest of the world."

"Very smart," I said. "I know I said you could plan dinner wherever you wanted after this, but do you mind terribly if we stop by Lewis's pub after we leave? He asked if we would. Said he had something for us."

"Of course, we don't mind." Lia took my hand as we started walking, explaining who Lewis was to her sister.

"We're all going to be one big happy family now, right?" Isabel asked. "Might as well meet him now."

My head snapped in her direction because I couldn't tell if she was being serious or if she was baiting me. But from the look on her face, she meant it, which meant Lia probably hadn't told her about our stop at my parents' farm.

"You don't need to ride with the team back to the hotel?" Lia asked.

I shook my head. "Cleared it with my manager because of Isabel visiting."

She smiled widely, and after my day, it was one small, sweet relief that I could still do that.

"Did you take the Tube out here?" I asked, holding the door open for them as we made our way to get a black taxi. Lia nodded. "Wasn't too bad."

"I love the whole *mind the gap* thing," Isabel said, sliding into the back seat. "I swear, in America, it would be like, don't fall on your frickin' face, and if you do, no one will help you up."

I laughed for what felt like the first time all day. "That can't be true."

She shrugged. "Maybe it's a slight exaggeration, but I do think Brits are more friendly than we are back home. To tourists at least. Even when they're trash-talking the Shorthorns, they're so pleasant."

I glanced sideways, and her face held a Cheshire cat grin. Lia nudged me with her elbow. "Ignore her. She's testing you because she's obnoxious."

Their teasing was so natural. And the entire drive to my brother's pub, it was bizarre to bear witness to how easy their interactions were. They had inside jokes. They laughed at each other and at themselves so effortlessly. They spoke of their family, of holidays, of watching games together. How Isabel flipped a table once when she lost a seven-hour-long match of Monopoly to their nine-year-old nephew. It was a glimpse into how our child would be raised, and it dug like a burr underneath my skin.

When it was just me and Lia inside the little bubble we'd created, it was easy to ignore the dynamics she might have with her family. And even as I recognized that my child would be raised around a loving, supportive family, it only served to dig that sense of uselessness down even further. A splinter I couldn't pluck out, so much more painful than it should've been.

Because of traffic leaving White Hart Lane and just London in general, it took us a while to head back south toward the pub. By the time we pulled up to The Red Lion, we were all quiet—Lia because she was hungry and tired, Isabel because she was still fighting the time change, and me ... well ... because that day was pure bollocks from start to finish. The rain had tapered off, and as I paid the driver, Lia and Isabel huddled together underneath the awning of the pub to ward off the chilly air.

Even that, keeping her warm, wasn't my job while her sister was around. And it was hard not to feel replaced.

It was a symptom of my day, to be sure, and another glaring reminder that I should've canceled. All of it. I stared at Isabel's arm around Lia's shoulders, saw her touch Lia's belly under the coat, and they laughed about something I couldn't hear.

I held the door open with a smile and waved when someone

wearing a Tottenham jersey yelled from his car window, "Thanks for the win, McAllister."

Isabel's eyebrows raised a bit.

"You get used to it," I told her under my breath.

"Do you, though?"

I thought about that question as they preceded me into the pub. It was busier than the night I'd met Lia, and I slipped a black hat out from where I kept it tucked in an inner pocket of my coat and covered my head. No, I never got used to it.

Fans yelled all sorts of things at players. Some were funny, some were understandably aggravated, some were horrific— racially charged slurs that got them banned for life from the matches of their favorite team. And to a certain extent, no I'd never gotten used to that. On the good days, it was easier to block out the noise, easier to mute the negative voices, and focus on the fans who carried the game in their blood.

But on days like this one, I simply felt really fucking tired.

Which was why I decided to answer Isabel honestly. "Not really, no."

She paused. "But it's worth it?"

"It's worth everything," I answered immediately.

That made her smile with what was probably the warmest facial expression I'd seen from her. "All the great ones say that."

"I don't know how great I am anymore." I shrugged, gesturing toward the back of the pub where Lewis usually saved a more private table when he knew I was coming.

"I don't know if Lia told you what I do," Isabel said as we skirted a long table.

"You're a personal trainer of sorts, right? At a boxing gym?"

She nodded. "We get a lot of athletes who come to our place, some because of my connection to the Wolves, and some because of my boss, Amy, and the number one thing I've learned from watching them is that their greatness never really fades. I trained someone in his sixties last summer who used to be a baseball player. Hurt his shoulder and had to retire before he wanted to, but that man, even though he's more than twice my age, had a fire in him that blew me away." Isabel shrugged, glancing over her shoulder at me. "I think what makes the great *great* is something inside them. Even when their body betrays them, it's still there."

A burst of laughter behind us made it so I couldn't answer her, but as we approached the back, I couldn't stop thinking about what she'd said, trying to decipher if it even felt true for me.

Ahead of us, I saw Lewis come around from behind the bar and greet Lia with a hug and friendly smile. No surprise that she'd won him over when they'd watched a match together. But I also saw the shock on his face when she embraced him, the way he tried not to look down at her stomach, visible behind the form-fitting Shepperton hoodie she was wearing.

"Bloody hell, fucking shit," I whispered under my breath.

Isabel's gaze snapped to me. "What?"

"I, uh, my brother doesn't know Lia's pregnant yet, and I think he just puzzled it out."

"Ahh." She lifted her chin. "Oh wow, so we get to meet the whole family?"

My stomach dropped out when my parents stood from the table in the back, regarding us warily as we approached.

I glared at Lewis, who held up his hands. "Jude, Mum told me what happened when you stopped by. It's past time you three have a decent conversation."

"And you thought tonight was the best time for it?" I hissed. I waved my hand at Lia and Isabel, who were standing by the bar, waiting to approach my parents until I was with them. "I'm not in the mood, Lewis."

He raised his eyebrows slowly. "Are you ever? I thought with her here, maybe you'd actually manage to be polite, and if they were expecting to see you, they could attempt the same." He shook his head. "You're all so bloody stubborn it makes me sick."

Slicking my tongue over my teeth, I tried to breathe through what their unexpected presence did to my mood.

Lia gave me a sympathetic smile when I slid my hand up her back.

"Sorry about this," I told her.

"Don't apologize to me. I wouldn't mind getting to know your family better, but …" Her voice trailed off as she gave my parents a quick glance under her lashes. "I don't know if this is the best way to do it."

Isabel looked between us. "What am I missing?"

"You're about to find out," I exhaled. "Come on, might as well get it over with."

Lewis muttered something to my parents, and my dad gave him a tight nod.

My father looked older, just as my mum had, and he gave me the same nod he'd just given my brother. "Jude. Nice to see you."

My mum was staring wide-eyed at Lia's stomach. There was no part of her even attempting to hide it.

"Dad, Mum." I motioned to Isabel with my free hand, the other was occupied by holding Lia's like she was a bloody life preserver. "Isabel is here from the States. She's Lia's sister. Mum, you remember Lia."

She nodded, giving Lia a small smile. "Hello again. It's … it's nice to see you."

Lia smiled back, her hand reaching up to rub her stomach. I'd seen her do it so many times but never had I been so aware of it. For her, it was probably a comfort, to be able to reach down and feel that warm curve of flesh as I'd done all the times we'd been in bed together.

My dad's forehead wrinkled when he watched her. "I was working when you two stopped by the other day. Lewis thought we should make a trip down and try to … talk."

Isabel and Lia pulled out heavy wooden chairs, and I did the same once Lia was seated to my right. Upon sitting, she slid her hand over my thigh and squeezed. Isabel looked at Lewis. "A pint would be great."

"Of course. Would you care to see our tap list?"

"Nope. Just ... any kind will be perfect."

I looked away, a feeling of shame coating every part of my skin. On the drive here, they'd been all warmth and ease.

And then there was my family. Dysfunction and discomfort.

My dad whispered something to my mum before he met my gaze. "How was your match tonight? Did you win?"

Lia blew out a slow breath as Isabel hastily grabbed the beer Lewis brought back for her. I inhaled slowly, then exhaled even more slowly. It didn't help.

"No. We got our arse kicked."

Mum frowned, and Dad looked away. Lia's hand squeezed on my leg again, and I looked over at her.

"*Try*," she mouthed. "*Please.*"

For the first time since I met Lia, I was furious at her. She was asking me for something without any bloody idea of how much it might cost me. But that was the point, wasn't it? She had no idea because I'd never told her.

It deflated most of the fiery righteousness that fueled my anger. But the frustration, the underlying sense of uselessness didn't dissipate. Maybe because it wasn't fire. It wasn't hot, something that could be stoked and tended.

What I'd been feeling all day was more like a fog. Murky. Dark. Everywhere.

Nothing you could touch, but it absolutely swamped the senses.

Fire could be extinguished, but fog ... it had the ability to destroy everything in its path if you didn't watch carefully enough.

I swallowed, laid my hand over hers, and looked up at my parents.

"This may surprise you," I said lightly, "but football is actually the last thing I'd like to talk about right now."

My parents exchanged a loaded glance. "All right," my dad said. His hands, big and rough and hardened from the farm, curled around his glass of water. "That's fine. What would you like to talk about, Jude? We're …" His voice stumbled slightly. "We're here to listen."

Lewis finished setting waters in front of Lia, Isabel, and myself and sat in the last free chair at the table, eyeing us carefully.

"Maybe Lewis should tell us why he scheduled this family event," I said.

My brother gave Lia and Isabel a sheepish grin. "Can I blame being drunk at the time?"

I rolled my eyes. "If you drank more than a beer a week, I'd believe that."

"Maybe it was a really strong beer."

"Lewis." Mum sighed. "It's not the time for jokes. Your father and I drove a long way to come down here, took time away from the farm. You said it was important."

"It is." He spread his hands wide. "This is our family, and we're doing a shit job of acting like it. You hate that he plays football, we get it. But he's been playing for over a decade. Bloody hell, move on already."

My brow furrowed at his vehement defense. I'd never heard Lewis—the happy one, the man in the middle of our little mess —speak up for me like that.

He turned to me. "And you, quit walking around like you've got a war to fight every time you see them. They don't understand the game, they don't understand how good you are, and you don't bloody need them to in order to do your job. Let it go."

I clenched my jaw tight and stared down at the table.

"We understand how good he is," my mum said in the loaded silence that followed. The pub wasn't silent, but our table was like a graveyard for how deathly quiet it was. "But you're right, Lewis, we don't understand his life. We don't understand how you can sacrifice all the things that really matter for a game that won't be there for him. Once he's done, once the crowds stop cheering his name, what will he have left? He's pushed away anyone who loves him for the empty praise of strangers."

My eyes lifted slowly to hers, and I felt that fog cloud over my vision for one moment.

From the corner of my vision, I saw Lia and Isabel trade a look. Isabel's beer was gone already. But I never pulled my eyes away from my mum.

"Is that what you think of me?" I asked quietly.

"It's what we know, son," Dad answered. "You changed. And not for the better. You may be a god to them, but to us, you're just the son we don't even recognize anymore."

"Dad," Lewis said sharply.

Lia leaned forward while I struggled to catch my breath. "How dare you speak to him like that," she said in a frigid tone. Icicles hung from her words. "Shame on you."

My parents stared at her in stunned shock. Hell, so did I.

"I know you're in a relationship with him," my dad said stiffly, "but you've no part in this, Miss."

"She's having my child," I said.

A bomb could've gone off on the table with less dramatic impact than what I'd just said. My mum's eyes fell shut, and my dad's widened. Lewis rubbed his forehead.

"She's a bloody part of this because she's having your first grandchild. Congratulations to both of you," I said smoothly. "And I'll tell you why what you've just said can't touch me, Dad. Because that child will have every-fucking-thing that you never gave me. I will give support. I will give encouragement. I will give anything they need or want because I've learned from you what not to do."

I curled my arm around Lia, whose shoulders were stiff as a plank.

"If my child wants to play football, I'll be at every bloody game. If they want to be a painter, I'll buy every single print. If they want to dance or sing or ... be a farmer, I'll be there every step of the way. Because that's what a good parent does. And you taught me how to be a brilliant one." I shrugged, feeling the fog roll insidiously off my body with each word I hurled at them. "All I have to do is not be like you, and I'll be the best fucking father in the world."

My mum wiped a tear from her face as she stood from the table. "I won't sit and listen to this."

My dad followed, as he always did, giving me a stunned look of defeat.

Lewis sat with his head in his hands. Isabel had a hand covering her mouth, eyes closed. And Lia, she was frozen next to me.

"I'm sorry you had to endure them like that," I told her, rubbing a hand on her back.

I'd hardly had time to blink, and she stood so fast that her chair fell backward.

"Lia?"

"I have to go." She looked at her sister, and whatever was on her face, Isabel nodded. Lia slipped her coat back on and I noticed her hands shaking.

"Wait," I stood. "Is it about them?"

She wouldn't look at me as she hooked her bag over her shoulder. Lewis still hadn't moved.

"Lia," I said more firmly. "Talk to me." When she did look at me, the look in her eyes was haunted. I wasn't even sure what word to use to describe it. But it made me take a step back, shaking my head. "Wait, talk to me. What's going on?"

She turned to leave, and when I moved to follow, Isabel held her hand out, just shy of my chest. I held my hands up.

"You're going to let her walk away right now." Her eyes, the same blue as Lia's, were fierce and bright.

I breathed out through my nose, hard. "I just want to know what's wrong. I can't *fix it* if I don't know what's wrong."

"Men," she murmured, pinching the bridge of her nose,

before glancing back up at me. "I don't judge anyone for having family issues. But I promise you right now, you don't want to push me on this because you will lose."

"What the bloody hell are you talking about?" I hissed. "It's not about pushing or losing. I just want to talk to her. I don't *want* her to be upset."

Isabel held my gaze. "I don't give a flying fuck about what you want, Jude. You will give my sister a minute to breathe, okay?"

My jaw was so tight, I could feel it all the way down my neck. But I nodded.

"We're staying at the Leonard Hotel by Hyde Park. She'll talk to you tomorrow."

It took everything in me not to shout her name again, but I let them walk out of the pub.

Why did my insides feel all twisted and knotted tight? Something was wrong, something yanked in a direction it shouldn't have been when she turned her back on me. Something that recognized, even before I did, that she and I were supposed to be facing the same direction. But there I was—standing still while she walked away.

If I thought I'd felt useless before, it was nothing to how I felt at that moment. I sank into the empty chair at the table and realized there were worse things than being benched or losing games. There were worse things than having terrible parents.

It was fucking up with the first woman to find herself in my miserable excuse for a heart.

Chapter Twenty-Three

LIA

ISABEL USHERED me out of the pub and immediately snagged a passing black cab. She didn't say a word after we settled on the bench, and for that, I was thankful. All I wanted to do was get back to the hotel and crawl underneath the blankets. Once I did that, once I was safe there, I could nudge open the release valve on all the tension that was building, building, building.

Through the panoramic moon roof of the cab, I stared numbly at the beautiful lights of London as we slowly made our way toward Hyde Park. My fingers were the first part of my body to shake, and Isabel wove hers through mine and held fast as though she could give me her strength through osmosis.

How had I made it this long without being by anyone in my family?

The voice that used to whisper questions I didn't know how to answer was right the F there. *You blocked out everything unpleasant, everything hard. You ignored the things that hurt to think about. And you were able to do that because Jude doesn't know you well enough to push you.*

And you don't know him either, was the next horrible thought. *I didn't know him at all.*

My legs started bouncing next, and I blew out a slow breath as we curled around the darkened streets. It felt like a womb inside that car, and with my free hand, I rubbed over my stomach. Hopefully, I wasn't transferring my stress or my anger to little peach.

And oh, I was angry.

At myself. And at Jude. Definitely at his asshole parents.

The anger was what was in the slowly growing vibration of my body. It reminded me of when Logan first married Paige. I'd sit on the kitchen island while she made homemade pasta. It was a mess. Noodles hanging everywhere as they dried. But my favorite part, aside from the eating, was watching the water start to boil.

No matter what the temperature of the water was when she set it over the flames, it always started the same way. Tiny little dots, hardly visible, as they moved in dancing lines up to the surface. The dots grew, but only if you were watching very carefully. And that was my job, watch for the big bubbles that finally made the water churn angrily.

Right now, I was the pot of boiling water, and the moment someone lifted the lid, I was probably going to friggin' explode in a mess of tears and hormones and tight-lidded tension.

Isabel tightened her hold on my hand. As different as the four of us girls were, one thing we had in common was that we were very calm and collected. Until we weren't so calm and collected. Then we needed to get the F away from everyone because all the feelings were about to explode in a messy burst. Until Logan, we'd learned to keep those feelings locked down tight because our mom just ... couldn't be bothered.

"Almost there," she murmured.

I nodded but felt the tingling at the bridge of my nose, the burning press at the back of my eyes.

I tried to focus on the lights, the architecture, the arches on doorways and beautiful columns in rows, anything to keep Jude's voice out of my head as he spoke to his parents.

My eyes pinched shut.

"We're here, Lee," Isabel whispered. I got out of the cab

while she handed over a crumpled wad of pounds through the window. "Keep the change."

He whistled. "Cheers."

With her arm wrapped around my shoulders, we ascended the steps into the hotel and made our way through the quiet lobby to the small elevator. Everything—hands, arms, chin—was shaking by the time Isabel got the door open. The first tear was hot on my cheeks. The second came down more easily. My teeth were chattering by the time she had us inside.

"Holy shit," I gasped, tears slipping immediately down my face. "Oh, holy shit, did you hear them? How they spoke to each other? I didn't know about *any* of this, Isabel."

"I heard," she said slowly. "That was ... that was brutal, Lia." She pulled off her coat and laid it over the chair by the desk as she shook her head. "I thought we had some awkward family dynamics."

I laughed, but the sound that came out was pathetic and watery. I pressed both hands to my chest and tried to breathe down my rising panic.

"I c-can't do this," I stammered. "I am not ready to do this."

Isabel stood in front of me, sliding her hands up and down my upper arms. "Look at me, let's take a couple of deep breaths, okay? In through the nose."

I did as she asked, but my inhales were shaky and my exhales quick.

"Do you think selfishness i-is genetic?" I asked on a choked sob. "Like, is little peach totally, royally fucked because I come from Brooke, and J-Jude and his parents—" my voice broke.

"No," she interrupted. "No, you don't even go there in your mind, okay?"

"How are you so sure, though? It's not like people *try* to screw up their kids. He and I haven't talked about anything important. W-We just ... ignored it all, and I don't know how you're so sure we'll be able to do this."

Isabel's eyes got suspiciously bright, but she blinked a few times, and it disappeared. "The reason I'm so sure is because selfish people don't wonder if they're selfish. They do what they please and don't think about the consequences of their actions. Brooke left us because she thought she'd be happier. She thought life would be easier without us. And fuck that ho, she was probably right. We were little savages sometimes, but I guarantee you she never worried about what damage she left behind, because she was—is—selfish to her core." Isabel pressed her forehead to mine, wrapping me in a tight hug. "You are not like her because right now, after something hard, you're worried about what this means. You will be an amazing mother, okay?"

"Okay." I squeezed her back, letting the hug fortify any part of me that felt ill-equipped for ... well ... any of it, really. I sniffed. "And Jude?"

She exhaled a laugh. "Well ... I think Jude needs two things."

"What?"

"An excellent therapist and a kick to the balls. He should've warned you."

It felt good to laugh, even if it was through my tears. I sank onto the bed, wiping my cheeks. "I think parents need the kicking even more than their son."

She nodded. "I can't imagine saying those kinds of things to your son."

I buried my face in my hands and took a deep breath. "I shouldn't have stormed out like that."

"No, probably not." Isabel was quiet for a second. "Why did you?"

My cheeks puffed out on a hard exhale. "I swear, my body moved before my brain knew what I was doing. I just wanted ... out. I didn't want to face how little I knew about him, and them, and the kind of family this baby is being born into."

She hummed, rubbing a hand down my back as she sat next to me.

"The stuff that was good between us, Isabel, it's so good. The parts that are just me and him. I was falling in love with him before I even knew it was happening." She sat next to me, and I lowered my head to her shoulder. "I think that's what made it so easy to ignore all the things that were ... I don't know, separate from us. It sounds so immature when I say it like that. A hot guy made my head spin, so I forgot to talk about what would happen when our child was born."

"You didn't forget, Lia. You're barely into your second trimester." She nudged me with her shoulder. "Go easy on yourself. You're in a different country, away from family, and he made you happy. Right?"

I nodded.

"Did he ever mention the future?" she asked.

"Not really. I mean, he mentioned the fact that he'd be done with the season and could travel to Seattle for the birth, so we both knew that I'd be home. But I think he counted on my understanding the demands of his career, you know? It's not like he can just ... press pause on the season and come hang out in America and watch me get puffy ankles."

"No," she said cautiously, "he can't. He must have thought about it, though."

"I think he did." I stood, snagging my water bottle off the nightstand to take a long sip. Emotional outbursts made my throat all scratchy. "I remember he asked me something odd, when we were watching the Wolves game a couple of weeks ago. He asked me what it was like to see my family doing what they did."

Isabel hummed. "That was it?"

"It's like ... it's like he never had true support, so he doesn't understand the family as a unit, you know? And aren't we our own little team? The Wards?"

She snorted. "The Wards are like their own *gang*. We'll defend each other to the death, and once you're in," she said ominously, "you can never get out."

I missed them. Our team. With the exhaustion of the day settling in like an iron cloak around my shoulders, all I wished for was the power to blink and find myself back home. Find myself surrounded by all the people who knew me best. Normally, I lived life wanting to see and do and go. But all of this, the newness and novelty, it made me crave home.

For the first time in my life, I craved the routine I had there and the sameness that I'd left.

Even though whenever I went back home, whether it was with Isabel or a couple of weeks later, I wasn't returning to the same life.

Everything, my entire life, would be different. And I couldn't ignore the parts that were hard, the parts that scared me anymore.

"What's that look on your face?" Isabel asked quietly.

"I think it's what Claire would call self-realization, or whatever the counselor speak is." I sighed heavily. "I have to talk to Jude."

She rubbed my back. "What are you going to say?"

I shrugged one shoulder. "I figure it'll, I don't know, magically appear in my head when I see him."

Reaching for my purse, I dug out my phone, and there was his name, in a series of texts.

Jude: I'm sorry about my parents. They're raging arseholes.

Jude: Your sister asked me to give you tonight, and I'll respect that.

Jude: But I didn't want to be across London at the hotel with the team, so I booked a room at the same hotel you're staying at. If you want, I can come to your room in the morning, or I'm in 327 whenever you want to talk.

I shook my head. "Pushy-ass footballer, used to getting his way."

"What?" Isabel looked over my shoulder. "Oh my gosh, he did not."

Standing up, I risked a glance in the mirror and cringed.

"It's not that bad," Isabel said.

I pointed at my face.

She grimaced. "Okay, you get a little splotchy when you cry. But if you plan to talk to him now? A plus for impact, I'll tell you that."

Rolling my eyes, I tapped out a text to Jude telling him I was on my way to his room.

"You sure you want to go there?" Iz asked.

I nodded. "It gives me control of when I want to leave. I don't want to have to ask him to go ... if it goes badly."

"Want me to come with you?" It was a token invite; I could see it on her face. I knew and she knew I needed to do this myself. "I can wait out in the hall, if you just ... want to know I'm out there."

I smiled, dropping a kiss on the top of her head. "No, but thank you. I'll be back soon."

When the hotel door closed behind me, I took a moment to take a deep breath before I went down the flight of stairs that separated his room from ours. There was no magical moment when I knew what I should say to him, the first moment of reckoning between Jude and me.

Actually, I realized, that wasn't precisely true. We'd had one before. When I told him I was pregnant, and in that split second before he could filter his reaction, the words that came out were selfish. Thoughtless.

And the words that came out of mine were angry.

Yes, I could understand his reaction, given the nature of his job. And I could understand mine because no one wanted to be called a lying ho. But as I walked down the hallway, I knew the inescapable truth. Our instincts in this, the desires that ruled our reactions, that ruled our interactions and tangible chemistry, needed work. At least if we were ever going to co-parent in a healthy way. Co-parent. No more sleeping together. No more making out on his couch. No more holidays in the English countryside.

A few stray tears escaped the corner of my eye when I thought about all of those things, and how I'd allowed them to cloud my judgment for months, simply because we had a talent for making each other feel good. Making each other forget.

When I arrived at his door, I let out a slow breath. Before I could even raise my fist to knock, he swung it open. Jude, in just the short time since I saw him at the pub, looked wrecked.

His hair was a mess, like he'd been running his hands through it.

"Lia," he exhaled, "I'm so bloody sorry."

Without a word, I walked into his room but didn't sit. He stood across from me after the door enclosed us into the space together.

"I'm sorry too," I told him. "I shouldn't have run like that." I tilted my head at him. "What are you sorry for?"

He blinked. "F-for my parents. That was ... well, it was awful."

Nodding, I gave him a careful study. The words, it seemed, were there, right when I needed them. "It was. They shouldn't speak to you that way, and I can only imagine how badly that's hurt you over the years."

He averted his gaze. "Doesn't hurt me anymore. They lost that power years ago."

Denial and shame often went hand in hand. One of the random things I remembered about helping Claire study for some of her psych classes. I was familiar with both because there were so many things I hadn't told him either, all the ugly parts of my own past. The fears I'd confided in Isabel had still been held out of reach for this man I'd been falling in love with, and I couldn't ignore that anymore.

"Jude, I need to know something important."

"Anything," he answered fervently.

That fervency had me tearing up again. I didn't want him to make this harder by being amenable. I didn't want to ask him these questions, but that was the point. It wasn't about me anymore. I slid my hand up over my belly, and his eyes tracked the movement, almost helplessly, like he couldn't look away.

And when he did watch, he looked miserable. It took me a second to voice the question in my head.

"Do you see where we went wrong?"

His face went blank in part confusion, part shock. "Have we?"

My hands shook slightly, and I knit them together in front of me. "I had no idea what kind of stuff you were dealing with, with your parents."

"It's not exactly my favorite topic," he answered evenly.

"And I get that." I licked my lips. "But ... at their farm, when we stopped, and then tonight, I was kinda tossed headfirst into the fire, you know?"

"Believe me, if I'd known they were at the pub, I never would've come."

I felt my brow wrinkle as I studied him—the set of his jaw, the line of his mouth, the tension in his shoulders. "Yeah, that was ... awkward."

"Again, I apologize for how my parents acted, if that's why you're upset."

He was at a loss, that much was obvious. Jude wasn't entirely sure what he should be saying, and maybe I didn't know either. But what I did know was that we'd done a stellar job of burying ourselves in each other while ignoring all the things that swirled just outside of that bubble.

I ran a hand over my belly. "I don't even know if upset is the right word, Jude."

"You looked pretty upset when you walked away from me without another word." He lifted his eyebrows, and my face warmed in embarrassment at how I'd acted. "And when you did, I saw that side of Isabel you warned me about. She looked like she wanted to feed me my bollocks from a blender, just for going after you."

It was the kind of thing I wanted to smile about, but even that felt too hard.

"She'll never not protect her family, even if she disagreed with me leaving like I did."

He swallowed. "That's a good trait to have in a family member."

I nodded.

"I don't quite know what that's like," he said quietly.

"The things your parents said to you," I paused, shaking my head, "and the things you said back … it was awful. I wish they could see how selfish they're being."

"Me too."

I chose my words carefully. "But I think it just all felt like a giant blinking sign of how little we really know about one another."

His jaw clenched.

"My time here, Jude, it's like … it's like being on vacation, you know? It's fun and exciting, and I'm doing something I love to do, but it's still not real life."

"It felt pretty real to me," he said in a rough voice.

The look in his eyes was full of unsaid things. And maybe my gaze was the same. Something big and important changed when we slept together, and he felt it too.

"I know. A lot of it did. But this whole time I've been here, the whole time we've been making up the little rules that gave us permission to do what felt good and right, we were avoiding everything hard and scary."

He exhaled a dry laugh. "I don't know about you, love, but I've come face-to-face with a lot of hard in the past few months. Do you think it's easy to get your arse benched?"

My mouth fell open. "Today you did?"

Jude slicked his tongue over his teeth before answering, but eventually gave me a reluctant nod.

"Oh, Jude," I whispered, "I'm so sorry."

As he propped his hands on his hips and stared at the ground, my stomach churned uncomfortably because I had to come to grips with the fact that Jude hadn't confided in me about anything important. Not one thing.

Not about his job.

Not about his family.

On an elemental level, the part of us that was instinctual and immediate, I knew him.

How he looked when he woke up in the morning.

How he smiled when a fan approached him.

How he kissed me.

How he made me feel, how thoughtful he was, how easy he made it to fall in love with him.

But all the foundational things that made him that way ... they were a complete mystery.

"I know not everyone likes to talk about what's stressing them out," I said carefully, "or how they feel about it. But Jude, you didn't even tell your brother I was pregnant, and you like him. I wish you'd see that not everyone is like your parents. There are people who want to know what you're going through, so we can support you, so we can know you."

Jude stared at me; his thoughts hidden. "You think you've got me figured out then?"

"I want to, Jude." I held my arms out. "But we've talked about nothing. We've ignored all the important things, and we ... we just ..."

My speech-making skills faltered, as thunderclouds formed on his handsome face. "We just, what? Got to know each other naturally? That's how you categorize all the nights we spent together. Wasted. Nothing. Unimportant."

"No," I said in a rush, "no, I just mean ... we didn't talk

about anything. Your job, your family, my family, the *future*. What are we going to do when I go home?"

"Well, you've got it all cleared up, I suppose. Why don't you explain to me how this whole *sharing* thing works, and I'll follow the bullet points as best I can." He held up a hand. "Just make sure the words are small. Not all of us go to Oxford."

He was like a lion, sitting back with a bloodied paw, swiping at anything that came close. Maybe I hadn't been the one to injure him, but in his mind, I was digging straight into the wound all the same. All I could do was shake my head. Anger wouldn't help right now, even if I wanted to tell him he was acting like a freaking child.

"Tell me what you want to hear, love, and I'll say it."

"Don't call me that," I snapped. "Not like that."

He pushed off the desk, where he'd leaned his weight. His eyes had a strange flatness to them. They were cold, behind the normally warm color. "Maybe it's best you're leaving soon then."

I sucked in a breath. "Why are you acting like this? Jude, we have to be able to talk to each other about the hard things, and I-I avoided that because it's what *I* do. I storm out when I should stay and I don't push to have uncomfortable conversations. I'm not perfect."

"You felt pretty perfect to me," he said silkily. Like he was wearing a mask, his lips curled up in a slight smile, but I wanted to slap it off his face. "Don't worry, love, all the distractions were my fault. Not the best idea, I'd wager, considering it just mucks things up now when we have to be adults."

Disappointment was ... I wasn't even sure what it was. It wasn't a rock in my gut because it felt so, so much bigger and more painful than that. I wasn't a poetic thinker, but all sorts of dramatic proclamations ran through my head because like I'd told Isabel, I'd started falling in love with him before I even realized it happened.

And maybe this, this version of Jude that was smooth and slick and studied—was armor, but I didn't want the man I gave my heart to, the man who I'd made a child with, to use that armor with me.

I rubbed my forehead. "Jude, maybe I came in here wrong, but I just ... I don't want our issues to bleed into this new life. You've got yours, and I've got mine."

"Oh, I'd wager mine wins, love."

"It's not a competition," I said, with an edge of frost in my words, "and you know *nothing* about what my family has been through."

The mask dropped, just for a split second, and it was the regret in his eyes that tempered my immediate flare of anger.

He held up his hands. "You're right. I don't. Because *you* haven't told me much either."

Embarrassment and shame warred mightily in my chest, because I had no choice but to concede his point. I was just as much at fault as he was, maybe even more, since only one of us bolted from the pub.

I didn't want it to be like this anymore. And there was only one way to change it.

"My mom left a few years after my dad died." As I said the words, Jude's forehead creased, his eyes taking on a curious light. I shrugged one shoulder. "That's why Logan raised the four of us. Why my family is so important to me. And I *hate* talking about it, so I get it, Jude. I get it more than you can imagine. I just ... don't want to make things worse by doing the same things over and over simply because they're easier."

"You're right." He sounded exhausted, and I took absolutely no pleasure in hearing the words.

In the wake of his concession, I deflated. Everything on my body felt like it dropped an inch, simply because I couldn't hold up the weight anymore. "Now what?"

Jude's gaze tracked over my face, which was probably still splotchy and red and awful looking. "I think, love, that you go home and be with your family. I'll finish my season. We'll talk every week, yeah? We'll figure out all those unanswered questions."

I swiped at a tear that leaked out. What a rude little tear, I'd given no permission to cry in this conversation.

It wasn't like I wanted him to know that I'd fallen in love with him, or that I was closing a door by ending things like this.

He watched the tear, which I'd missed, and a muscle clenched in his jaw.

Noisily, I sniffed. "Okay."

Jude's fists clenched, but his face smoothed out. "Do we ... shake hands? Hug?"

I tried not to think about whether it was smart, but I stepped forward. Immediately, he opened his arms. They folded around my back, and while he held me, chin resting on the top of my head, I allowed one more tear.

"You changed my life, Jude McAllister," I whispered. His chest, warm and broad and strong, expanded slowly. "I'm glad I met you."

He didn't answer right away, but I felt the whisper of his mouth against my hair. "I'm glad I met you too, Lia Ward."

If I looked up at him, with the loaded, rough tone to his delicious voice, I'd probably want to kiss him. How stupid I was when it came to this man. So, I pulled out of his arms and walked out of the room.

A few doors down, Isabel stood in the hallway, looking down at her phone.

She glanced up when I exited. "You okay?"

I shook my head.

Isabel held her hand out, and I took it. We walked back to our room like that, and by the time I curled up in bed, she'd booked my tickets home with her in three days time.

I didn't cry myself to sleep, but I curled a hand around my stomach and promised my little peach we'd be okay. All of us.

Chapter Twenty-Four

LIA

I DID okay packing up my things. No tears were shed as I packed the brand new suitcase I'd purchased to accommodate the new items I'd purchased the past few months. Even my Shepperton hoodie and winter hat made it into the suitcase with dry eyes, which I was pretty ecstatic about. Isabel helped some, but I also forced her to do a few of the touristy day tours she'd booked.

My paper, once it was polished and printed and bound into a hardcover binder, had been delivered to Atwood's office earlier in the week, as well as via email. The beautiful thing about the way we'd structured my semester cohort with her was the flexibility in my schedule. My flat was empty and clean, Isabel gone early from her Oxford B&B to do a day in Bournemouth. Originally, I'd planned to go with her, but Atwood had availability in her schedule and emailed me a cryptically short message that had my stomach twirling with nerves that she hated my paper and I'd end this entire semester with no credit.

When I knocked on her office door, I felt the first stirrings of emotion that I wouldn't be doing it again.

"Come in," she called.

Peeking around the corner, I gave her a tentative smile. "Ready for me?"

Professor Atwood watched me over the edge of her glasses, and I felt the weight of it like a wool cloak, something that in the right situation could be warm and wonderful. Or hot and oppressive.

I took my usual seat and saw my bound paper on her desk, next to her ever-present teacup. "Well, you didn't burn it. That's a good sign."

She smiled softly. "No, definitely not."

Nodding, a sigh escaped my lips in relief.

Atwood twirled an expensive-looking pen in her hands, briefly tapping it against her desk before she spoke again. "Your final product was quite lovely, Lia. I'm proud of you."

"Thank you." I exhaled. "I was worried you'd hate the change I took with the end."

She shook her head. "On the contrary, I thought it was a wonderful shift in perspective and shows the understandable change you've undergone in your time here."

"It felt right, I guess."

Atwood picked up the binder, flipping to the back. "This is the part that I highlighted. *Discontent is a powerful motivator for change and a fuel of ingenuity, but only when it's coupled with an unwavering sense of self. When applied through a lens of the past, the indomitable spirit of the independent female is wonderfully subversive, a concept that only thrived in secret, printed on words claimed by male monikers. But when that concept is viewed in light of the present, with a clear-eyed glance at the future, we find Brontë's words equally applicable. Not only that, but their intelligence, her own discontent, provides the reader with a timeless benchmark for how to apply change in their own life, even when choices seem few.*"

My face felt warm at her smile when she set the paper back down.

"I'm quite proud of you, you know," she said.

"Thank you." I laughed. "I swear, I'll say something else at some point."

"It will be incredibly easy to email your advisor at the

University of Washington with a rave review and to heartily sign off your credit for this semester."

My eyes welled up. "I'm so appreciative of everything I learned from you."

Atwood waved that off. "That's the beauty of teaching upper-level students. You don't need as much teaching; you need guidance to see the information you already know at a deeper level. Flesh out the layers of what's already up there," she said as she tapped her temple. "I don't know if you've given much thought to what you'll do when you finish, but I think you'd make a marvelous teacher, Lia."

"Really?"

"Really." She took a sip of tea, carefully set the cup back down. "You have the energy students would respond to. Give it some thought as you do your last couple of classes. Whenever you get back to them." She looked pointedly at my stomach.

"I should be able to finish the last two classes during the spring semester," I told her. "I'm not due until early June."

"I'm happy to hear that." She stood. "Is it inappropriate to ask for a hug before you go?"

I shook my head, getting up and walking easily into her embrace. She patted me on the back, brisk and firm. When she pulled back, her eyes were bright, but her smile shaky.

"Off you go. If I get weepy over every student that came through this office, I believe they'd revoke my tenure."

"Thank you for everything." I held my hands out, then let them drop by my sides. "This whole experience ... I'll never forget it. I could never repay you for the chance you gave me."

"Catherine is a lovely name for a girl," she said with a raised eyebrow.

I laughed. "I'll keep that in mind."

With a small wave as I left her office, I walked back to my flat from her office for the last time.

I'd never gotten a strong sense one way or the other whether I was pregnant with a boy or a girl, and as I took my time studying the buildings I'd gotten used to seeing, I started thinking about names.

Fourteen weeks in, and I found myself smiling at the thought of a little girl named after an English professor, despite how hard it was to acknowledge that I'd be doing things like that without Jude once I was home.

My phone had been quiet since I left his hotel room in London, which I expected, especially knowing he was playing regular matches, plus additional midweek games for various European cups that I still didn't really understand.

The distance between us was something I'd have to get used to. He said we'd talk once a week, and that was smart, but it might take me a while not to think about him as often in all those quiet days in the middle.

I found myself, as I did the final sweep of my flat and left the key with the building manager, making peace with the fact that it simply would've been too easy of a story if we'd ridden off into the sunset.

"Think about it," I told Isabel the next day as we settled into our seats on the first leg of travel. "This is the connection I needed to make."

She stretched her arms over her head and groaned. "I'm thinking ..."

"I avoided all this stuff, right? I avoided discussions and questions and worries because it felt easier, and I didn't want to face all the things that freaked me the hell out about becoming a mom. But what I needed was the discontent, right? It's like I put in my paper, and it's what Atwood was trying to get me to understand, about fixating on the past as a way to avoid facing the future. I needed the fuel to change. Getting pregnant wasn't a choice I made, but it was what I needed to change."

Isabel grinned. "Look at you, making big girl realizations."

"You do it too. The fixating thing."

Her mouth fell open. "I do not."

"Oh, please." I hooked my neck pillow over my shoulders

and closed my eyes while people filed past us into their seats for the nine-hour flight to the East Coast. "You absolutely do, but that's not the point."

When she grumbled something under her breath, I ignored her.

"Remember when Claire and I were in like fifth grade, and we had to take something to school from our parents' jobs?"

Isabel burst out laughing. "Like I could forget. You almost got suspended."

Glancing at her through tiny slits in my eyes, I tried not to smile. "I didn't almost get suspended."

"You took a poster-size picture of Paige's *Sports Illustrated Swimsuit Edition* cover to a fifth-grade classroom. She was topless, Claire."

"And do you remember what Logan said to the principal when he came to pick me up that day?"

Isabel sighed. "Does this have a point?"

"Yes. Logan said, *I hope you're not shaming my wife for what she does for a living or Lia for being proud of her for it because she's teaching an entire generation of girls that you can be beautiful and smart and sexy and respected, and none of those things cancel the other out.*"

Iz smiled. "Of course, he did."

"The radical and subversive celebration of the indomitable independent female spirit!" I shouted.

She widened her eyes when people turned to gawk at my outburst. "What the *hell* are you talking about?" she whisper-hissed.

I started laughing at her expression and couldn't stop as the flight attendants made their announcements, and the plane took off. Like when you're in church and you know whatever the thing is, it's not actually that funny, you just know you shouldn't be laughing. The entire time, Isabel was regarding me warily, like maybe she should've sat somewhere else.

When I finally got my giggles under control, I was wiping tears from the corners of my eyes.

"Yeah," Isabel drawled. "I wish Claire was here right now because you've lost your friggin' mind, Lee."

I took a deep, cleansing breath and stared at the ceiling of the plane. "I think maybe I have too, Isabel."

She handed me a water bottle from the side of my backpack, stuffed safely underneath the seat in front of me. After I took a sip, I handed it back to her.

It took a couple more minutes for my thoughts to fully form. But when they did, I didn't feel much like laughing.

"When we get to Seattle in a hundred hours," I said quietly, "we will be greeted by a veritable army."

"True."

"But I don't think, until this week, I really ever thought through that I'd be a single mom. Independence is a pretty concept, a topic for speeches and posts and flower quotes, but the truth of truly doing something on your own is ... not always so pretty. It means long days and nights, of facing a lot of battles on your own. Yes, I will have so much help, but in the middle of the night, when I haven't slept well in weeks, I can't roll over and tell Jude to take that feeding or rock the baby to sleep because I'm exhausted." I exhaled slowly. "I can do it. And I will do it. But it's not a fun truth to face, and that's not always something I'm very good at."

Isabel hummed. "Are any of us good at that, though? I think you need to give yourself a little grace, Lee. What you're going through is really fucking tough. And it's understandable that this part—the closing of this door—is bringing up a lot."

The closing of the door. With Jude.

"I still miss him," I said quietly. "And I'm a little annoyed with myself about it."

"Be nice to my sister," Isabel insisted. "She got boinked by a hot footballer with an accent, resulting in a child that will probably be so genetically blessed that all who gaze upon it will turn into a walking happy sigh emoji."

I laughed even as I struggled not to go all weepy again. Pregnancy hormones were so weird. "You're right."

Isabel leaned her head back and closed her eyes. "I'm always right. It's my best quality."

I leaned my head on her shoulder with a smile and tried not to think about the growing ocean of space between me and Jude.

I tried not to think about what it would be like when I talked to him next.

I tried not to think about when I'd see him next, probably waddling around like a giant, puffy-ankled mess.

And as we watched movie after movie after movie, took more naps than I thought capable of in one long day of travel, I tried not to think about how long it would take me not to miss him.

When the plane touched down at Sea-Tac, and I powered my phone back up, I felt my heart skip a beat at the sight of his name.

Jude: Let me know when you've made it home safely. Precious cargo and all.

"What an ass," I whispered as my eyes welled up. He was not going to make any of it easy, and he couldn't even help it. He was sweet and thoughtful and stupid and sorta damaged, and I wanted to hug him as I waited to get out of my seat. I liked it better when I was trying not to think about it. When I was thinking about the army of people about to greet us with screams and tears, and oh, my word, they were going to be so obnoxious, and I couldn't wait.

But there I was, staring at his text, feeling my eighty-fourth emotion for the day. And a long day it had been.

Isabel helped me stand and kept a tight grip on my hand as we got off the plane and made our way down to where they'd be waiting.

I saw the balloons first. Isabel shot me a grin.

"It's gonna be so bad," she said with utter and obvious glee.

Everything I'd worried about, everything I'd been sad about, everything I'd been trying to hold in poured out of my stupid, pregnant eyeballs as I saw the *Welcome Home Lia and Baby* sign next. The screams and squeals started as soon as Claire and I made eye contact, and by that point, I was openly weeping.

She broke away from the group and reached me in a few long strides, about knocking me over when she flung her arms around me.

"You're home. Oh, you're *home*," she cried into my shoulder. My heart felt complete like it hadn't since the day I left. "We're having a *baby*!"

I couldn't even talk. I made no sense. Whatever words tried to come out of my mouth for the next few minutes were incoherent babbling and snot.

But they passed me around all the same. First Molly, who cupped my face and told me I was gorgeous. Emmett clung to my waist and informed me he'd grown two inches since I left.

Paige came next, tears coursing down her face (which did *not* go splotchy when she cried). "I hope you're okay with me hugging you a thousand times for the next two days."

"Y-Yes, please," I hiccuped, holding her so tight that my arms ached. "I missed you guys so much."

"Oh, sweetheart," she whispered. "We missed you too."

Paige pulled back and slid a motherly hand over my hair. "I think your brother has waited patiently enough, huh?"

I nodded, wiping super attractive ugly-cry snot off my face with the back of my hand and saw Logan behind us, his hands jammed tight in the pockets of his dark jeans, and his eyes suspiciously bright.

When Paige let me go, he looked at my stomach, and his jaw clenched. Then he held his arms open. "Come 'ere, kid," he said in a rough, uneven voice.

He folded me into his arms, and I left about a gallon of

everything in that hug. All the fear, the disappointment, and heartache went onto my brother's shoulders. Someone rubbed my back, but I wasn't sure who. I didn't care.

"It'll be okay," he whispered into my ear, tightening his hold on me. My big brother could hold up the entire world with those arms, and if I'd ever doubted it, I didn't doubt it now. "You're going to be the best mom, Lia, and that kid is already so loved."

I heard sniffling from behind me.

Or maybe that was just me.

I was home. And that was all that mattered.

Chapter Twenty-Five

LIA

"BUT IT DOESN'T MAKE SENSE," Emmett said, staring at the fruit basket.

I grinned at Paige, then finished my bite of oatmeal. "What doesn't?"

"The whole fruit thing." He held up an apple and a banana. "How can the baby be compared to these two incredibly different fruits and still have it make sense. One is a sphere, and one is oblong."

My eyebrows popped up. "Mighty big word for a nine-year-old."

"We do have to learn 3D shapes, Lia. I'm almost ten."

Paige snorted, holding out his backpack once she had his lunch finished. "Does that mean you're going to start paying rent soon?"

"You're changing the subject." He pointed at my stomach. "You're telling me that right now it's a ..."

"Sweet potato," I supplied helpfully. "I felt a hiccup yesterday too."

Paige gasped. "You did? When?"

"Last night." I rubbed my bump. "Super weird."

Emmett ignored Paige's oohing and aahing. "And in a few

weeks, it's going to be a carrot, Lia." He held out his hands. "A frickin' *carrot*."

"You're right." I sighed. "It doesn't make sense."

"Thank you." He grabbed the backpack from Paige and hugged her around the waist. "Do I need my coat today?"

She pointed at the windows overlooking the backyard. "Do you see the snow outside? It's January, bro."

"Is that a yes?"

I laughed into my last bite of oatmeal. Paige walked to the mudroom and shoved his winter coat over his giggling face.

"That's a yes. I don't need your school sending your ass back home because I'm an inept parent." She yanked a winter hat over his head once his coat was over his arms. "Especially since I'm just around the corner from being a non-grandma grandma," she cried.

I shook my head while Emmett dissolved into laughter at her mock-crying. Paige was having an identity crisis over what her "grandparent name" was going to be, as she'd unilaterally dismissed the actual label of Grandma.

"Language," I said.

She blinked. "What did I say?"

"Ass," Emmett answered, pushing the winter hat up his forehead.

"That hardly counts," said Paige.

The school bus driver honked her horn from the front of the house, and Emmett shouted his goodbyes to us, then disappeared.

"I frickin' love that kid," she said, peeking out the windows by the front door as the bus drove off.

"Me too." I picked up the apple he'd discarded and started slicing it up. My new rule was one piece of fruit for every sweet or carb I wanted to shove in my face.

"What's on the calendar today?" Paige asked.

"I have some reading to do. I've slacked off this week since I finally started organizing all that stuff from Christmas."

"All that stuff from Christmas," she mused happily. "Your face was priceless."

The apple was crisp and sweet and crunchy, and I finished swallowing before I answered. "I'm going to have to move out simply because there's not enough room in the house for me, little Sweet Potato, and all the shit you're buying for it."

Her face shuttered, and I had a momentary pang of regret for bringing it up again. But I made a promise to myself the first week home from England. No more avoiding the hard. It was not allowed.

Not like I minded living back at home for the past month.

The first week had been a lot of naps, a lot of Feelings Baths (where I cried in Logan and Paige's sunken jet tub in their bathroom, surrounded by mountains of bubbles), and a lot of subpar non-British scones because I swear, they baked differently in the States.

The second week went better. Christmas kept us busy with lots of food and laughter and shopping and cuddling under blankets on the couch while we watched all the movies we loved. I only sobbed once during *It's a Wonderful Life*. Fine, twice. Claire held my hand under the blankets. And my family spoiled Little (at the time) Avocado with more gifts than should have been allowed, considering the kid wasn't even born yet.

Blankets and footballs and books and a bassinet with beautifully carved wood that I suspected Logan and Paige spent a fortune on. It would fit perfectly into my old bedroom. But the thing that made me lose it, sitting on the floor by our ten-foot Christmas tree, was the small box that bore marks of being shipped from the UK. Jude hadn't warned me he was sending anything, but when I sliced open the packing tape and folded back the white tissue paper, I saw the impossibly tiny Shepperton jersey bearing his number, and underneath it, a tiny board book about soccer. I cried quietly while Emmett laid his head on my shoulder and rubbed my back.

That was the first text between us since I'd returned home

that gave me the first kindling of hope that we could get through this in a good place.

Me: Thank you for the present. It's perfect (a little big this year, but that's okay)

Jude: Whenever it fits, I can't wait to see. How was your day today?

Me: Good. More chaotic than usual this year. Molly is home with Noah, and Washington doesn't play this Christmas Day, so they could be home. Claire and Bauer were here too. Tomorrow they'll be with his family, though. What about you?

Jude: Not quite chaotic, but Rebecca forced me to her house for dinner. Her husband is a Man City fan, so it was a rocky start.

Me: LOL. Well, we can't all be perfect.

Me: It's late for you. Don't you play tomorrow?

Jude: If I play like rubbish again, you'll know why then. I best try to sleep. Merry Christmas, Lia.

Me: Merry Christmas, Jude.

I dreamed of him that night for the first time since being Stateside. Waking alone, in the middle of my old bed, in my old room, was disconcerting. And the hazy memories of how he'd kissed me, dirty and deep, underneath the Christmas tree lingered for days, a strange ache that mixed into finding a new normal with my family.

But as week two slipped into week three, a quiet lull between holidays spent playing games and watching the Wolves beat Green Bay, watching Shepperton tie against Leeds United 2-2, the new year came and went with very little fanfare, considering I found myself sound asleep by ten on New Year's Eve, curled up underneath the bright purple comforter that I'd used in high school.

That was the first time I'd mentioned where I might live after the baby was born.

"Why not just redecorate the whole room?" Paige had asked. "And you know you can turn Molly's old room into a nursery once the baby is out of the bassinet."

Logan glanced carefully at my face when I didn't respond as we'd eaten dinner that night.

I don't know if I can do this. The thought came and went quick and quiet. But that was the thing. I would not let those thoughts escape anymore. That was my promise to myself. I'd grab them by the tail and yank them back, so I could take the time to figure that out.

That night, I'd answered her diplomatically since I didn't have an answer yet. "I don't know if that makes sense since I'm not sure what my long-term plans are, but I'll think about it."

And just like she had that night, when I mentioned it again now, fully entrenched in week four with all of us back at work and school now that the holidays were behind us, Paige's hands froze in the middle of what she was doing. It took her a long moment to make eye contact with me.

"Do you want to move out?" she asked.

I took another bite of apple and snagged a stool by the island, thinking carefully as she refilled her coffee. As it was most every morning, it was just me and Paige at the house. Logan was gone to the Wolves practice facility, and once Emmett went to school, it was just the two of us.

"I don't know."

She nodded and took a seat across from me. "I think ... I

think I just assumed you'd want to be here to have help with the baby. And I mean, it's not like we don't have the space."

They did, in spades. It was the house that Logan bought when Brooke first dropped us all on his doorstep, metaphorically. He found the five-bedroom house in the suburbs and bought it the same day, a place we could grow into and make our own. And it bore the strong handprint of our family in the way we'd molded it to fit whatever phase of life we were in. It was so much more than four walls and a roof; it represented a second chance for all of us in different ways.

"I know," I told her. My thumb tapped on the granite, and I fought the impulse to change the subject and see if she wanted to go shopping or go for a walk or go work out. "But I'm almost twenty-three, Paige. I'm in my last semester of school. And ... and I think I need to consider the fact that just because I *can* live here after the baby's born doesn't mean I should."

She sighed. "I hate when you guys make sense about shit like this."

"I know you do," I answered with a smile. "You'd have us all here forever if you could."

"Hell yeah, I would. What does it say about me that the crazier this house is, the more at peace I feel?"

Paige and I were so similar, and it was the kind of shared trait that made my heart grow about two sizes because even though there wasn't a shred of shared DNA between us, and I was practically stepping into my teen years when she married Logan, she held a piece of my soul. Just like I held a piece of hers.

"I think it says we need to find something to do today," I told her. "I haven't made up my mind yet."

"Deal." Her face lit up. "Can we start working on your registry?"

"Isn't my shower supposed to be like, a month before I give birth?"

"What's your point?"

I laughed. "Let's circle back to that next month, okay?"

That conversation helped bridge a previously untouched gap in my relationship with Jude in our weekly phone call.

Paige had left to run errands, so I sat in the family room under a blanket with my phone on my lap and Jude on speaker.

"Is it stupid to move out if I have a free place to live?" I asked him.

He hummed. "Not stupid, no."

There was a slight hesitation in his words that had me smiling. "But ..."

"But," he said, "I think I'd want my own space. If it were me. But I've been on my own since I was seventeen, so I might not be a good person to help you make that decision."

"Seventeen?"

"Mm-hmm. Moved to Germany to play in the Bundesliga, which is their national league. That's where I got my start."

I shook my head. "That's so young to be thrown into a world like that. I can't even imagine."

"I learned a lot," he said ruefully. "On and off the pitch. And for a kid who came from a bloody sheep farm, it was nothing I could've prepared myself for."

My fingers twisted the edge of the blanket. "Is that when your parents ... started disapproving?"

Jude let out a slow breath, and I found myself holding mine before he answered. "They started a few years earlier than that, when I took a job outside of the farm to make enough money to keep myself in the youth clubs." Jude went quiet, and I held my breath, waiting for anything else he might give me. "My dad, especially. I was the eldest son, yeah? And it was my job to take over the farm, just as he'd done with his own father. But I think ... I think they saw how serious I was, working myself to the bone to play a game they didn't understand."

Relief was sweet and unhurried as I listened to him talk about his time in Germany. What he loved about the independence he found, and what he didn't. He asked me, in a slight subject change, about living with Claire in college and what that had been like. He asked me about Finn, who I'd only managed to see a couple of times since I moved back, busy, busy boy that he was.

"What do they all say?" Jude asked when we fell quiet. Most of our weekly calls lasted around thirty to forty minutes, but I'd been on the phone with him for over an hour. "Do they think you should move out?"

"Logan and Paige want me to stay. Probably because they'll worry less. Claire isn't saying one way or the other, but ... I know what she's thinking."

"Twin thing," he teased.

"Sometimes. I can't like, read her thoughts, but it's like hearing your neighbors talk through thin walls. You get impressions, you know? And I get the sense she thinks it would be good for me to live on my own." I spread my hands over my belly. "So, your vote is to move out?"

"For whatever it's worth," he murmured, "yes, that's my vote. But I'll support whatever you choose."

The gloomy days of January, only a few of them cold enough for snow to stick on the ground, gave way to slightly warmer, just as gloomy days in February. Lia and I turned twenty-three, and split a giant platter of pink and white cupcakes after a family dinner. My class, considering it was one of the last before I finished my program, felt like it was the least of my stresses. I read and wrote and had discussions with small groups. My family, all busy with their own lives, found time to carve out pockets with me when possible.

Molly traveled about half the month, and when she was back, she always took me out for time with just the two of us, considering she'd made it her mission to find me the best scone in the greater Seattle area.

I'd taken to texting Jude updates amid our search.

Me: This one was pretty good. Not as good as Rebecca's, though.

Jude: It looks dry as cardboard.

Me: Maybe not CARDBOARD. But it needed a lot of cream. Can you eat one of hers for me? Or just send me a picture of one? Or a video so I can pretend I'm sniffing it?

Jude: Good Lord, you sound like an addict.

Jude: Here. It's got currants in it.

I laughed when I saw the picture he attached, him shoving half the scone into his mouth. The sight of him wasn't a punch to the heart or anything, one side effect of being able to see him on TV every week when I got the chance to watch one of his matches. But this was a different Jude than the one I saw on the pitch. Despite the silly picture, he looked tired. It was in the dark circles under his eyes, the lines on his face that hadn't been so prominent when I'd last seen him.

Molly sipped her coffee across the cafe table and watched me. "It's going okay with him?"

I shrugged. "As good as it can, I suppose."

"Do you miss him?"

My eldest sister was the only one who dared to ask me about him. Maybe because she was the most romantic to her soft little heart. She'd tamed her big beast of an athlete in Noah, and I knew she was holding out hope that I'd still be able to overcome ... everything ... when it came to Jude.

Staring at the picture, the scruff along his jaw and the mess of his dark hair, I rubbed my thumb over the image, and then cleared it away so I wouldn't obsess.

"Yeah." There was no point in lying to Molly. And I

wouldn't have lied to anyone else either if they'd asked, but along with the realization that I was very skilled at moving through life restlessly was the fact that my family was used to that. They probably thought I'd brush them off with a *It's totally fine, guys, look at how completely fine it all is.* "But I don't think missing him is the problem. It's figuring out what we're like outside of missing each other. He's finally talking to me about stuff, but it's not like I can just hop back over to England because the thought of him makes me heartsick."

"Makes sense," she said. "No one is perfect, but you already know that, and I don't think that's what you want from him."

I shook my head. "No. I don't need perfection. I think my problem was that it felt so good when we weren't worrying about anything else, and now that everything else has surfaced, I can't think about how good it was between us until those things are better, at least. And they may never be."

Molly watched with a soft smile when I curled my hand over my stomach. A soft bump greeted me, and I motioned for her hand. She slid her chair closer, eyes widening. "Can you feel it moving?"

"Yeah." I took her hand and set it along the top of my bump, and we waited. I tried pushing on the side, and then felt it again.

Molly gasped. "Ohhhh, hi little Banana, I'm your favorite Aunt Molly."

I laughed as she tucked her head down beneath the table and kept talking to my stomach. A couple passed us, not even trying to hide their WTF faces. I waved.

"And we're going to do so much fun stuff," she kept going, rubbing the top of my gently moving stomach with her palm. "And I just love you so, so much." When she sat back, her eyes were bright. "Goodness, that's amazing."

"You should have one," I said slyly.

Her cheeks went pink almost immediately. "Noah said that the other day."

"Really?" I squealed. "Oh please, please, please, get knocked up so we can have babies grow up together."

She laughed. "I caught him looking at baby Wolves stuff the other day, and I think it's Jude's fault for sending that jersey at Christmas. It got him thinking about, I don't know, everything. We're so happy and so busy, but if you wait for life to be the perfect time to do things like get married or have babies or travel, you'll never do it."

"Very true." I thought about Jude, and how if it hadn't been for our night at the bar, and my shitty memory with birth control, he'd still be alone. I was young, so it was different for me. "Do you think Noah will propose soon?"

Her eyes sparkled happily. "I do. I overheard him asking Paige something about her ring, and he didn't realize I was in the next room."

"Molly!"

It was her turn to squeal. "I know!"

"Promise me something," I said, gripping her hands with mine.

Her eyes got big at my grave tone. "What?"

"Please try not to get married like, the week of my due date. Because then my options are being as big as a whale in your wedding pictures or missing it because I'm in labor and I don't particularly like either option."

She laughed. "How about we wait until he proposes first, then I can worry about setting a date." Molly nudged me under the table with her knee. "Look at you, Lee, planning ahead and everything. Did you swap personalities with Claire?"

"I know, I know."

"Ready to go?" Molly asked.

"Yeah. I told Paige I'd help her make the dough tonight for family dinner."

"Oooh. Pizza?"

I nodded. "Little Banana wants some."

"Another reason me and that kid are going to get along just fine."

I followed Molly out of the cafe and found myself glancing back at my phone screen. Wanting that glimpse felt a little bit like his tease about being addicted to scones. Two months away from Jude, and I still craved the pieces I could get. Even though the picture was in thumbnail, I stared at his face, wishing that any planning I did could include a clearer picture of what role he'd have in my life, in Little Banana's life.

But as February came to a close, and March dawned a little warmer, a little less gloomy, we stayed exactly in the same place —getting to know each other—and I knew that I'd have to be okay with that.

Chapter Twenty-Six

JUDE

I'D LEARNED a lot as winter thawed into an early spring in England. Not all things I wanted to learn, mind you, but I'd learned them all the same.

First, it was entirely possible to sit out of a game and still feel the amount of pressure you felt when you were starting. And losses hurt just as bad from that vantage point as well.

Second thing I learned was that I yelled. A lot.

The starting players began calling me Boss, and not necessarily as a term of endearment. My manager normally just looked back at me with raised eyebrows as he calmly watched us navigate through the middle of the season in complete and utter fucking mediocrity.

"Get your head out of his arse, Williams," I bellowed. "Learn how to clear the ball."

"Do you want to stand here?" Conworth asked dryly with a quick glance over his shoulder.

"No, but if you don't do your bloody job, I will," I muttered. The young player next to me must've heard me because he snorted.

I gave him a look, and his cheeks reddened.

Third, I learned with complete and utter fucking clarity that

Lia might've been thousands of miles away from me, but I couldn't get her out of my head for a single second. It was hell.

And the reason it was hell was because I couldn't do anything about it, except try to forge a friendly truce until the season was over.

In the locker room after the match, a 1-1 draw against Aston Villa, I sat on the bench in front of my cubby and stared down at my phone.

She'd started sending me "bump pics" as she called them. Always right in the middle of our weekly phone calls.

I hated them.

I loved them.

She was changing, somehow getting more and more beautiful with each centimeter she grew, and I felt very much like I was staying the same.

"What's got your balls in a bunch?" Declan asked, tossing his dirty kit onto the floor and tightening the towel around his waist. "You yelled even more than normal today, which is impressive, considering how much you yelled the week before. Conworth is going to be out a job not because he can't win, but because you're going to take it from him."

I ignored that because I didn't want to coach. I wanted to play. I didn't want to be sitting on the bench in any facet of my life, and I seemed doomed to that position.

Waiting on an opportunity to play

Waiting for calls.

Waiting for pictures.

Waiting for something to happen so I could shove the door open and see what was on the other side.

I scrolled back up to the last few pictures she'd sent, all in front of the same long mirror in a big bedroom with a fucking terrible purple cover on it. I stopped, realizing she'd missed a week, and I hadn't even noticed at the time.

"Did you know that a baby at twenty-four weeks' gestation is the same length as sweetcorn?" I asked.

He froze, glancing at me with wide eyes. "Err, no. I wasn't aware."

"Well, it fucking is, all right? An ear of corn. I didn't get a picture that week. I missed the sweetcorn."

Declan pulled some trousers up and discarded the towel. "And what week are we on currently?"

"Twenty-six."

He nodded. "Right."

When I didn't speak, Declan carefully lowered his big body onto the bench. "And this is the American?"

"Yeah." I tossed my phone back into my duffel. "She's back home now."

"Congratulations," he said dryly. "Relationship issues are difficult, mate. If you need the name of my therapist, he's a bloody miracle worker."

I groaned. "Just what I need. Someone to make me lay on a couch and purge my feelings. I've already got one person telling me I've got the emotional IQ of a potato. I'm not sure I should add a second."

"You'd be surprised how much it helps."

I eyed him.

Declan smiled, completely un-self-conscious. "How do you think I manage you lot without punching people in the face all the time?"

"Never given it much thought, really."

Declan elbowed me. "Glad to know it's that, if I'm being honest."

"Why?"

"Here I just thought you were in a shit mood because you haven't been playing well enough to start anymore."

I gave him a dry look.

"Well, you haven't. If you were doing the job correctly, you'd be out there, not sitting off to the side." He slapped my back as he stood. "Nobody ever wants to bench the best person for the job, McAllister, and if that's you, then bloody prove it."

I rubbed a hand down my face, wishing I could ignore the truth of his words. "And if it's not?"

He shrugged a shirt on, his expression thoughtful. "Then move aside for whoever is and teach them what you know."

Those words, those bloody words from that bloody great grump of a captain stuck with me for weeks.

Every time I got a few minutes to play, I heard them in my head. I scored in stoppage time against Wolverhampton and earned myself more playing time in the next match. And in that game, I played them on a loop when all I managed was a yellow card and an epic yelling match with the linesman.

I heard them in my head all the time, it seemed, like a puzzle piece I couldn't quite fit into place.

When I practiced.

When I tried to sleep but thought of her instead.

When I worked out, and my thoughts waffled between football and Lia and the baby (now a bloody cauliflower at twenty-seven weeks).

When she and I talked on the phone, about her appointments and class and apartment search and family.

When I'd get a picture or text between phone calls and had to think on exactly how to respond so she wouldn't realize just how horribly I missed her in my life.

Sometimes I did better than others, matching her tone easily when we'd text about meaningless things. Foods we liked, and things we'd done that day. And others, I didn't do as well.

Lia: Are you still awake?

Of course, I'm still awake. It's still early enough that I'm in the lying in bed, staring at the ceiling, contemplating how I'd gotten my life so bloody off course *portion of my evening*, I almost answered.

Jude: Yeah. What's up?

I almost fell off the bed when she started a FaceTime. Fumbling with the bedside lamp, I answered the call once I had it switched on.

Her face filled the screen, and I almost fucking wept at the sight of her broad smile. "Hi!"

I cleared my throat. "Hello."

Her eyes tracked down to my bare chest, and her cheeks pinked immediately. "Sorry, I know it's late, and I didn't give you any warning."

"You never to apologize for calling, lov-Lia." I caught myself just in time, and she didn't seem to notice my almost slip. "What's up?"

Her eyes glowed. "You have to see this."

Lia pulled the phone away from her body, so I could see her bump from the side. She was lying in her bed too.

My ribs felt tight seeing it. "It looks so different than in the pictures you send."

"Shoot, it stopped." She tugged up her shirt, and my heart started hammering at the sight of her bare stomach. Then something moved. "Did you see that?"

"Bloody hell," I whispered. I practically jammed my nose against the screen to see it better, laughing incredulously when something pushed along her tight skin. "What *is* that?"

She laughed. "I don't know, it feels like an elbow maybe?" Lia's hand drifted over that spot, and her fingers pushed. When she pulled back, the baby moved again, and I found myself laughing.

"Did he just push you back?"

"Yeah." She sighed. "This is the weirdest thing ever." After one more small roll underneath the surface of her skin, Lia tugged her shirt down and moved the angle of her phone so I could see her face. "You said he."

I traced every part of her face, documenting the changes since I'd last seen her. "Did I?"

Lia nodded. "I'm trying not to guess."

"Why not?" I settled back against my pillow, in no rush to end this conversation. I'd talk to her all bloody night if she'd let me.

She tucked a stray piece of hair behind her ear. "I don't know. It feels like ... how often do we get this big of a surprise, right? There's nothing else in life, no bigger moment when you could find out news of this magnitude. I like not knowing, not expecting. And when they come ..." Her voice trailed off, and she got a dreamy expression on her face that about had me fucking crying. "Then I'll get that moment, you know?"

"What moment?" I asked, so fully entranced by her.

"When you meet the most important person in your life, and your soul can go, Oh, yes, you're the one I've been waiting for."

This.

This was the danger in us talking face-to-face.

I wanted to spout words, poetic and emotional and impossible to take back. And I think she knew it because she was looking at me carefully in the silence that followed what she'd said.

I cleared my throat. "I like the sound of that moment."

She smiled. "But it's okay if you want to guess what it is."

"Truthfully, I don't care whether it's a boy or girl." I shook my head. "Though I'll probably be a rubbish girl dad."

Lia laughed. "Why do you say that?"

"Because I'll want her to conquer a world that won't make it easy for her to do so."

"Oh." She sighed, her whole body going soft. Then her eyes teared up.

"Shit, I'm sorry, please don't cry."

Lia waved a hand. "Don't mind me. I'm just ... hormonal, you know? I cried yesterday when Emmett made me a fresh chocolate chip cookie because he heard me say it sounded good."

"I'd cry if someone made me one too."

She smiled widely.

I decided to risk one small confession. "I miss seeing you eat things you love."

"Do you?"

I nodded, holding her gaze steadily. "That's one of the things I miss."

Lia's eyes got sad, and her mouth opened, then closed.

At that moment, for the millionth time, I thought about what Declan had said. *Nobody ever wants to bench the best person for the job, McAllister, and if that's you, then bloody prove it.*

This was the first time we'd done a FaceTime, and in our weekly phone calls, we'd done so well, shared so much of the things that must have been important to her. And if this was my shot, then I'd take it.

"Maybe I shouldn't have said that," I started, "but I do miss you, Lia. Very much."

She let her head fall back with a sigh, against a dark gray upholstered headboard, and her eyes never wavered from mine. "I ... I don't know what I should say to that, Jude."

"Why don't we start with what you *want* to say?"

Her eyes closed briefly, and I saw the struggle in the pinch of her brow and the lines that appeared on her forehead when she was deep in thought.

"I wish I could," she whispered. "I wish I could tell you those things without worrying about the consequences that might come with it."

I rubbed a hand over my forehead and again, cursed the distance between us.

"I almost didn't even call you," she admitted.

"Why not?"

"Seeing your face …" She paused, sucking in a slow breath and then letting it out through pursed lips. "It's hard, Jude. Because it makes me wish we could be back like it was before. And I'm happy being back home. I'm happy to be with my family. I was afraid you'd make me wish I wasn't. And even though I know it's the right thing to be home right now, I was afraid you'd make me wish I was still there with you," she admitted quietly.

Frustration ebbed and flowed inside me, not in any great giant waves, but a low simmer that was out of my hands just as much as it was out of hers. It was the truth of our situation that she couldn't stay in England forever, and I was in the middle of a season, unable to even contemplate what changes the next season might bring.

But still, there was an irrational spark of hope at her softly spoken confession. Could I yet prove that I was the best man for her? I wanted to. That much was clear.

"And have I made you wish that, love?" I asked. The moment it was out of my mouth, I knew what a selfish question it was. And I saw in her face that it was the perfectly wrong thing for me to say.

She sighed. "Oh, Jude."

"I'm sorry." I shook my head. "That was stupid."

"No, I'm muddying things too." She covered her face with one hand. I wanted to rip that hand away. I wanted to kiss her fingers and palm. I wanted to taste her mouth again and cover my body with hers, see how it had changed and how it felt now. But even more than that, I found myself wanting to take away whatever brief flash of pain I'd just caused her with my stupid pride.

Wasn't that always my problem?

My unrelenting need to prove myself valuable, prove myself worthy had cost me so much more than it had gained me. Especially in the past few years.

"Look at me," I told her gently.

She lowered her hand.

"I won't do that again," I vowed. "I think I was momentarily weakened by the mental image of you eating a freshly baked cookie. I know what sounds you make when that happens, and I'm only human, love."

Lia smiled so brilliantly, bloody hell, it hurt to look at. I'd do anything to see her smile like that, I realized. Even if it cost me.

She bid me a quiet good night, and we disconnected the call. For a long time after, I stared at the ceiling.

Maybe that was what she'd been trying to show me when she walked away all those months ago. It cost her to walk away from me, but she'd still done it. There was strength in putting someone else first, like she'd done with our child. I knew that now. I was far enough removed from the bloody dinner that my own selfish words echoed like a broken bell in my mind, discordant and harsh. Yes, my parents said some bloody terrible things, but in my choices that night, in my complete inability to be honest with people about the things I was struggling with, I'd made Lia suffer as a result.

Lia's strength had been showing me what love looked like when you asked someone to be accountable for their actions.

If she'd cared less, she wouldn't have minded half as much how I was acting. Her leaving proved something that I hadn't been able to see at the time.

And not once in my life had I ever had that modeled for me, not until her.

It was the edge piece I was missing, where Declan's words provided the full image I'd been puzzling over.

Sometimes, you proved your worth by showing what you were willing to give up.

What Lia was asking of me was a selfless love, not a parade of proof or a litany of accomplishments for why I'd earned her priceless favor. Not even for her, but for our child.

They were both priceless, a legacy that I could never have built by myself and never could have earned. But if I could pull my head out of my arse, I just might yet be able to.

I pulled out my phone and sent two messages. The first asking for a phone number. The second asking for some time.

Chapter Twenty-Seven

LIA

WITH A VERY DRAMATIC ARM MOVEMENT, I whipped back the dressing room curtain.

I turned to the side, then the other. "Well?"

Claire grimaced.

"Oh, come on," I groaned. "That bad?"

"You just look a little bit like ... like Nana's old kitchen wallpaper puked all over you."

I glanced down at the dress. The purple and blue flowers on a cream background had seemed so cute on the hanger, and then she had to go and say something like that.

"Shit."

She winced. "Sorry."

"I'm so sick of trying on dresses, Claire," I whined. The comfy chair in the corner of the dressing room held my weight when I sank back into it, sticking my legs out to rest on the poufy ottoman in front of it. Maternity dressing rooms were the shit.

"Hey, we can stop. You'll just have to show up to your shower naked."

I rolled my eyes.

She started ticking off options on her judgy little, non-pregnant fingers. "The blue option was cute. It was comfortable, the color looked really good on you, *and* most importantly, it was machine washable."

"Only you would list that as the most important feature."

"How happy are you going to be when you stain it and have to bring your pregnant ass to the dry cleaner?"

"Wellllll, since I'll probably only wear this dress once ..."

"What about the next time you're pregnant?"

My gaze zipped to hers. "Holy shit, I never even thought about that. I might have another *kid* someday."

"People do it all the time," she answered gravely.

"And my kids might be like, ten years apart for all I know."

"They might be."

My eyes widened. "And I have to keep stuff for those ten years, don't I?"

Claire held her hands out in a magnanimous gesture. "You are welcome."

"I thought I was doing so good at thinking ahead too."

She walked into the dressing room and lifted my feet so she could sit on the ottoman, then lowered my feet into her lap. "You are. You looked at that apartment for a second time last week. That's really good, Lee."

"I liked it," I told her. "It had so much light, and the bedrooms were big. Only ten minutes from Logan and Paige's too."

Claire smiled. "So why the hesitation? You said that Little Cabbage was moving like crazy while you were in there."

"Is it so weird that all I can imagine is a Cabbage Patch Doll now?"

She nudged my feet. "You need a dress. Your shower is next week."

"I know." I let my head fall back against the chair. "I don't know why I'm hesitating."

"Don't you?"

"What's that tone?" I asked, without lifting my head. "You're shrinking me. You know how I feel about that."

"I don't know how many times I have to tell you that I'm not a shrink, but a little bit, yes."

Claire, with her infinite patience and ability to see through me like I was made of Saran Wrap, waited quietly. Truly, it was her superpower.

"The season ended today," I said. "Jude's."

She hummed.

"We've been texting a little more during the week. All friendly stuff, nothing too deep, you know. After that FaceTime last month, it was ..." I stopped, shaking my head. There were a host of things I could've said.

It was hard because seeing his face turned my heart inside out.

It was impossible because even if he'd changed some, we still had the same issues.

It broke my heart because of how much he tempted me when he looked at me like I was his entire world.

"It was difficult to move past," was what I settled on. "It was the first time we even tiptoed past our friendly truce since I came back."

"That makes sense," Claire said, smoothing a hand over the top of my foot. "How does that tie into the apartment?"

I swallowed. This part was hard for me to admit out loud. The big unanswered question that would only be answered when he and I were face-to-face again.

"What if ... what if he comes here, and I'm making all these strides to move forward, and he's moved forward too, but ... but I'm still in love with him?"

"Would that be a bad thing?"

My eyes burned with unshed tears. "Not if he loves me back, no. But what if he doesn't? You know? What if all this distance I asked for, that I insisted on, is the one thing that ends up pushing him away? And at the end of this, he's like ... fixed and happy and healthy, and I'm just"—I sniffed, trying not to choke on the words as they came up my throat—"alone."

When I could finally meet Claire's gaze, her eyes were bright with tears too. "You'll never be alone, Lee. But I also know that's not the kind of loneliness you're talking about."

"No." I wiped at my face. "I left and I don't recognize anything about my world now. So much of it is good, you know? Molly is practically engaged, and you and Bauer are stupid happy, frickin' Finn is working ninety hours a week in his residency and he still manages to find a perfect girl, and I think, I think I still thought Jude and I would come to the end of this, and it would work out. That this distance would help us get closer."

"It still might," she said gently.

"But what if we don't end up together?"

She reached forward and grabbed my hand. "Then he's not the one for you."

"I'm nervous to see him."

"That's okay too." She smiled. "When will he get here?"

"He said he'd try to get a flight out in the next week so he can make it for the shower. Logan is hooking him up with one of the apartments they lease for players when they need a place to stay, said they may have him run some sort of clinic for the players or something so he could get it cleared."

She stood from the ottoman. "Well, if he's going to be here for that shower, then the blue dress won't cut it."

"Thank you."

"But we also don't want wallpaper dress."

I rolled my eyes as she started digging through the pile that I'd brought into the room.

"Oh, yeah," she said. Then held the hanger on her pointer finger. "This one."

"Yeah?"

Claire nodded. "Definitely."

I touched the hem of the dress with a tiny smile. When I

did, Little Cabbage did a massive somersault that knocked my breath away.

"Whoa," I gasped, rubbing over an elbow or knee or something. Claire pressed her hand down on the spot with a grin.

"See? Cabbage Patch agrees with me." She leaned down. "Don't forget, I'm your favorite aunt, okay?"

JUDE

"Bloody fucking bollocks, this is stupid."

The soothing voice came through my car's Bluetooth system. "It's okay to be nervous about this, it's a big deal."

"Don't coddle me right now, all right? I need you to tell me I'm not about to walk into a trap."

My therapist—whose number I'd gotten from Declan—did not make me lay on a couch, but he did make me talk about my feelings, and often in the past four weeks, I'd hated him for it.

"From what you've told me, I don't believe you're walking into a trap." I could hear the smile in his voice, the wanker, and I wanted to punch him for convincing me this was a good idea.

I yanked my car to the side of the country road, staring out the windshield at the rolling green hills and hedges. "I'm not ready."

"Talk to me about what changed then, Jude." He was always so bloody patient. "Yesterday when we met, you'd had a good talk with your brother and a good phone call with your parents. Based on what you talked about with both of them, you told me you were ready to go out to the farm."

I gripped the steering wheel until I could've sworn my knuckles were going to pop out of my skin. "Yeah, it was easy to say I was ready while sitting in your bloody beige office with your soothing music and fucking oils in the air making me relaxed."

"What's scaring you right now?"

I pinched my eyes shut. I hated that question. For the past four weeks, twice a week, he'd asked me all these blasted questions that I hated answering. Sometimes more than others.

"Right now? How much I want to punch something."

He chuckled. "Fair enough. But you aren't punching anything, which is excellent. What else?"

Blowing out a hard breath, I finally opened my eyes. "I'm afraid that I'll go to the farm, and it'll be just like the last time I saw them at the pub. My dad will say something awful like he did, and I'll lash out like I did, and we'll be right back where we fucking started." I slammed my palm against the steering wheel. My heart was ramming against my chest like I'd just run for a bloody hour. "And if that happens, then all of this was a waste, and Lia was right that I don't know how to talk about shit, and I'll never change, and the woman I love and my child will be halfway across the world, happy without me, and I'll be empty and alone with no one to talk to about anything because I've shown over and over that I don't need it when I really do."

The car was deathly quiet at my admission. I could hardly believe I'd admitted anything that big.

Quietly, thoughtfully, he hummed. "Bravo, Jude. Excellent."

I ran a hand down my face. "Bloody hell," I muttered. "I feel like you just yanked my guts out."

He laughed. "I didn't do anything but ask a few questions. The truth is that you already have changed. You're seeking help in seeing the damage that your parents have inflicted, that you've inflicted in turn. You've recognized that Lia's absence, her ability to walk away for the health and well-being of your child and your ability to parent that child in a healthy way, is a boundary she needed to erect in order for you to seek that change."

My head dropped back on the driver's seat, something unlocking in my chest. A pressure eased that I hadn't even been aware of, even though I'd probably been carrying it around for half my life.

"I know. But it's still not a choice I would've made."

"No, but think about what you can choose within this situation."

I rubbed my forehead.

"Jude," he continued, "you can't force your parents to change any more than Lia can force you to change. You can choose to work on these things. So can they. It's all connected. But if your parents are willing to try, then there's hope. Maybe that's the reason Lia and this child are in your life."

His words, even though they were freeing, unraveled a domino effect inside me. I missed her so bloody much and seeing her was just out of reach. My flight for Seattle left the next morning, and this stop was something I had to do before I attempted anything else with Lia.

Terror and hope were so inextricably entwined, and I'd never been so fully aware of it until I was on the cusp of everything I wanted.

A life with Lia, if she'd still have me, gave me so much hope, but I couldn't really achieve it until I faced this monster, one that was partially of my own creation.

"I can do this," I said quietly.

"You are doing this," he affirmed.

"Thank you, Kendrick." I grinned even though he couldn't see me. "You're not so bad."

"High praise indeed. Send me an email if you need to schedule a session while you're in Seattle. We could do a virtual appointment."

"I will."

We disconnected the call, and even though I needed to put the car in drive and finish the rest of the five-minute drive to the farm, where my parents were expecting me, I decided to take a moment longer in the still and calm.

Glancing down at the passenger seat, I picked up the small

sheep, dingy with age. But still, it was soft in my hand, and I ran my thumb over the face, imagining it in the small, uncoordinated hands of a child with Lia's eyes and maybe my smile.

The sheep was set carefully on the dashboard of my car, a symbol guiding me forward to a place where hopefully I would find a small measure of peace in my past and establish a foothold to the future I wanted.

With a deep breath, I eased the car into drive and moved forward.

Chapter Twenty-Eight

JUDE

EYES GRITTY and back sore from a long day spent traveling, London to Chicago, where I spent a sleepless night waiting for the first flight out to Seattle, I wasn't feeling my best as I approached the arrivals area at Sea-Tac airport. There would only be one person waiting for me there, and it was up in the air whether he'd greet me with polite reserve, a warm welcome, or a kick to the bollocks.

Were I in his position, it'd probably be the latter.

I didn't have much in the way of luggage, as three large boxes of my belongings were being shipped by Rebecca, who'd made me swear a blood oath that I'd do a FaceTime with her when the baby was born. And I felt like that was a good thing when I turned the corner and saw Logan Ward for the first time.

He was tall—taller than me—and solid muscle, arms crossed forbiddingly over his massive chest. His eyes were shaded, a Washington hat pulled low over his forehead. I found myself swallowing heavily as I approached. We were interrupted briefly, a pause button on our little showdown, when a small boy approached him.

Logan softened immediately, the change in him so profound

that I blinked. He crouched down with a smile and shook the boy's hand after they exchanged brief, quiet conversation, then allowed a picture when the boy's mother asked for it. The whole thing lasted only a minute, just a shade more, but it established an immediate kinship.

His grin was wry as he stood back up. "Never know when that'll happen, do we?"

"We don't." I held out my hand, and immediately, he took it. His grip was firm but not overbearing, and I breathed just a tad easier that he'd decided against the kick in the bollocks. "I appreciate you being willing to pick me up."

"I wasn't going to at first."

We started walking, me following Logan's lead as he steered us through the milling crowds toward the car park

"What changed your mind?"

"Lia's sister," he admitted, with a small shake of his head.

"Not Isabel, I'm assuming."

Logan cut me a look. "Claire."

"Ahh."

"Why do you say it wasn't Isabel?"

"The last time I saw Isabel, she threatened to de-man me, I believe."

Logan laughed heartily. "Yeah, that sounds like her."

I pointed at a Starbucks. "Mind if I stop for some coffee?"

"Go ahead."

While I got the largest Americano they'd sell, Logan waited, tapping away on his phone. The smell hit my bloodstream before I took my first mouth-scalding sip. He eyed me carefully as I approached. "No tea?"

I answered with a wry smile. "Sometimes even the British need more caffeine than tea will give us. And this is one of those times."

We walked out of the airport and into the car park quietly, and I appreciated him allowing me a few moments to let the coffee hit my system.

Logan's truck was large and black and carried a Washington Wolves sticker in the back window. He opened the back of the truck for me, and I hesitated before sliding my suitcase in.

"What's wrong? Do I need to like, lift it for you?"

I gave him a look. "No, I just want to make sure it's safe back here. I've got ... a gift for Lia, and I'd hate for anything to happen to it."

His eyes were inscrutable, his facial features all but carved from rock as he gave me a good old-fashioned stare down. It was hard not to fidget underneath the weight of it, but I met his gaze square on.

"I'm in love with her," I told him. "And I'll do my best to prove that, even if I have to wait."

Logan inhaled slowly, then exhaled in a hard puff. "You can put it behind your seat. There's room."

"Thank you."

Once in the truck, he paused before pulling out of the parking space. "Claire told me I have to give you a chance, no matter how wrecked Lia was when she got home in December."

My jaw clenched, but I kept my mouth shut. I'd not seen the fallout, of course. Which he knew.

"And she reminded me that because we all love Lia—and this baby—so much, that if you are the best thing for both of them, then it would be worse for me to do or say something I'd regret in a moment of anger."

I should have brought a gift for Claire as well.

"And I feel like it's important that you know that before I say what I'm about to. This is not coming from a place of anger or thoughtlessness. I don't know exactly what happened between the two of you," he continued. "I didn't ask for the details. They're not important. But I'll warn you, McAllister, that this family—my family—is everything to me. If you don't have the fortitude to stick this out with her, with the baby, then tell me now, and I'll buy your return ticket home before she's any wiser."

Slowly, I turned my head and met his stony gaze. He bloody well meant it.

"I'm not going anywhere," I told him.

Logan searched my gaze before he nodded resolutely. "Good."

He put the truck in reverse, and I exhaled slowly.

"Lord, you're an intimidating lot, aren't you?"

Logan smiled. "We don't mean to be. But we've learned to close ranks when it's necessary."

"Why?"

"Did Lia ever tell you how they came to live with me?"

Feeling horribly sheepish that I didn't know, I shook my head. "Just the bare minimum."

He glanced over at me before turning his gaze back to the road in front of us. "We share the same dad, the girls and I do. But my father remarried a woman much younger than him when I was starting college."

"Lia's mum," I said.

Logan nodded. "Brooke. She was—for lack of a better term —a trophy wife for my father. Beautiful, bubbly, the life of the party. Charmed everyone, as long you were only around her for small doses. Our dad died of a heart attack when the twins were young. And Brooke"—he frowned, his grip on the steering wheel visibly tightening—"she didn't much love the idea of being a single mom when there wasn't as much money as she originally thought."

"Bloody hell," I murmured. I rubbed my forehead, each bit of information offering further clarity. "She left them with you."

"On my doorstep." Finally, he smiled. "I probably aged ten years the first six months they lived with me, but they're the greatest gift anyone's ever given me. A couple of years later, my wife and then my son got added into the chaos, and now ... apparently ... we keep adding their men too."

He sounded so disgruntled about it that I found myself smiling despite the terrible story that had led to their family.

"Lia was ... ten, yeah?"

Logan nodded. "Tough time to have your mom bail. Any age is, I guess. I always wondered if they heard her that day she left."

When he fell quiet, I glanced over at him.

"Brooke always wanted the fun, the excitement, the adventure. But we'd always known that about her. It wasn't anything new. But leaving them ... I never saw that coming. Right before she left, I asked her why she was doing this." He shifted in his seat. "She looked back at me and shrugged, then she said, 'I have one life, Logan, and it's already been hard enough. Why would I spend the rest of it being miserable?'"

"Fuck me," I murmured. Even if Lia hadn't heard her mum, everything made so much sense, looking at her through that lens. "Thank you for telling me."

"It's something you have to understand. Anyone who's going to love one of those girls needs to. You don't experience someone leaving you like that without scars. And Lia might hide those scars well, but they're there. She'd never let anyone make her child feel the way Brooke made them feel."

I mulled that over, each thing he told me only serving to make me love her even more.

"She'll be an excellent mum, won't she?"

"I have no doubt about it," Logan said.

I stared out at the mountain peaks, still capped in white despite the warm May air. I thought of what Lia had said driving through the English countryside, about paying attention to your surroundings when they were unfamiliar, and I smiled. Each mile closer, it wasn't even so much the scenery that had me overwhelmed, but the idea that I was so near to her after so many months.

"And you're sure you're ready for all this change?" Logan asked. He flipped his indicator on to take the next exit, and my heart raced in anticipation. We were close.

"I am."

He nodded but didn't say another word as he wove through a few streets, taking us farther from the noise and busyness of the highway. At a small curve in the road, I saw a beautiful building set back in a clearing. Long balconies stretched in front of a dozen sliding glass doors on each of the three stories with parking underneath the building. The landscaping was lush and green against the white stucco.

"2B," he said quietly. "She thinks I'm picking her up for the shower in a little bit. I told her I'd hit the buzzer three times so she knew it was me."

Logan parked his truck and held out his hand.

I took it for what it was—an olive branch and a blessing. I wasn't entirely sure I deserved it yet, but I'd bloody well try.

"Thank you," I told him again. "For everything."

He clapped me on the back. "You fuck it up, and I'll rip your balls off, Brit."

"Fair enough," I answered dryly.

I pulled my suitcase out of the truck and gave him a small smile before I walked to the main entrance. The building had a small entryway behind glass doors, and I was happy to see security cameras affixed all around. Quickly finding 2B on the panel, I gave the button three quick bursts and held my breath.

LIA

I EYED the clock on the wall above the couch, pressing the button to let Logan up. "Come on up. I'm almost ready."

From my living room window, I'd seen the back of his truck parked in front of the building, so I knew it wasn't a serial killer or anything.

A stack of boxes sat next to the door, and I moved the top one over so he wouldn't knock into it when he came in. The apartment was sparsely furnished and only half unpacked, but it already felt like home. The May sunshine streamed in through the sliders that led to my balcony, and I hummed along with the music playing in my bedroom.

My hand reached down, but I couldn't reach the buckle on my ankle. "Shit," I whispered. Mildly awkward to ask your big brother to do it, but hey, pregnant people had to do what pregnant people had to do. And as I was learning, Baby Pineapple, with its low center of gravity over my hips, made just about everything harder most days.

Including dressing. Thankfully, I'd been able to slip on one of my nude, open-toed sandals, showing off the bright red pedicure that Paige had treated me to in honor of my baby shower. But the other buckle came unhooked when I tried to wiggle my puffy little foot into the left shoe.

I heard the door to the apartment open, and I called out over my shoulder. "In my room. Can you help me with my shoe, please?"

His heavy footsteps slowed in the living room, and I sat back on the bed, adjusting the neckline of my dress. Claire had been right, the deep V, slightly off the shoulder neckline and pale pink color were perfect. The dress hugged my stomach and hips, ending just above my knees.

It was as sexy as I'd felt the entire pregnancy, with my hair curled, a full face of makeup, and a body with curves I'd never, ever had before. Honestly, my boobs were amazing.

As long as Jude's flights weren't late, he promised he'd be there before the shower ended.

Maybe not ideal to see him for the first time after so long in front of my family and friends, but I was just excited to see him.

Logan approached, and I stuck my foot out. "I can't re—"

My voice broke off at the sight of him, big and tall, filling the doorway of my bedroom.

Jude's eyes drank me in hungrily, and in a daze, I stood slowly.

"Jude," I whispered.

The strong column of his throat moved on a visible swallow when his eyes landed on my stomach, his lips curving slightly. "Hello," he said, voice low and sure and oh, his accent saying that one little word.

I didn't dare move when he closed the remaining distance between us because I couldn't believe he was in my bedroom. His hand rose carefully, and when I knew what he was doing, I gently took it, laying it over the top of my sizeable stomach. A gentle roll rippled the surface of my stomach, and he huffed out in amazement.

"Holy bleeding hell," he whispered. "Look at how beautiful that is."

I laughed, my eyes pricking with happy tears. "I wish you could feel it from my end. It's so crazy."

Jude's other hand slid up my back, and he leaned over to press a gentle kiss to the top of my head. "You look incredible, Lia."

My fingers curled into his forearm as we stood like that, his hand on my belly, the other on my back between my shoulder blades. The room was filled to the brim with palpable tension, the kind that slowed your movements and forced you to breathe it in deeply, like the kind of electric, crackling air before a storm or a first kiss.

I turned into him, wrapping my arms firmly around him, and he did the same, exhaling heavily when I was fully folded between those strong arms.

Tilting my head up, I studied his face. He looked good. Tired, but his eyes glowed like I'd never, ever seen. "You're here."

Jude grinned. "I may have fibbed about my arrival time."

"So ... Logan picked you up? I saw his truck out there."

He nodded, carefully pulling away but leaving his hands to smooth up my upper arms so he could look at me again. "I managed to get his phone number through my agent, and then his agent."

I covered my face with my hand and groaned. "Did he like ... do the scary big brother thing?"

Jude laughed. "Terrifyingly well, yes."

And still we stood there, my hands resting on his waist, his on my arms, and suddenly, I felt a flurry of self-consciousness. Carefully, I extricated myself, fidgeting with my hair while he looked at my queen bed and upholstered headboard, then smiled at the bassinet in the corner next to the ivory-colored glider that Molly and Noah bought me as a housewarming present. "My apartment isn't really ... ready yet."

"Do I get the tour?"

I smiled. "Yeah." My arms spread out. "My room, obviously."

"Big windows."

"It's what I loved about this place. When we do get sun, I wanted as much of it as possible. And it's only ten minutes away from Logan and Paige's house."

He glanced into the room that would be the nursery, now only filled with the white crib and dresser, a wicker lamp in the corner, and a fuzzy white and tan rug spread along the floor. Boxes of diapers were stacked in the corner, and empty frames sat propped inside the closet in which hung a long row of small white hangers.

"It's a work in progress," I told him. "I'll get a lot of stuff at the shower today."

He stared at the crib for a few seconds, then blinked, his attention returning to me. "I love it."

"Thank you." My face warmed under his praise.

"I, uh, I have something to add to it, actually."

My head tilted, a smile spreading across my face. "You do?"

"It's in my suitcase." Gently, he took my hand, and even if it wasn't smart, I curled my fingers through his and let him lead me into the family room. I found a spot on the couch and watched him curiously when he immediately crouched in front of me. Then his fingers brushed over my ankle, and I sucked in a breath. So, so carefully, he closed the buckle on my shoes with his big fingers, allowing his palm to rest briefly on my ankle when he'd finished.

"Thank you," I whispered. Where, exactly, had my voice gone? Apparently, it flew out the window with my reserve upon seeing his face. His scruffy, exhausted, handsome face, which I wanted to grab with both hands so I could kiss the absolute shit out of him. There was something coming from him that made me feel a little bit less crazy for feeling that way.

Something in the way he was looking at me.

Something in the way he was touching me, with such care and such reverence.

Jude, for the first time since I'd met him, was looking at me like I could crush the heart in his chest if I said the wrong thing. And that was the difference, I realized, as he gave me a secretive smile before unzipping his sleek black suitcase. Shifting perfectly rolled clothes aside, he fished out a box, perfectly wrapped in gold foil wrapping paper, then another smaller one.

Taking a seat next to me, he took a deep breath before handing the smaller of the two to me. On the label, scrawled in his masculine handwriting, was my name.

"This is from Rebecca too," he admitted.

My mouth fell open. "Did she ... is this ...?" I held the box up to my nose and took a whiff. "Oh my gosh, you didn't."

Like a kid on a frickin' Christmas Day, I tore into the present with glee, causing Jude to laugh heartily when I tossed the paper at him and ripped open the top of the box.

Scones. Beautiful, beautiful scones sat inside the box, enclosed in a plastic bag.

"As fresh as I could manage," he said. "She finished them a couple of hours before I had to leave for the airport."

I pulled one out of the bag and held it up to my nose. "Oh, I love her," I groaned. I took as delicate of a bite as I could manage since I already had my lipstick on. Eyes closed, I sank back on the couch and savored every perfectly not-fresh crumb. "My soul is so happy right now."

"It would seem so," he said, voice full of amusement.

After one more bite, I sat up, giving him a shy smile. "Thank you."

"I'm sorry I couldn't manage some clotted cream in there." With a smile, he watched me take another small bite and then move that box aside. When my lap was free again, he slid me the second box. On that label, it said Little Pineapple. My eyes met his, and he grinned.

With careful fingers, I pulled open the wrapping paper. It felt more important to go slow with this one, and it was almost never my instinct to go slow on anything. But as I folded the edges back, I knew what he was trying to do. He was trying to create something special. Something meaningful. It was why he came earlier than he told me and why he reached out to my brother.

When I pulled the top of the lid off, three objects were wrapped in white tissue paper, one large and square, one medium and squishier looking, and one flat and small.

"Any particular order I should open these in?" I asked.

His eyes were smiling as he watched me, and I felt it in my heart.

"Left to right is fine." He pulled out his phone. "I have a video that goes with the second one."

"My goodness," I murmured, picking up the first. It felt like books, which made me smile. When I pulled off the tissue, I laughed in delight. It was a stack of board books, all baby versions of classic literature. On the top was *Jane Eyre* with a bright illustrated cover. "Jude, these are amazing."

Underneath *Jane Eyre* was *Pride and Prejudice*, *The Wizard of Oz*, *Alice in Wonderland*, *Sherlock Holmes*, *The Jungle Book*, and *Romeo and Juliet*.

"So that you can teach our child all the wonderful things you know so well," he said.

I clutched *Jane Eyre* to my chest like it might contain all the happy I was feeling. "Thank you," I said, completely overcome.

"Next," he urged.

I set the books aside and picked up the next package. It was soft but firm. Before I could pull the tissue off, he handed me his phone. The screen was dark, a play arrow in the middle of it.

"Video first?" I asked.

He nodded.

I hit the button. I didn't recognize the dark table or kitchen where Jude had set the phone. His face filled the screen, and I could immediately read the nerves in his expression.

"Hello, the present you're about to open isn't just from me. I had some help in getting this to you and to the baby." Jude turned the screen, and I saw his mom wave nervously. I gasped, a hand coming up to cover my mouth. I only spared Jude a quick glance through my lashes, but he was watching me with a slight smile.

"Lia," his mom started in a wavering voice, "Jude's father and I wish very much we could be there to give you this in person. And I'd like to start by apologizing for what happened at the pub the last night we saw you. We have no excuse for our behavior, and"—she looked over at Jude—"it's something that we're working on as a family, to overcome. I hope you can forgive us because we'd love to meet our grandchild someday soon. And if there are any mistakes on the gift, it's because Jude doesn't take direction very well. But I did try." In the video, Jude gave his mom a smile, and she returned it. It was awkward, and they both looked unsure, but I felt a tear go down my cheek all the same. "Take care of that little one for us."

The video cut off. I couldn't even risk a glance at him before I opened the next package.

It was two small creatures made from the same soft wool of the sheep I'd found in his room. One was a similarly shaped sheep with a lopsided head and one leg. Through my tears, I traced the other, a black and gray wolf.

"So our families can teach our child all the things they know as well," he said in a rough voice.

His eyes were filled with tears, and I cupped the side of his face, smoothing a thumb underneath his eyes. "You talked to your family?"

"We are very much a work in progress," he said, clasping my hand and pulling it down so he could lay a kiss in the center of my palm. "I won't say we're all the way there, but with the help of a therapist," he said with a wry smile, "and a few tense phone calls before my visit, yes, I'm talking to my family."

I wiped at my face. "I'm going to have to redo all my makeup, and I can't even be mad about it."

He grinned. "One more, love."

"Oh, geez." I set the small toys aside with just one more soft touch to the wolf. With a grin, I knew this would win Paige over in a heartbeat. She'd love him.

I found myself holding my breath as I unfolded the last bit of tissue. My forehead creased in confusion when I saw a small jersey. It was a different blue, with different logos, but my heart skipped dangerously when recognition clanged like a noisy bell in my head.

"Seattle?" I whispered. "You ...

He settled his hands over top mine, which were clutching the Seattle Sounders jersey with shaking fingers.

"One-year contract," he said, holding my gaze steadily. "My agent thinks I've lost my bloody mind for doing this, but I couldn't stand the thought of being across the ocean from the two of you."

I shook my head. "Jude, I don't even know if I can say this delicately because my emotions are like ... gone right now," my voice wobbled, "but isn't this a massive step down for you?"

"Yes." His grip tightened. "And while you were gone, I realized there are worse things than not playing in England. There are worse things than not being the player I used to be. There are worse things than not having my family understand me." Jude cupped my face the way I'd cupped his, and I leaned into that touch. "I will be happy playing here because the worst thing I can imagine is being away from my heart. That's you, love. Both of you." He slid closer, resting his forehead against mine, and took a deep inhale. "I don't know what I did to deserve finding you that night because you were the catalyst, Lia. Whatever hope I've found for the rest of my life started with you. I know how closed-off I was, how selfish I've been, and reparations begin now. If it takes you a month, a year, two years, for you to trust what we have, I'll wait."

A sob escaped my mouth, and I was hardly able to see him through my tears. The warmth of his hand on my face caught plenty of my tears, and I knew he meant it. And my heart was so full of the truth of that I couldn't find a single word as he held me. My hand gripped his shirt when he tried to pull away, and he laughed under his breath.

"My love," he said, wiping my tears with sure movements of his hands over my skin, "I'm not going anywhere."

"You're not," I replied.

"Not as long as you'll have me." He grinned. "You were so right about us, Lia. And as much as I missed you, this time apart was good for me. We needed it to do this right. Because now, I know that our future is built on something unshakeable, yeah?"

"Yeah." I couldn't stop touching him. "You'd really wait that long?"

His thumb touched the center of my bottom lip. "If that's what you need."

When I pulled in a shaky breath, my tears finally cleared from my eyes, and I slid my hands behind his neck and into his hair. "You know patience isn't my strong suit, right?" I whispered, tugging him closer.

"Is that right?"

I nodded. "Especially when I know what I want."

As his mouth descended achingly close to mine, he laughed. "I'm so bloody in love with you."

I let his words wash over me in a warm, contented sweep. Our lips touched once, twice, and then he tilted his head with a groan, fitting his mouth firmly to mine.

Winding my arms around him, I slid my tongue against his, relief lighting up every nerve ending in my body. I hiked up my dress as high as it would go and tried my damnedest to straddle the beautiful man's lap.

He laughed into my mouth when I couldn't pull it up higher. "Look at you," he murmured. He tugged the dress up over my hips in one sharp tug, gripping my ass and sliding me closer as he sat back on the couch. His hands caressed my thighs, my stomach, and as we traded kisses, his fingers tangled into my hair.

I pulled back and stared at him, one hand over his mouth when he tried to kiss me again. "Is this real? I'm not having one of those really vivid pregnancy sex dreams, am I?"

He nipped at my fingers. "I'd love to hear about those, but no, this is quite real."

I sighed, running my hands over his chest. "I love you too," I whispered, his heart thumping strong and steady and sure under my palm.

His lips—those wonderful, talented, devilish lips—curled up into a smile. "Shall we fix you back up now? Or are we going to be late for your party?"

I ran my nose along his, grinning when he licked at my bottom lip. "They can wait a few more minutes."

"Bloody right, they can," he said against my mouth, his hand cupping my breast. My hips started rolling along with the clever circular motion of his thumb, and Jude's other hand gripped me tightly, fingers digging into my bottom, directing me with a firm motion. "That's it."

That ... was when my cell phone started ringing. "Noooo," I groaned. The shrill sound, coming somewhere from my bedroom, was Claire's ringtone.

He looked dazed, his hand pulling slowly away from my chest. "Right. Good. No, we should stop."

I gave him an incredulous look. "We should?"

"Come on, love, up you go." With a tortured sigh, he helped me to stand, staring intensely at the black lace underwear I was wearing as he carefully pulled my dress back down.

"What? Why? Why are we stopping?"

Jude laughed, kissing my forehead after he'd stood from the couch. "Because the last thing we need is to miss your shower, and me meeting your family."

Ugh. I pouted, which made him laugh. He wrapped me in a hug.

"I know you're right," I said, my head resting in the center of his chest.

He smoothed a hand down my back and leaned his head down. "We can wait a bit longer, love. We have forever."

Chapter Twenty-Nine

JUDE

Seven weeks later

"This is not going to work," Lia said between helpless bouts of laughter.

"You doubt me?"

She tried to turn, which was quite a feat in her current condition—one week past her due date. "Yes!"

"What a terrible mistake on your part," I whispered in her ear once she was comfortably on her side.

On my knees over her, I marveled at the expanse of naked skin in front of me. My hands coasted over her stomach, and I smiled when I felt the hard press of an elbow or knee. When I dropped down to kiss that very spot, I caught her mouth curving in a smile.

Since the day I arrived, it had been like this between us.

Peace, sublime and sweet happiness that rolled from day to day, all wrapped up in a mind-blowing amount of time in bed.

She kept me up later than I was used to, chatting happily about her days, hearing about mine, and most nights ended with us on the couch, her head in my lap, where I could trace my fingers along the gentle lines of her face and body into the soft length of her hair.

We went out to eat, wandered the sights in Seattle, and she shrieked with laughter when I almost turned us into oncoming traffic given that Americans drove on the wrong side of the bleeding road. We talked about her upbringing and mine.

Together, we pieced together our home in the bright apartment and planned for a future one after her initial one-year lease was up. At Lia's insistence, I didn't pay more than half of the rent, but I told her I got to make the deposit on our next home.

And now, a week beyond where our little watermelon was supposed to make its appearance, we were quite preoccupied with hastening their entrance into the world.

Spicy food hadn't worked.

Neither had long walks.

And so far, the sheer maneuverability of sex was becoming an issue, if that was supposed to help.

I kissed the side of her breast, and Lia stretched herself out fully with a soft sigh.

"Still doubt me?"

"Entirely." She exhaled. "I'm huge."

"You're perfect," I murmured into the slope of her shoulder, just as I eased behind her. "Lift your leg over mine, love."

"Shit."

I froze. "No leg? Shall we try standing in the bathroom like last night?" My thumbs coasted lightly over her chest because I knew how sensitive she was, but she smacked my hands away. My eyebrows lifted. "Or not, that's fine."

Lia looked over her shoulder at me, eyes wide. "Either I've lost all bladder function and I just ... peed a little, or my water just broke."

Blinking, I glanced down. "You ..."

Lia sat up. "I think maybe I should put some clothes on."

Then a brilliant smile dawned on her face. "And maybe you should too, champ. Nice work." She held out a hand for a high five.

I flew out of bed, stark-bollock naked, and grabbed her hospital bag from where it sat just next to the door. "What clothes do you need?"

Lia scooted to the edge of the bed, a small smile on her face. "That blue shirt on the dresser is fine. And the soft black shorts in my top drawer, please."

I tossed them at her and barely glanced at what I pulled over my own body.

Lia paused once, a strange expression on her face. "Oh, hey there."

I froze as I was shoving a phone charger into the side of her bag. "What?"

She grimaced. "Contraction. Weird."

It was that grimace that kicked my heart into a gear I hadn't previously known existed.

Through any doctor's appointment I'd attended with her, the birthing class—which was terrifying—and all the books she read from, I'd never fully realized how bloody terrible it would be not to bear a single bit of this pain for her.

And with the realization came sheer terror at the reality of this new life we were bringing into the world.

Lia cupped the side of my face and smiled. "It'll be fine."

I clutched her in my embrace, pressing a fervent kiss to her lips. "I love you."

"I love you too." Her face straightened. "But I need you not to be a sissy right now, okay? It will be fine, and if you get that Lost Boy look on your face, I'm going to worry about you, and if you're going to do that man thing where you pass out at the sight of the epidural needle or my placenta or something."

"I'm not going to be a sissy," I said in a completely affronted voice. "Also, I don't plan on looking at your placenta."

"Great." She clapped her hands. "Now, let's go."

The drive to the hospital was a blur, and occasionally, she'd let out a slow, even breath when another contraction tightened her belly. With each one, though they were still fairly spread apart, my hands involuntarily tightened on the steering wheel.

Lia sent a text to her family and made a phone call to Claire, who was planning on being in the delivery room with us.

Quite soon, we'd be overrun with Wards, and in the approach to the hospital, I found that I was okay with it.

It was a surprise that this massive, chaotic group allowed me to slip seamlessly into their impressive ranks.

"Claire is on her way," Lia said, sliding her hand over my thigh. "She should be here in about an hour."

I smiled over at her. "Good."

"Are you ready?" she asked me quietly.

Sucking in a deep breath, I pulled Lia's hand up to my mouth and pressed a kiss to her knuckles. "As ready as one can be, I imagine."

And by that, I felt completely unprepared. I felt inadequate. Humbled. Excited.

"I'm scared shitless," she admitted.

Laughing, I kissed her hand again. "Feel free to yell at me if it helps distract you from it. Call me names. Break my hand with your grip. Whatever you need."

As directed, I pulled the car up to the Emergency Room entrance, and she sighed. "I love you, Jude. I'm not going to call you names."

LIA

FIVE HOURS LATER

"OH, YOU SELFISH PIECE OF SHIT," I groaned. "If you eat one

more piece of food in front of me——" My voice broke off when another contraction knocked the breath from my lungs.

Claire laid a washcloth over my forehead, speaking to Jude in a soothing, quiet voice. "Maybe you should set the apple down, Jude. Or eat it out in the hallway."

"Or choke on it," I said through gritted teeth.

Jude tossed the apple into the trash and approached the other side of the bed. He kissed the crown of my head. "Apple's gone, and I know you don't want me to choke, love."

The tension eased from my body, the monitor next to my bed showing the contraction as it eased. "I know. I really don't."

Taking his seat on the stool, he smiled, but I saw the tense lines around his eyes and mouth. "In all fairness, I never should have asked that question, so I can't blame you for feeling ..." He paused, searching for the right word.

"Murderous?" I supplied helpfully.

Claire rolled her lips in to smother her smile.

Jude—who I loved to a scary level, who I trusted with my heart, who I wanted to spend the rest of my life with—about got himself castrated when he asked the pregnant girlfriend on the bed, as she was writing in immense pain, what a contraction felt like.

Folks, he almost didn't survive it.

Another contraction rolled over me, and I felt my legs draw up helplessly.

It was impossible at that point to talk through them, so I didn't even try. Jude moved the washcloth and spoke something soft and sweet into the damp hairline of my forehead.

Eventually, it ebbed, and I could suck in another deep breath.

Claire held my hand tightly on one side, Jude on the other, and the doctor entered the room with a smile. "How are we doing?"

"If they don't get that giant ass needle up here and in my back, I'm going to go find them myself," I hissed.

Jude grinned. "Bloody hell, you're marvelous."

As the doctor laughed, I pulled Jude down for a soft kiss.

"I don't feel marvelous," I admitted. "But thank you."

"You've got quite the group out in the waiting room," the doctor said as he pulled his little stool up right between my spread legs.

When people said you lost your modesty in labor, they were not fucking around, because I would've flashed the entire hospital if it would've helped get my child out of my body sooner.

"Are they being obnoxious?" I asked, wincing when he measured me.

Claire sighed. "The last time I went out there, Paige was on her *I cannot be called Grandma* thing again. She's real worked up about it."

I laughed.

Jude's brow furrowed. "I thought they decided on Gigi and Papa."

Claire and I shared a look.

"What?" he asked.

Claire stood to refresh the washcloth. "This is what she does. When Paige is nervous or excited, she gets a little ... twitchy. She hates feeling helpless when one of us is hurting, so she fixates on something she can control."

Jude gave me a soft smile, his thumb tracing over my knuckles. "Now that I can understand."

My heart, already totally gushy from the general emotions of the day, swelled just a bit bigger. "Kiss, please."

He accommodated me happily and spoke against my lips after he pulled away. "I like it better when you're not threatening my death."

"Me too," I whispered.

The click of a photo being snapped had me blinking. Claire smiled at us, her phone aimed in our direction. "Sorry, guys. Couldn't resist."

"I hate to interrupt," the doctor said. "But unfortunately, we're too far for an epidural."

I blinked.

Jude leaned toward him. "What?"

The doctor threw away his gloves. "You've dilated very quickly since our last check. You're already at an eight, Lia."

Claire snapped her mouth shut and gave me a tremulous smile. "I'm sure it'll be fine. It'll go really fast, Lee."

I burst into tears just as the next contraction hit me.

***

Jude

Two hours later

If I could've given every penny I'd ever earned, traded every accolade, every award, every trophy in the entire world to trade places with Lia, I would've done it in a heartbeat.

My hands were all but crushed in her bruising grip as my other hand held the back of her thigh.

And my heart, it was a mangled, horrible useless heap behind my ribs from what I'd watched her go through the last handful of hours. How any woman ever did this more than once proved why they were the superior sex in every definable category.

Don't be a sissy, she'd made me promise. And so far, I hadn't broken that promise.

"Come on, Lia," the doctor said, face set in concentration. "Give me another push."

"I can't," she sobbed. Her hair was soaked, her face exhausted.

Claire made small soothing noises, moving another washcloth over her sister's sweaty forehead.

"Come on, love," I told her. "You're so close."

"I've heard that for the past two hours," she groaned.

"Here we go," the doctor said. The two nurses busied themselves with ... something, but as I'd promised not to look at anything that would make me faint, I couldn't tell what it was.

Lia gritted her teeth and emitted another soul-shriveling sound of pain and agony and exhaustion, and I shit you not, I could feel the bones in my hand as they were crushed into dust.

"One more, Lia, you're doing amazing," one of the nurses said, positioning herself just next to the doctor. "I can see a head of dark hair."

Lia sobbed. "He has hair?"

I pressed my forehead to hers. "One more, my love. One more."

And with an effort that had me holding my breath, and Claire emitting an audible gasp when she looked down, Lia gave one more glorious push, and the room filled with the most incredible sound I'd ever heard in my life.

A baby crying.

"You did it," I told her, eyes and heart and soul overflowing. Lia sobbed openly, and I kissed her forehead, her cheeks, her mouth.

"It's a boy," the nurse said with a wide grin. "Congratulations, Mom and Dad."

In the next moment, we were all crying because they laid him on Lia's chest as she wept.

With shaking hands, the nurse told me how to cut the umbilical cord.

Everything around me felt like it was moving slower somehow, like my heart now existed in these three separate segments. One behind my ribs, one in Lia, and one in this marvelous, wriggling, wailing thing that was lying in Lia's embrace with a shock of dark hair and button nose.

Claire took pictures as I curled my arm around Lia and kissed the top of his head.

"He's perfect," she said, tears coursing down her face.

"He is." I kissed her cheek. "And you were so bloody incredible, Lia."

The nurse smiled at us. "If you want to help me clean him up and weigh him, Dad, they'll handle Momma."

Lia looked up at me, her chin wobbling. "Take care of him, okay?"

Her thumb was on my face then, wiping away another tear.

"Always," I promised.

LIA

TWENTY MINUTES LATER

"THIS IS SO WEIRD," I whispered. My finger followed the line of his nose and the perfect bow of his lips.

"Right?" Paige asked. "Like they're all slimy and covered in this crazy shit from inside you, and *boom*, just like that, you'd just die for them."

I met her knowing eyes and grinned. "Basically."

Jude smiled at me from where he stood next to my brother.

"Ready to hold him, Logan?" Paige asked, rocking the baby gently. The little man was sound asleep because hey, it was quite the exhausting event to be born.

My brother nodded. "As long as Momma doesn't need him back."

I laid my head back on the pillow and smiled at him. "Go ahead."

My sisters all crowded in the room, snapping pictures over Paige's shoulder.

Isabel quietly wiped at a tear she didn't think we saw. Molly winked, then pointed at herself, "*Favorite*," she mouthed.

But we all watched raptly as Logan first kissed Paige on the top of the head, then clenched his jaw as his wife stood and carefully transferred the baby into my brother's huge arms.

Basically, I was just going to cry my way through the entire day. No way around it. I sniffed loudly before I realized that every single other person in the room, save for Jude, was doing the same thing.

Logan stared down at my son and let out a shaky breath. When he looked up at me, his eyes were bright with unshed tears. "You did real good, kid."

Jude set a hand on Logan's shoulder before he approached the bed.

"You did," he said quietly, wiping my face carefully. "A bloody warrior."

I smiled up at him. "Should we tell them the name?"

Jude kissed me softly. "Go ahead."

My family looked at me expectantly, except Logan, who was staring at the baby again. I smiled. "We'd like you guys to meet Logan Gabriel Ward McAllister."

Paige covered her mouth, sniffing noisily. "Welp, here I go again."

Logan's eyes flew to mine. "What?" he whispered gruffly. "You named him after me?"

I nodded. "We'll call him Gabriel." I slid my hand into Jude's and smiled up at him.

Logan's jaw clenched, and he feathered a hand over Gabriel's fluffy black hair. "Thank you. Both of you."

Isabel rested her head on Logan's shoulder, Molly held Isabel's hand, the diamond of her newly acquired engagement ring winking on her finger, and Claire was next to Molly, an arm around our eldest sister's waist.

Logan cleared his throat. "All right, I need someone to take him before I start ugly crying."

"My turn," the sisters said in perfect unison.

I laughed as they argued over who got him next.

With Jude at my side, his hand curled around mine, I felt almost impossibly happy and impossibly overwhelmed.

It was amazing, I thought, where you could end up when life gave you something you didn't choose for yourself.

Maybe that was how it was supposed to work. We could make all the plans we wanted, but ultimately, the exact right path for us was the one we'd end up on.

And this was mine.

Epilogue

LIA

8 WEEKS LATER

"Hush little baby, don't say a word," I sang, rocking Gabriel in his nursery, "Momma's gonna go have private time with Daddy, and I'll buy you a freaking pony if you stay asleep for the next hour."

The words didn't fit with the melody, but I was so deprived of sexy times with Jude and sleep, in general, I could not have cared less what came out of my mouth as long as it got Gabriel to go down for his nap.

My darling little angel stared up at me, but his blinks got slower and heavier, and when he finally, *finally* conked out, I breathed out a sigh of relief.

Honestly, I loved him so much it was terrifying, but he was the worst sleeper in the entire world. As I laid him down in his crib, I smiled. His hair, still as dark as when he was born, stuck straight out from his head like he'd stuck one of his fingers into a light socket.

Just like when Emmett was born, my son was continually fought over by every single member of my family, and the horrible side effect was a child who only got to sleep when someone was rocking him. I blamed Paige because she'd been known to knock people over in order to reach Gabriel first.

I turned on the white noise maker on the dresser in the nursery, and tiptoed out of the room with my newly acquired ninja sneaking skills, something I was told you inherited upon birthing a light sleeper.

Jude had the day off, and since it had been hard to find time for a little "Mom and Dad alone" time once I cleared the six-week mark, we'd blocked out an hour on our calendars so no one could schedule any meetings and no one could infringe on something we both craved.

With the nursery door closed, I exhaled loudly. "Hallelujah."

I whipped off my top and grimaced at the sight of my super sexy nursing bra. Then I shrugged because I knew one person who wouldn't care in the slightest, and that was Jude. He loved the curves I still hadn't quite lost since Gabriel had been born, something he reminded me of every time he slid his hands around my hips or ducked his head to kiss the tops of my gloriously huge boobs.

The door to our bedroom was cracked open, and soft music played from inside. It had taken me a bit longer to get Gabriel asleep than I planned, but I told Jude to keep the bed warmed up and ready for me.

Slowly pushing the door open with one hand, I peeked in and grinned.

Sprawled in the middle of bed with no shirt on and one hand on his beautiful, beautiful chest was Jude. And he was fast asleep. I wasn't even too surprised. He'd been working himself hard since he started with Seattle. In the team, he'd found a supportive group of guys. Some, like him, used to play in England. Some were young Americans, and some from other parts of the world who just wanted to play, and were fine with a little less pay and not quite as many people in the stands.

Even though the stakes might not have been as high, Jude found a team that he was starting to love, even if it wasn't Shepperton, a place that was home for so long. It probably always would be, given he decided to keep his house so we always had a place to stay when we visited.

Ninja-skills activated, I tiptoed into our bedroom and crawled onto the bed. He made a low sound, but his eyelids never opened. Even as I tucked myself up against his half-naked body, he didn't stir. Lifting my head before I laid it down on his chest, I glanced at the clock on the wall of our bedroom. Our hour-long block was almost half gone, and I had plans that night to go wedding dress shopping with Molly, Isabel, Claire, and Paige. Big sister was finally getting hitched, and I couldn't exactly bail on those plans because I wanted to bang my hot British baby daddy.

I sighed, laying my head against his shoulder and my arm over his waist. Even though my movements were gentle, it was enough to ... rouse him, as it were.

"Oh, bollocks," he murmured, turning to me, his muscular arms wrapping around me tightly. "I'm sorry I fell asleep."

"It's okay." I lifted my mouth to his for a soft kiss. He went back in for one more, longer and a little deeper, humming when I pulled away. "You've been working yourself pretty hard."

"I'm still not used to having a giant, crazy family and their giant, crazy plans keeping me busy outside of work."

With a laugh, I slid my hands up his chest. "Oh, come on, building that treehouse for Emmett wasn't your idea of fun?"

He gave me a look. "I'm quite sure whoever puts together those assembly instructions is sent straight from hell, and Bauer agrees with me. He almost lit the thing on fire when we realized we'd done the first half wrong."

I cupped the side of his face, and he turned to kiss my palm. "Thank you for doing that. Emmett will love it. And some day," I said softly, nibbling along the edge of his hard jaw, "Gabriel will play in there too."

Jude hummed. "Maybe he'll have a brother or sister by that time."

His hand slid into the back of my shorts and started pushing them down my restless hips. I laughed into his mouth. "You looking to knock me up again, McAllister?"

"Someday," he answered ruefully. "But not quite yet. I'd like to marry you first, I think."

My head snapped back, eyes wide, mouth hanging open. "Are you proposing to me right now? I did not imagine this happening while I was wearing a nursing bra and granny panties."

He grinned. "No. But make no mistake, future Mrs. Lia Ward McAllister, it will happen. And you won't see it coming."

I narrowed my eyes. "I bet I will."

Jude slid down, placing sucking kisses along my neck, then the tops of my breasts. "No, you won't. But it will be so fun to watch you try to figure it out."

With a shove to his shoulders, I rolled us until he was on his back. My leg swung over his hips, and I held him down. His big hands slid up my thighs.

"I don't think you'll last another six months, mister." I leaned down to kiss him deeply. He groaned into my mouth.

"I love you," he said between kisses. "But I cannot wait to watch you squirm while you wait."

"I love you too," I returned, digging my hand down into his shorts, biting onto my bottom lip when his eyes rolled back in his head. "But I think you're mistaken about who's going to do the watching right now."

He laughed, and it was perfect. Everything about the life we were building was. It was exhausting and busy and sweet and perfect. Just how I liked it.

SECOND EPILOGUE

ISABEL

THE GYM WAS dark when I walked in, which suited me just fine. I'd memorized every inch of the place years earlier, so the weak light of the sunrise was more than enough for me to navigate back to my office. As it was my day off, I wasn't actually supposed to be there, but my boss, Amy, was never too surprised when I came in. I took a sip of my coffee and stretched my free arm over my head with a wince. Went a little too hard in class the day before, and I groaned loudly when my muscles screamed in protest at the movement.

The groan is what had the door to Amy's office opening, the light of her small corner lamp illuminating the space. The shades were drawn over the glass that looked out over the gym, which I hadn't noticed earlier. Amy's head popped out. "What are you doing here?"

I stopped. "Why do you look nervous about the fact that I am?"

I'd worked for her and known her for too long to tiptoe around anything.

Amy sighed, her face falling in a look that had my stomach falling too. This was it. As soon as she looked over her shoulder and spoke to someone in her office, I knew this was the thing I'd been dreading.

A new owner.

A new boss.

I hated change. It made me all twitchy and uncomfortable.

But that was nothing on how I felt when Amy turned back to me and gave me an apologetic smile.

"I was going to do this tomorrow a bit more formally, but I should've known your ass would show up before sunrise on your day off."

"I needed to do inventory," I murmured, watching as she moved aside, and *he* filled the doorway.

I almost dropped my friggin' coffee, which would have been a shame for how little I slept the night before.

Before either of them said another word, I knew.

Honestly, I knew so much about him, it was ridiculous. I knew he was six-three and in his prime fighting days, he weighed in around two forty-five, tiptoeing him into the heavyweight class that he dominated for years.

I knew what it was like to watch him fight because I'd watched every one.

I knew his eyes were dark, and his mouth never, ever curved up into a smile.

I knew he'd retired a couple of years ago, after the death of his wife, in order to care for his daughter.

Amy cleared her throat, and it broke the connection between his gaze and mine.

"Iz, you might as well be the first to know." She gestured toward me. "This is my gym manager, Isabel. She's indispensable."

He took a step toward me, mouth flat but not mean, eyes dark and curious, and when he held out his massive hand, I inhaled shakily before slipping my palm against his.

When our hands touched, his brow lowered and his gaze held on that single connection point. Slowly, I pulled my hand back, hoping he didn't feel the tremor in my fingers.

"Aiden Hennessy," he said.

Like I didn't fucking know his name.

When he opened his mouth again, I almost slapped my hand over those lips because I didn't want him to say it. But my hand stayed at my side, and he spoke the words anyway, all low and dark, and I felt a shiver of foreboding at how my life was about to change.

"I'm your new boss."

Forbidden, the fourth book in the Ward Sisters series, is coming June 2021!
Preorder Now

Author's Note

Oh, my goodness, my first foray into writing a character who lives/was raised in Europe! I fell completely in love with Great Britain when I visited in September of 2019, I couldn't wait to bring Lia's story to life. Even though I hired a British editor, I did make a conscious choice to use American English, other than Jude's dialogue. Also… if I used 'bloody' too much for your taste, PLEASE forgive me. It's just so fun that I couldn't help myself. Any mistakes are mine and mine alone. I did my best! Thanks for reading.

Acknowledgments

Thanks so very much to the 'usual suspects'- my husband and boys for putting up with me and a weird 2020 writing schedule, Fiona Cole for being my writing buddy in the year of virtual school (AKA THE SHITSHOW), Kathryn Andrews for her wonderful feedback and brainstorming.

To Najla Qamber and Regina Wamba for the beautiful cover.

To Kelly Allenby for being my "Brit Checker".

To Michelle Clay for reading through to make sure I didn't jack up the story in revisions.

To Jenny Sims and Janice Owen for edits and proofreading, and Pauline Cassie for doing one last read-through.

To my wonderful reader group and review team for all their support.

And a special shoutout to my husband's friend Kenneth … he'll never see this, but introducing Premier League into our lives (and turning me/my husband/boys into Liverpool fans) was what gave me the idea to do this book! THANK YOU!

Faith is confidence in what we hope for and assurance about what we do not see.

Hebrews 11:1

Also by Karla Sorensen

Washington Wolves

The Bombshell Effect (Luke and Allie's story)

The Ex Effect (Matthew and Ava's story)

The Marriage Effect (Logan and Paige's story)

The Ward Family Series

Focused

Faked

Floored

Forbidden

Published through Smartypants Romance

Baking Me Crazy

Batter of Wits

Steal my Magnolia (available February 9, 2021)

The Three Little Words Series

By Your Side

Light Me Up

Tell Them Lies

The Bachelors of the Ridge Series

Dylan

Garrett

Cole

Michael

Tristan

Stay up to date on Karla's upcoming releases!

Subscribe to her newsletter

About the Author

Karla Sorensen has been an avid reader her entire life, preferring stories with a happily-ever-after over just about any other kind. And considering she has an entire line item in her budget for books, she realized it might just be cheaper to write her own stories. She still keeps her toes in the world of health care marketing, where she made her living pre-babies. Now she stays home, writing and mommy-ing full time (this translates to almost every day being a 'pajama day' at the Sorensen household...don't judge). She lives in West Michigan with her husband, two exceptionally adorable sons, and big, shaggy rescue dog.

Photo credit: Perrywinkle Photography

Made in the USA
Monee, IL
17 February 2025

12434991R00173